Edwin Lassetter Bynner

Tritons

A Novel

Edwin Lassetter Bynner

Tritons
A Novel

ISBN/EAN: 9783337031466

Printed in Europe, USA, Canada, Australia, Japan

Cover: Foto ©Andreas Hilbeck / pixelio.de

More available books at **www.hansebooks.com**

BY

EDWIN LASSETER BYNNER,

AUTHOR OF "NIMPORT."

———

BOSTON:

LOCKWOOD, BROOKS AND COMPANY.

1878.

CONTENTS.

TRITONS.

CHAPTER I.

AN OLD COMEDY WITH A NEW HERO.

IT was one fair night in midwinter, eighteen hundred and — no-matter-when, that Dorothy Dighton and her mother went alone to the theatre. Alone,—that is, in each other's company, but without the usual male appendage that society demands.

It happened that evening, that Mr. Curley—I refer to Mr. Samuel Curley, of "Curley & Bros.," the well-known East India merchants—was unexpectedly called from home, and Mrs. Dighton, without a second thought, gave up the theatre as a matter of course, although three of the best seats in the house were taken, and there was nothing else to hinder.

Dorothy, on learning her mother's mind, cried out:

"Let's go alone, then!"

"Go without an escort, my child?"

"Why not? It's a clear night, the carriage will take us to the door; besides, it's an old comedy, a fine cast, and I'm dying to see it. Come, you needn't be afraid, Rhody, I'll take care of you!"

"You are a lawless girl," returned the mother with a look of yielding.

"And you are a dear, indulgent little mamma, who is going forthwith to get on her finery while I order the carriage."

"But, my dear"—

"There, there, but me no buts; come, now, say 'Yes' for once, plump and downright!"

"What would your uncle say, Dorothy?"

"Uncle Curl? Why, he would echo your 'buts' from now till cock-crow if he could be consulted, which, thank fortune, he cannot; when it's all over he may say what he pleases."

All further breath of objection was driven from Mrs. Dighton by the speed at which she was dragged, or rather bowled through the hall and up the winding stairs by her eager and irreverent daughter. And, indeed, before she could collect her wits for further protest, she found herself arrayed in her dress-bonnet and wraps, snugly tucked away in the *coupé* and rolling off to the play. Seated there, in the sumptuous carriage, settling her lace neck-gear, smoothing the last suspicion of a wrinkle from her fresh gloves, what with her trim figure, soft skin, and shining hair, she looked rather like the elder sister than the mother of the tall, fair-haired girl by her side.

Arrived, they find the house filled with a fine audience. Fine? Why, yes; there is beauty, health, intelligence and gayety enough to make it fine—nay, even to give it an apparent splendor. Of course, like other such assemblages, it is not wanting in a certain grotesqueness—rather moral than physical—which we are tempted to call its most striking characteristic, as we note yonder a smiling, unconscious dowager marshaling her tender chicks under the eye of the worst rake in town; here a beardless boy-broker, dependent on to-morrow's gambling for his flashy clothes, elbowing a portly millionaire; there a young belle, reveling in the conquests of her first season, flirting with the club bachelor with his back-lock combed carefully over a growing bald spot; here a faded beauty, made up to the proper touch of youthfulness, talking with desperate archness to her friend's husband; and yonder a sober, white-haired father of a family sitting cheek by jowl with a queen of the demi-monde.

Society here has simply come forth out of its class lines and become shaken together; but nobody thinks of excepting to his neighbor, so long as his neighbor is well-dressed and behaves himself.

This audience, moreover, is indigenous to its earth and clime; it belongs to the spot it inhabits, to the air it breathes; it has, like certain kinds of fruit and wine, a soil flavor; it is made up of people of whom our first thought is that they are gay, fashionable, and somewhat overdressed, but whom we presently discover to be also keen, shrewd and intelligent; of people evidently critical withal, who, if they are not very esthetic, have unerring common sense; who are in the main discriminating, who cannot be humbugged, and who will not be bored; who are not over-awed by great reputations, and who are apt to be rather iconoclastic in their tendencies, but who will, nevertheless, on occasion, submit to an amount of clap-trap that is almost incredible.

Physically too they have their distinctive traits: the women are unusually beautiful, the men are lean and careworn; the young men especially are largely of the terrier type — small, slightly-

built, and nervous, with an alert, precocious look;
while, altogether, there is about the whole assem-
blage an amiable, *blasé*, I 've-seen-the-world-and-
know-it 's-hollow air.

We need hardly add that this audience was
gathered in one of the fashionable theatres in the
greatest city of the New World.

We all know the fascination of sitting in a fine
theatre and looking about upon the people, for
we feel that here, far above the darkness and
coldness of the glebe, far above the coarse tangle
of stalk and leafage, we see life in its bloom and
perfume; that here is the upper air of existence;
here is luxury strained from squalor; prosperity
from want; happiness from misery; light and
health from miasma and disease.

Mrs. Dighton and Dorothy felt this same fascination as they seated themselves and took a
survey of the house; and now if we were as rude
as some half-score idle men and as many curious
women, who immediately leveled opera glasses
at the new-comers, we might do the same and
receive the impression of a well-preserved, middle-
aged gentlewoman, daintily and quietly dressed;
and a tall, half-stately, somewhat immature-
looking young woman; and we might persuade
ourselves that in the elder lady we discover an

expression of unusual intelligence, with that fleeting suggestion of slyness always found where
such intelligence is not balanced by commen-
surate courage. We might further fancy that
there is not the same penetrating look to the
younger face, and yet we might be unwilling to
exchange its frankness, generosity, fearlessness,
goodness, and native dignity for the more brilliant trait. We might fancy we had discovered
all this, and we might nevertheless be very much
deceived; opera glasses are not trustworthy,
neither are first impressions — but there goes
up the curtain, and so let us attend to the stage,
where the chambermaid and *valet* are industri-
ously brushing through the opening scene, and
giving a hint of the plot.

The play progressed; the curtain rose upon
the third act, the action became more rapid, the
characters more defined, and the interest grew
with every scene. The audience, thoroughly
absorbed, sat with attention riveted upon the
stage, when, lo! out of the sky, out of the air,
out of the mysteries of nowhere and nothingness,
came a spark of *dementia*, that fell with appalling
effect upon one and all. One word, one thought
in one moment changed that fair assembly of

rational, well-bred, sympathetic men and women
into a panic-stricken mob — craven, selfish, and
cruel. A terrible word, a terrible thought indeed,
that in one swift instant could sweep away every
higher attribute and leave men but their brutish
part.

" Fire ! Fire ! Fire ! "—the horrid cry came
ringing through the air, echoed on every side by
stentorian lungs, and the scared multitude rose
with one accord. They who a moment since
thrilled in sympathy with the mock ills of the
stage, applauded its courage and magnanimity,
despised its meanness and cowardice, now one
and all, forgetful of every better impulse, yielded
themselves up wholly to the basest of human
passions.

The narrow doors were quickly choked by the
rushing crowd ; exit became impossible ; the
very fury of the fugitives defeated its own end.
Climbing over each other, the stronger trampling
down the weaker, they fought, pushed, scrambled,
and tore at every obstacle like a herd of wild
beasts.

A score or two of people, more cool or cautious
than the rest, or perhaps more afraid of the
crowd than of the fire, were left thinly scattered
in the wide auditorium. Among these were

Dorothy and her mother. Mrs. Dighton clung
to her daughter in an agony of fear, and Dorothy's
own cheek was pale enough, but she was otherwise composed as, clasping her mother in her
arms, she said stoutly : —

" I'm afraid we can never get out alive, Rhody ;
but we can die together ! "

Standing in the aisle not far from where they
had been seated, regarding with absorbed attention the movements of the crowd, their deserted
situation attracted the attention of a party of
young men who were hurrying past on their way
to the rear entrance of the theatre. One of the
number turned back and came to them.

" Fire's gaining headway, ladies ; there's not a
moment to spare ! You're lost if you stay here ! "

The voice was quick and imperative ; Dorothy
turned and saw a slightly-built young man whose
foppish elegance of dress was in strong contrast
to the vigor and energy of his countenance.

" We are lost in any case then," she said.

" Perhaps not. Come with me,—I may save
you ! "

" Go, Dorothy, go ; leave me, hurry, hurry, my
child ! "

" Hush ! mother, don't be absurd ; we will
both go."

The stranger, seeing that Mrs. Dighton was almost overcome with fear and excitement, threw down his opera glass and cane, drew her arm through his own and hurried away, bidding Dorothy follow.

Making the best of their way through the dark corridors, they reached at length the stage exit only to find that also blocked up by a struggling mass of men and women, at sight of which Dorothy instantly stopped and drew back.

As the stranger stood looking at the mob, hesitating what to do, an actress suddenly emerged from the darkness behind them, with her arms full of her stage wardrobe. They recognized in her the soubrette of the play.

Instantly seeing the hopelessness of escape by the regular means, she whispered to them : —

" Come with me; if you 'll lend a hand I know a way to get out ; — only be quick and still ! "

They turned and followed the nimble actress across the stage, up some steps, and along a narrow corridor connecting with the box-office ; proceeding some dozen or more paces the woman suddenly stopped and said : —

" There's a little window along here somewheres, if you can find it. It don't open ; 'twas

only made to light the passage, but you can
smash it in."

The corridor was full of blinding smoke;
nothing could be seen; the young man groped
about, guided by the frightened actress. Soon
there was a crash; he had found the window and
broken in the sash.

At the same moment a rush was heard from
behind — a half dozen men came trooping through
the passage — they felt the breeze from the open
window, made a concerted scramble for it,
knocked the young man down from the window-
seat, crawled through themselves, carrying broken
glass, sash and all, in their furious course, and
jumped frantically a distance of thirty feet to the
ground. One big poltroon brought up the rear;
he threw down and trampled upon Mrs. Dighton
in his reckless fright. The stranger flew to her
aid and grappled with the ruffian. They fought
in the dark, like tigers; their voices grew distant
down the smoke-filled passage; it was impossible
to tell who was prevailing. Mrs. Dighton called
aloud for help, but one voice was nothing in the
uproar; the air was filled with an infernal clamor
of snorting engines, rushing feet, hissing water,
and the cries of the escaping multitude. Everybody
and everything seemed possessed with a separate

fury ; even the little actress at length lost her head, dropped her bundle, climbed through the window like a cat, and sprang screaming to the ground.

Dorothy, with her mother clasped in her arms, stood in the stifling passage, hesitating what to do, when their strange friend returned — his antagonist had escaped. *He* did not hesitate ; his decision and movements were quick as thought. His words were short and sharp, but his voice was perfectly controlled and his presence of mind evident. He quickly dragged Dorothy and her mother through the little window, where they found a secure but narrow foothold upon the outside sill. He looked keenly about for a moment, bade them wait for him, then hugging the wall he stepped boldly around a projecting buttress, reached a water-pipe, and, swinging downward hand over hand, was quickly lost in the darkness.

Here, what with the flying sparks, the sight of the roaring flames, and their perilous position, Mrs. Dighton grew giddy. Dorothy instantly blindfolded her mother's eyes and shut her own.

The suspense now became almost intolerable ; the five minutes they waited seemed as many days. At length voices were heard below. Dor-

othy opened her eyes and saw some dark figures
adjusting a ladder; a moment more and their
strange friend came climbing into the air. He
seemed now a friend of years. He spoke a few
words of encouragement to Mrs. Dighton, who
tremblingly prepared to go. He stood ready to
protect her from below; Dorothy helped from
above, but the poor woman's nerves had been too
severely tried; the moment she found herself in
mid-air on the swaying ladder, she swooned quite
away. The stranger immediately caught her and
bore her down; Dorothy quickly followed. They
reached the street and found a Bedlam which
the impotent police were vainly trying to control.

The stranger, however, fought his way through,
the crowd falling back a little at sight of his
burden. He got a carriage and placed Mrs.
Dighton in it. Dorothy gave the address and
they rattled off. Stopping at the nearest drug-
gist's, the stranger rushed in and came back with
his handkerchief drenched with cologne for the
sufferer; it was then that Dorothy saw for the
first time that his face was smeared with blood,
that his clothes were torn, and his hat was gone.

Mrs. Dighton revived somewhat before they
reached home, but was still so weak and faint
that she had to be carried in. The excitement

of their coming set the whole household astir.
Dorothy accompanied her mother up stairs and
attended to her comfort.   She was gone perhaps
fifteen minutes.   She had left everything below
in bustle and confusion.   On going down she
found the hall still and deserted, and the servants
locking up for the night.

"Where is the young gentleman who came
home with us?" she asked in the greatest astonishment.

"Oh, he is gone, Miss!"

"Gone?   Did he leave any message?"

"He left his compliments."

"The compliments of whom?"

"He did not say, Miss."

2

CHAPTER II.

THE CORNER OF A POCKET HANDKERCHIEF.

"GOOD morning, Uncle Curl!" said Dorothy, coming into the library before breakfast, and going up behind a busy little person who was unpacking something from a large hamper, and who might have been easily mistaken for Mrs. Dighton masquerading in trowsers. "Morning, I say," repeated Dorothy, seizing the little gentleman about the waist and whirling him unceremoniously around in a waltz.

"There, there, my dear ; good morning, good morning, that will do ; see, I've something to show you, just arrived by the English steamer. Look at that !" he cried, holding up a china jug.

"What is it ?"

"Cloisonné ; *isn't* it a beauty, eh ? Look at this, and this, for instance !" said Mr. Curley, as he pointed to details in the decoration.

Mr. Curley's library was already so crowded with pottery of every description, with old furniture, Japanese stuff, statuary, Chinese carvings in

wood and ivory, and hangings of every variety,
that it looked more like an auction-shop than
a private room, and Dorothy asked naturally
enough as she regarded her uncle with a quizzical look : —

"Very fine ; but what are you going to do
with it?"

"Oh, I shall find a place for it somewhere ;
but stay, my dear, wait a minute ; I haven't
shown you the gem. Ah, here it is! There,
what do you say to that?" he asked, holding up
a tiny cup and saucer; "that's real *Capo di
Monté*; and, isn't it dainty, eh?"

"Oh, I dare say it is well enough, Uncle Curl,
but put away your crockery now, and let me tell
you of our adventure last night!"

"Adventure! Ah—h—h," he cried with a
long-drawn expression of delight, holding up a
plate decorated with a sprawling figure in blue
and yellow ; "look at this lovely piece of Italian
faience!"

"How many times," began Dorothy, severely,
"have I been lectured for that very"—

"Beg pardon, my dear ; so it was very rude,
I'll allow; pray proceed! — 'Adventure,' you
say," he continued, attentively studying the signature on the bottom of the plaque ; "did you

find a mouse in the closet, or did the cook come home drunk again?"

"Oh, nothing so terrible as that; we merely went to the theatre and were nearly burned to death by fire, stifled with smoke, and drowned with water; and a heroic young man with dark eyes and a commanding air came to the rescue with a ladder, and dragged us out of a window; and it was all as fine as a fiddle, or as Mrs. Radcliffe herself."

"Dorothy, Dorothy, what a reckless chatterbox you are!"

"No such thing; I'm only making a clean breast of what you are bound to find out sometime, and explaining why poor Rhody is not ready for breakfast and bids us not wait for her; so please give me your arm; I presume you haven't the slightest idea that the bell rang fifteen minutes ago, and that the breakfast is spoiled by this time."

"Dorothy, what does all this mean?" asked her uncle, studying her face with a puzzled air. "Is anything the matter with your mother?"

"Oh, nothing much; she's a little tired and stiff after such hair-breadth escapes from fire and flood, as a matter of course; I am myself."

"Do you really mean that you went to the theatre without me?"

"Certainly!"

"And that there was a fire?"

"Yes, indeed, here's the morning's paper full of it. I've been looking to find our names among the victims. But there are no victims; that is, nobody is killed; only a few bones broken. The building was saved, too; so, you see, it didn't amount to much after all."

"But the ladders and the rest of it?"

"Plain unvarnished fact!"

"Well, my dear, I should have expected nothing better from *you;* but your mother must have taken leave of her senses."

"Why, bless your heart, so she did, I tell you; fainted dead away and was brought to and brought home by the aforesaid cavalier."

"And is she — are you sure she is quite well this morning?"

"Yes; I've been in to see her, and she'll be down presently and tell you all about it."

"And who was this young man?"

"Ha, ha; why that's the funniest part of it; I haven't the slightest idea. I went up-stairs to attend to Rhody, and when I came down to thank our fine hero, he was gone."

"And you crawled out of a window?"

"Yes; and ruined my dress in consequence."

"And were taken down a ladder?"

"Taken down? Not I; I climbed down by myself. It was poor Rhody — but here she is, to answer for herself!"

"Yes, here I am," said Mrs. Dighton, advancing to greet her brother, "and of course, Samuel, you think I was crazy and that it served me right for going off on such a wild-goose chase; and so I dare say it did, but we both wanted very much to go"—

"Oh!" exclaimed Dorothy, rolling up her eyes incredulously.

"I did indeed, my dear; I saw no harm in it, and it would all have happened just the same if your uncle had been there; it was simply one of those inevitable accidents that might as well have overtaken us at our own fireside, and our only duty now is to thank Providence we escaped as we did — but let us go to breakfast!" she concluded, leading the way as she spoke.

"I suppose Dorothy has told you all about it, Samuel, but no words can give you any idea of the awfulness of the scene. The people really behaved like wild animals, did they not, Dorothy?"

"They behaved like devils!"

"Tut, tut, my dear, not so strong!" said Mr.

"I certainly never expected to get out alive," pursued Mrs. Dighton, pouring the coffee; "and we never should have got out, had it not been for that noble young man — by the bye, my dear, I hope you thanked him properly?"

"I regret to say I did nothing of the kind."

"What *do* you mean?" asked Mrs. Dighton, in a little tone of exasperation.

"I mean, Rhody," returned Dorothy, cracking an egg, "that when we arrived home you were so used up, so out-of-the-combat, so whatever you like, that I had to attend to you first; and when I at length came down to see our cavalier, he had fled."

"But he left his name?"

"No."

"How very odd; now we cannot thank him."

"Just what he wanted to avoid, I think."

"Then there's his handkerchief, which he brought to revive me in the carriage; I have it up-stairs."

"He may possibly have others," said Dorothy, dryly.

"His name may be on it," suggested Mrs. Dighton.

"Of course it is, — name, age, and address in full; if it isn't we will put a card in to-morrow's

'Herald' as follows: 'The little fat old lady and the big bony young woman whom he helped through a window and carried down a ladder at the fire last night, would like an opportunity of thanking the heroic, dark-complexioned young gentleman, and returning his pocket handkerchief. Address Gratitude.'"

"Be still, Dorothy, you incorrigible girl!"

"The shabbiest part of it is, we left him to pay for the carriage."

"If we had only thanked him, I shouldn't care."

"Oh, what are a few thanks! I haven't a doubt he thought we overpowered him with thanks and rode home in such an exalted state of glorification that he thought about us only as the instruments of his exploit, and made an entry in his pocket diary to this effect: 'Great fire; saved the lives of two females!'"

"If we had only done *our* duty, it would make no difference what *he* thought."

"For my part, I was immensely relieved to find him gone; I didn't know what to say to him. I was thinking all the way down stairs whether I had better say: 'We thank you very much, sir, for your noble and disinterested conduct;' or, 'We are very much obliged to you for saving our lives, and hope to do as much for you;' but in my confusion I should very likely have wished him 'many happy returns,' or something worse, so it's just as well; and don't you go indulging any romantic notions about this handsome young man and his mysterious departure, Rhody!"

"Do, Dorothy, stop calling me by that ridiculous name; twice recently you have used it in public, and it is not at all respectful!"

"And who is responsible for that ridiculous name?" asked Dorothy, rising to hand her own coffee-cup, and seizing the opportunity to catch her mother around the neck, kiss her heartily, pinch her cheeks, and rumple her hair. "Who, I say, made up that ridiculous name but a ridiculous little woman who came from a ridiculous little State, and who was nevertheless so proud of it and boasted so much about her New England origin and her magnificent Rhode Island, that her ridiculous little baby caught the word and naturally enough applied it to her?"

"You are a ridiculous little baby no longer, my dear, but a very ridiculous young woman to keep up your baby tricks," returned Mrs. Dighton, trying to dissemble, by a mild rebuke, her maternal delight at the caress; "but about the young gentleman —"

"Still harping upon the Unknown!" interrupted Dorothy.

"Oh! don't borrow any trouble about him," said Mr. Curley, "it will turn out to be some fellow connected with the theatre, who will be around here shortly for a reward of merit, with a bill for the carriage."

"Indeed you are mistaken, Samuel; he was a gentleman — I wasn't so scared as not to see that — and a very unusual looking young man, too; was he not, Dorothy?"

"Yes, a delicious little dandy," said Dorothy.

"He was nothing of the sort; his dress was a bit fine, but there was real stuff to him; he was a young man of character, I am confident; — have you forgotten the way he fought the ruffian?"

"No; I approved of that. I wonder if I could have done it myself: the young man was not so much larger than I. Uncle Curl, will you let me take boxing lessons?"

"You had better take a few lessons in discretion and propriety!"

"How can I be wanting in those respects, when I am taking lessons all the time from two such dear, proper creatures as you and Rhody? But now," she continued, taking her uncle's arm as they rose from the breakfast-table, "I am going to make amends for everything by asking to see the new crockery."

" Yes, you may come if you will be quiet ; we will look over it together ; I hardly know what there is myself, yet."

" Now I am ready," said Dorothy, settling herself on a large Moorish rug on the library floor. "Go on, Uncle Curl ; I will bask in this streak of sunshine while you exhibit and explain."

" By the way, my dear," said Mr. Curley, as he rummaged among the straw, " I haven't told you my new ideas about decorating the drawing-room, I think—Delft," he said, interrupting himself to examine a plate, tapping it with his bent forefinger and looking critically at the signature ; " real old Delft," he repeated, as he handed it to Dorothy. " It strikes me the plan is very original."

" It will be a good deal more original to leave it as it is. Now pray, Uncle Curl, don't go decorating us out of that dear old room ! "

" Dorothy, you are hopeless ! — Italian, my dear, soft paste, sixteenth century. You don't seem to have naturally the least artistic sense.— Höchst porcelain, wheel and crown, and Oo-o-o what a beauty, too ! — No intuitive perception of fineness in art ; you always need to have the points of anything rare shown you ! "

"I know it ; it's dreadful ; but not having this 'intuitive perception,' as you call it, I don't pretend to have it, and so I am quite free to say that it will be nothing short of desecration to turn our dear old drawing-room into a tiresome curiosity shop."

"But it will be more logical to object to my plan when you know what it is."

"Certainly ; I am only taking Occasion by the forelock to protest against any change whatever."

"Why, my child, the drawing-room was furnished years ago, before there were any notions of interior decoration in vogue in this country.— Eh ! what, Etruscan — a real Etruscan, as I live !" exclaimed Mr. Curley, holding up a small vase and almost dancing with delight. "Well, this is a happy day ; there isn't the match to that in the city !— The drawing-room, I say, is not only out of date, but it is common-place ; it is inartistic."

"Heigho ! then, Rhody and I will have to retreat to the nursery."

"My design is — think, my dear, of owning a bit of Etruscan more than two thousand years old !" exclaimed Mr. Curley, regarding the little vase again with rapture. — "My design is, I say, to have the floor laid in marqueterie of different

varieties of Irish oak ; to have the walls covered
with Japanese stamped leather, with a dado of
ebonized cherry carved in cameo, after a mediæval
design, of hunting scenes and insignia for which
I have drawings ; the ceiling I shall have painted
in panels and cross-hatched with ebonized mould-
ings, while for the frieze I am going to have fac-
simile casts of the frieze of the Parthenon, actually
set in the wall. What do you think of that, my
dear ? "

"I think it will be a jumble of an Anglo-Saxon
castle, a Japanese palace, and a Grecian temple,
all shaken up and poured into a Yankee parlor,
and it will be frightful ; but then, you know, I
have no 'intuitive perception ;' so ask Rhody,
for here she comes ! "

"I have found it, sure enough," cried Mrs.
Dighton in a tone of satisfaction, as she advanced,
holding in her hand a fine cambric square ; "here
it is, neatly written in the corner ! "

"What, the name of the Unknown ?" asked
Dorothy, lazily.

" Yes."

" What is it ? "

" Ralph Dexter ! "

CHAPTER III.

PUTNEY PLACE.

A S there are men with negative faces, with pent, close-lipped looks, with an air of having battened upon secret and unknown things, so there are streets and neighborhoods of a like inscrutable character, — blank, expressionless, architectural riddles, surrounded by an atmosphere of respectability which we feel may be only specious, and of quiet which, on the other hand, we may be too hasty in deeming suspicious ; such a neighborhood was Putney Place.

It was a short street, holding not more than a dozen houses and ending in a blank brick wall ; a shady street in which the sun never rollicked with his garish beams, but only crept softly with his quiet, reflected rays. Its dozen houses were all in excellent preservation, but quaint and old-fashioned ; they had an old-time liberality of width, an old-time richness of ornamentation, seen in the elaborate cornices and the grotesque faces carved over the doors and windows, while

the brightly-burnished door-plates, the scrupu-
lously clean steps and walk, the stray glimpses
of rich window draperies seen through jealously-
closed shutters, told of ease and comfort, not to
say of elegance within.

Number Five was, outwardly, in no wise distinguishable from its neighbors — a plain, four-
and-a-half story brick house with a flight of
massive granite steps leading up to a quaintly-
carved old door, painted snowy white, on which
was a polished brass plate bearing the name,
" Madame Velasco."

Who Madame Velasco was, or what the particular mystery — if mystery there were — of
Number Five might be, was evidently no secret
to a stout middle-aged man who turned into
Putney Place and walked rapidly up to the door
one bright afternoon a few days after the fire
described in our opening chapter, — not that the
visit of the stout middle-aged man to Putney
Place has any necessary connection with the
fire, but as the finite mind demands limitations,
and that point of time is already conceived, we
refer to it for our passing convenience.

We have just time to take a rapid note of the
new-comer before the door opens. Dressed in a
fresh suit of black, with fine white linen, care-

fully polished hat and shoes, well-fitting gloves, and a gold-headed walking-stick engraved with the name, " Sydney Dexter," he is an excellent specimen of that class which a truly American newspaper would call " our first citizens;" but we are just coming to the conclusion, nevertheless, that he has an air of high living rather than high breeding, when the door is at length opened by a keen-looking mulatto woman, who answers the note of interrogation in his raised eyebrows by a silent nod, and makes way for him to enter.

" Take that to Mrs. Hoyt, and say that I am pressed for time !" he said, handing his card to the servant.

The woman presently returned with the request that he would walk up-stairs. He went up directly ; proceeded through the upper hall with an air of familiarity, and knocked at the first story front door.

" Come in !" said a feeble voice.

He entered a large, luxuriously-appointed room, of which a woman and a small child were the only occupants. The child was playing with some toys on the floor, and took no notice of the visitor ; the woman, evidently an invalid and still bearing traces of great former beauty, rose from the sofa on which she was reclining to receive him.

"Rebecca" —. "Sydney," the greeting showed that the two were not strangers.

A flush, it would be hard to say whether of pleasure or pain, swept across Rebecca Hoyt's face as she advanced half-eagerly, half-doubtfully, to meet her visitor, who endured rather than responded to her caress. The flush deepened in her cheeks, and a proud look kindled in her eye, as she resumed her seat and drew a soft wrap about her shoulders, pulling it tightly under her folded arms. As she sat thus looking steadily at her visitor, her whole attitude was one of repression.

"Well," exclaimed Mr. Dexter, seating himself in the nearest chair and speaking in a cool, brusque business tone, "I 've come to see what you want."

Sudden tears rushed to the woman's eyes, and it plainly required all her firmness to master her emotion as she replied : —

"Oh, do not, do not assume that tone! If I am nothing to you now ; if things can no longer be what they were ; if your great worldly success has hardened you and rendered you deaf to all the better promptings of your nature — oh, Sydney, remember at least what has been ! We may ignore, but we cannot blot out the past.

3

Remember what you were and what I was, when years ago I came here loving, trusting, — yes," she repeated with a suppressed sob, — "trusting you with my whole heart. I did not count words; I did not measure promises then; I believed in *you*. I thought I knew your heart and I trusted in that; trusted in it with a great faith, and I waited and waited with a great patience till — till " —

She stopped and again controlled herself by a resolute effort.

"But even when all hope was gone I forgave you. Yes, Sydney, and even now I pity you; for it was not you, it was the world's changeling that wronged me — I will not think otherwise; I cannot bear to think that in those early, happy days you were as false, as merciless, as — as — but no, no. Oh God, let me not judge you ! "

"This is the old story," said Mr. Dexter, impatiently, "and if you have brought me here to ring the changes on this, I will spare you the trouble. I have no time for such sentiment. Whatever you did in the past you did with your eyes open. You were a clever woman; you counted the chances and took the risk; so let us have no more penny-romance phrases; it is too late in the day for that ! You are here," he continued, harshly, "because you chose, of your own free will, to be here. I am willing to shoulder my part of the responsibility, and I have done it — and paid the penalty," he muttered aside.

The sick woman, still sitting erect upon the sofa with her arms tightly folded, still steadfastly regarding him, answered now in a proud, firm tone, although the unfallen tears still glittered in her eyes : —

" I *will* spare you such sentiment ; it is indeed too late for it. I pray you forgive this momentary weakness ; it is partly the effect of my physical condition. Forgive me for supposing that you could be any longer susceptible to such appeals ; forgive me for wasting your time in useless remonstrances and idle reminiscences ! I will spare you such allusions in the future. I will spare you everything but the briefest possible statement of my purpose in sending for you."

Her unwonted effort in speaking and the excitement of the interview brought on a violent and protracted fit of coughing, during which Mr. Dexter rose and impatiently paced about the room.

" Look at me," she continued feebly as she lay

upon the sofa, recovering from her exhaustion.
"You are a man of penetration; you have spent
all your life in reading men and forecasting
events. You cannot but see that I am a wreck;
the victim of a lingering and hopeless disease;
that my case is beyond all human help. The
few earthly interests I have left are centered in
my children; it is of their future that I think
with anxiety and foreboding. What lies for *me*
beyond the grave I do not trouble myself about
— it cannot be anything more remorseless than
the judgment of my own kind."

She paused and closed her eyes wearily,.as if
gathering strength to proceed.

"Sydney, my principal object in calling you
here was to claim the fulfillment of a promise
which you have made me so often and so seriously
that I cannot think you will refuse to grant now."

"Promises belong to the time when they were
made. I warn you to ask of me nothing that I
must refuse!" returned Mr. Dexter, nervously.

"I will ask nothing that you must refuse; I
will ask only what you have no right to refuse;
what demands of you no sacrifice, but what is so
dear to me, so necessary to my few remaining
days, that I have subjected myself to the trial of
this interview, to the pain of meeting you again

face to face, to beg of you this last earthly favor
— Sydney, I must see my son !"

Her voice softened as she spoke, and rising
painfully to a sitting posture in her earnestness,
she leaned forward and fixed her eyes eagerly on
her visitor, who, with averted face, gazed out of
the window, presenting only his harsh, inflexible
profile to her appealing look.

"Oh," she continued, in an imploring tone,
"pity a mother's weakness! Let me see my
child! Let me assure myself by the evidence of
my own senses that he is well and happy ! Let
me see him in the bloom of his young manhood,
and know for myself that all my hopes have been
realized ; that he has grown up ignorant of the
stain upon his birth, ignorant of his mother's
shame, proud and happy in the consciousness
of his innocence, proud and happy in the surroundings and advantages of his unclouded life
and future!"

"It cannot be," returned Mr. Dexter impatiently ; "I made the promise in an idle moment,
when wearied by your importunity. It would
hazard everything ; you cannot control yourself.
The boy is shrewd and intelligent ; it could not
be done without arousing his suspicions."

"Oh, do not so hastily, so cruelly deny my

last request! I have lived on this hope; it has
cheered me through sleepless nights and weary,
weary days"—

Interrupted by another severe and painful fit
of coughing, she sank back upon her pillow; but
presently getting her breath she started up
impetuously, crying :—

"I *will* see him. I am his mother. I do not
ask a favor; I demand a right !"

" Hush," cried Mr. Dexter, startled at her
vehemence; "be it so then ! Have your wish !
Jeopardize if you will the boy's happiness !
Indulge your own selfish whim and risk the
betrayal of the secret we have kept for so many
years !"

"It may be selfish," she continued more
quietly, "but I cannot help it; I have not
strength left to struggle against the temptation.
I have looked forward to it too long as the last
earthly solace remaining to me. But I will risk
nothing; I will betray nothing ! He shall never
know by one word, by one look of mine that he
has been brought face to face with his unhappy
mother. He shall go to his grave ignorant of
my person and my fate, and — Oh, dear, dear
boy !"— she cried, with a convulsive sob, "all the
happier for that ignorance."

There was a silence of several minutes, during which Mr. Dexter sat with frowning brow, gazing at the floor.

"It will not do," he said at length ; "I retract my consent. I will not risk it. He stands before the world as my legitimate son and heir ; he is to inherit my name and fortune. He is now well and happy, he has the pride of a gentleman, he has respect and honor for me — I will not risk the loss of all this to gratify a womanish freak!"

As he finished he regarded Mrs. Hoyt with a hard, determined look, as though steeling himself against an expected outbreak of passion. But nothing of the sort occurred. A strange flitting smile played for a moment about her compressed lips, a sudden fire came and went in her eyes, but that was all. Mr. Dexter evidently did not quite understand this behavior ; he watched her curiously.

"I ought not to be surprised," she said quietly, "I ought not to have expected a different result from this appeal to you. Your refusal leaves me now at liberty to take my own course — the consequences must be upon your own head."

"Pooh!" returned Mr. Dexter with affected contempt, but with manifest uneasiness, "if that

is a threat, I despise it! I have been actuated
in my course solely by my anxiety for the boy's
best interests; if you are capable of imperiling
the peace of his whole future life — do it!"

Mr. Dexter rose as if to go.

"One moment," interposed Mrs. Hoyt, without changing her supine position, "this is not all
I have to say; it is not quite all," she added with
a sudden sting of bitterness, "I have to ask of
you — I am encouraged to proceed."

Mr. Dexter turned and regarded her in silence.

"You see that child," she continued, pointing
her wasted hand towards the boy busy with his
play; "I have sent his sister on an errand that
she might be out of the way. What is to become
of them when I am gone?"

"That," returned Mr. Dexter, with a coarse
attempt at a jest, "is one of those dark riddles
of Fate that I invariably give up!"

Perhaps it was Mrs. Hoyt's involuntary look
of disgust at this ill-timed pleasantry, that led
him immediately to add half-sneeringly, —

"You are not gone yet ; it will be time enough
to consider that question when you are!"

"No," returned Mrs. Hoyt, firmly, "it will not.
I must see to it *now*, while I have strength and
intelligence left. I must have some guaranty for
their welfare!"

"Why do you consult me about it?"

"Consult you about it?" she repeated, rising upon her arm and regarding the questioner with a bewildered air.

"Yes, why do you single *me* out? Why don't you consult some of your other kind gentleman-friends?" asked the man, coolly.

"I — do — not — understand — you! — Consult *you?* — Single *you* out?" she repeated, breathlessly, as she rose from the sofa and stood trembling before her visitor. "Explain yourself!" she cried with a wild, scared, yet imperative note in her voice.

"You don't propose to try and convince me that I am responsible for these two also, I hope?" returned Mr. Dexter with a look of hardened effrontery.

Every vestige of color faded from the wretched woman's face. White as marble and well-nigh as rigid, she stood for a moment stunned and speechless. Then clutching a supporting chair she advanced a step forward and bending towards him said with blazing eyes and a voice so husky as to be almost inarticulate : —

"May God forgive you for this cruel, cowardly insult!"

Pausing for breath she regarded him with a

look before which even the stolid world-hardened
man visibly quailed. "Is it for *you*," she continued in a tone of terrible contempt, "for you
that I have endured this life of shame! To such
an one as you that I have been as true as any
wedded wife in all the land! For you that I
have forfeited peace, honor, respect, home,
friends — all — all that makes life worth having!
You that I have loved and trusted ; you that I
have honored and believed all these dreadful
years! And with your blood have these innocent
children inherited also your nature! — I should
hate them if I thought it. Hate them as I shall
hate you from this moment. Go!" she cried
with increasing vehemence, as her voice sank to
a hoarse whisper, "I would rather turn them
naked into the streets, dependent alone upon the
mercy of a pitying God, than trust them to your
care. Go!" she repeated, extending towards
him her trembling, emaciated hands with a look
of indescribable aversion ; "*you — are — LOATH-
SOME to me!*"

Her strength sufficed but for the last word ;
she tottered backward and fell senseless to the
floor, while a dark stream of blood issued from
her mouth and nose.

Mr. Dexter started forward with a look of

alarm, raised her unconscious form, and called aloud for help.

Help was at hand; the door opened almost immediately. Mr. Dexter felt himself pushed roughly from behind, while a sharp, imperative voice called :—

"Go away, stupid!"

He turned and beheld a deformed child with a shrewd, impish face, who with wonderful dexterity sprang to the sofa, got a pillow, and placed it under the sufferer's head, pushing him unceremoniously aside as she cried : —

"*You've* done it ; you've *done* it, you have!"

"Is she dead, Zilp?" asked Mr. Dexter, in a shocked tone.

"If she is, you've killed her!" returned the impish child, as she busily stanched the flowing blood with a handkerchief. "But she ain't dead this time — good enough for you if she was!"

"Where's the nearest doctor?"

"Don't want any nearest nor any furtherest doctor. Madame's doctor enough, good as any of 'em, an' *I* guess a pertickler good sight better. She's got a hem'rage ; that's what she's got ; she's had 'em afore an' she'll git over it, but she won't git over a great many more."

"What can I do to help you, Zilp?"

"You can clear out, that's the best thing *you* can do!" replied the uncompromising hunchback.

"Here!" exclaimed the conscience-stricken man, taking a bank-note from his pocket and laying it on the table, "get medical assistance if necessary, and see that she has everything she wants — you can keep a dollar for yourself."

"'A dollar for yourself,'" repeated the wrathful Zilp in a mocking tone, leaving her charge and running to the head of the stairs. "*My* tongue is not for sale. Sh — Bah! — Take your old money!" she cried with a hiss of contempt, flinging the bank-note after the donor down the stairs.

CHAPTER IV.

WINDMERE.

MRS. DIGHTON ordered her carriage, made an effective toilet, and started out on a round of calls. Like everybody else, who moves much in society, Mrs. Dighton had a long list of calls to be made ; like everybody else she scolded about the bore of making them ; but whether from native talent or long experience, it was generally conceded among her friends that Mrs. Dighton was an accomplished caller. She had a very fresh way of saying common things; she had a well-modulated voice, a cheerful manner, an excellent judgment, a sympathetic atmosphere, while above and beyond all, she knew the happy secret of tearing herself away at the most inter- esting moment, when she had told some neat story, made some happy jest, shed some kindly tear, or in some way made herself valued. This last detail of her method we offer as a valuable suggestion to all those who, without natural gifts of mind or person, aspire to shine in the social arena, whispering the added hint that sympathy avails more than wit, and that a good listener is by so much rarer than a good talker, as he is a creature of exceptional organization, who, without wag of tongue, can often say better things than the veriest gabbler of them all ; who can criticise, suggest, applaud, disapprove by the exquisite play of look and gesture.

But, however much Mrs. Dighton scolded about the trouble, as she always came home from these visiting expeditions with some amusing experiences and a fresh store of gossip, it had long been confidentially understood in her family, that she took a certain delight in the business. But if Dorothy or her uncle found anything pecu- liar in the fact that Mrs. Dighton, in this in- stance, followed up her calling day after day for an entire fortnight, they refrained from remark, and were only too glad to have the attention of their busy little mentor, for the moment, diverted from themselves.

One evening, however, it all came out. Mrs. Dighton took her seat at the tea-table in unusual spirits ; there was a little air of conscious triumph in the pose of her head, and an unnecessary matronly patronage in her tone to Dorothy. She was, however, far too adroit to reveal, at once, the cause of her elation. It only appeared after a while, and in the most graceful by-the-way: Mr. Curley was describing a painting he had picked up at auction.

"By whom was it painted, Samuel?"

"Don't know; some unknown."

"Oh, Dorothy, dear, that reminds me of our 'Unknown.' I had nearly forgotten to tell you. I have found him out."

"I expected you would," returned Dorothy, dryly.

"How so?"

"You always do when you start on a regular crusade."

"Crusade?" repeated Mrs. Dighton, with a little flush of mortification.

"There, there, Rhody dear," cried Dorothy, with a merry laugh, caressing one of her mother's hands as she spoke; "don't waste that air of innocence on me! You comical little creature, don't you suppose I know your dark and secret ways yet, and that you never take the war path so deadly in earnest unless there is a scalp to be had?"

"Dorothy, you are getting into a fairly dreadful way of talking," returned Mrs. Dighton, cleverly disguising her vexation at being found out under cover of a timely rebuke; "it is so extremely unladylike; so like a man — but, to come back to Mr. Dexter, I was calling at Mrs. L's,— you know what an enthusiastic creature she is,— and happening, incidentally in connection with the fire, to mention Mr. Dexter's name, [Demure Mrs. Dighton, she omits to say that during the whole fortnight she had been happening incidentally to mention Mr. Dexter's name, to give her friends an opportunity to say what they knew of him] she cried out at once : 'What, Ralph Dexter?' 'Yes,' I said. 'Oh,' said Mrs. L——, 'he is a very fine fellow and a ravishing dancer.'"

"I thought as much," said Dorothy, contemptuously, as she buttered a piece of toast. "Away goes the romance with the mystery, and I haven't a doubt all the heroes in poetry and history would share the same fate, if the daylight were let in upon them."

"I learned," pursued Mrs. Dighton, "that he is the son of Mr. Sydney Dexter, and one of the beaux of the town. And pray who is Mr. Sydney Dexter, Samuel?"

"A well-known millionaire, but otherwise, I believe, a respectable man," said Mr. Curley, waggishly.

"A beau and a ravishing dancer," repeated
Dorothy. "Think of being rescued by such a
dainty creature!"

"*You* would, no doubt, have been better
pleased, my dear, if he had been big and rough,
with long hair and the brawn of a Hercules."

Mrs. Dighton's judicious little lash of satire
had its effect, and Dorothy reddened as she
replied :—

"I should have been better pleased if he had
not assumed a grand air of Spartan insensibility
when, of ·course, his knees were knocking together with fright all the time."

"If he felt any fear he certainly controlled it
very effectively, and we have every reason to
think him a young man of spirit and character."

"I don't see that he could have acted any
differently."

"I don't know, my dear," returned Mrs. Dighton, shrewdly, "we saw a good many men that
night, who behaved very differently."

"I see you are bound to champion him, Rhody,
so have your own way — we wash our hands of
him, don't we, Uncle Curl? We are going to
decorate the drawing-room."

Two or three months after the above conver-

4

sation, Mr. Curley suddenly took it into his head
that he wanted a seaside home, and although
Mrs. Dighton suspected it was only in order to
give his hobby free rein in fresh fields, she and
Dorothy were both too fond of the sea to object.

In one of their house-hunting excursions to the
suburbs, they visited, one day — under the guid-
ance of the most voluble and energetic of real
estate agents — the little town of Windmere.
Taking a carriage at the station, a ride of two
miles brought them to the place they were in
search of. The beauty of the grounds drew an
involuntary cry of admiration from the whole
party as they turned into the fine avenue leading
to the house. Nature here had certainly been
lavish of her charms, and Art had wisely with-
held her hand. The house was situated near the
water and commanded a fine sea-view, with which
our party was so taken up that they failed to
notice the house itself, until they found themselves alighted and walking up and down the
broad piazza. Before the agent could ring, however, they saw a young man advancing—evidently
to meet them,—from the shrubbery that flanked
a large flower-garden on one side of the house.
As he leisurely approached them along the winding path, the ladies apparently busied themselves

with the scenery in the opposite direction, but
we are very much mistaken if either of them
could not have told you, without the slightest
hesitation, that he was dressed in a yachting suit
of navy blue, a pair of canvas shoes, and a rough
straw hat; that his skin was very much sun-
burned; that he was unmistakably a gentleman,
and that he was smoking a cigar, — and all this
without seemingly taking their eyes off the
distant sea, or ceasing a moment to discuss the
points of the view.

It was only when the young gentleman threw
away his cigar and began to mount the steps,
that Mrs. Dighton suddenly clutched Dorothy
and exclaimed : —

"Why, can it be ?—it looks like " —

"Who?" asked Dorothy, in the greatest astonishment.

" How do you do, Mr. Dexter?" said Mrs.
Dighton, advancing, " I thought I could not be
mistaken, allow me to introduce myself: I am
Mrs. Dighton, this is my daughter, Miss Dighton,
and this my brother, Mr. Curley."

Mr. Dexter politely took Mrs. Dighton's proffered hand, and welcomed the others with an
easy salute, but the puzzled look in his eyes
showed that he did not know, in the least, who

they were. A flush of vexation passed over Dorothy's face, as her mother proceeded to explain : —

"You wonder, of course, how I knew your name; and have forgotten, I dare say, that it was written in the corner of your pocket handkerchief."

Mrs. Dighton in a traveling dress in the open daylight, and Mrs. Dighton in opera attire under a softening gaslight were, doubtless, two very different looking people, but Mr. Dexter must be accused of a little obtuseness in still failing to recognize her.

"Mamma, you had better explain to Mr. Dexter that we have only met him once before, and that under circumstances which naturally gave him little opportunity to remark our personal appearance."

The moment Dorothy began to speak, Mr. Dexter looked up quickly, and a gleam of recognition shone in his eyes.

"Oh, the fire, to be sure — I beg pardon — I have been very stupid."

And pulling off his hat directly he shook hands with Mrs. Dighton again, and then with Dorothy in the heartiest manner.

"We have been waiting all this time to thank

you," continued Mrs. Dighton, "and I must call you to account for running away without leaving your name."

"Yes," returned the young gentleman, smiling, with a little look of confusion, "yes, I fear I — I behaved rather boorishly in that matter. I should, at least, have gone back the next day to inquire after you."

"We were very much mortified to have you go away without a word of acknowledgment or an offer of hospitality, but I was in such a state, and my daughter was so taken up with me, that there seemed to be nobody with their wits about them."

"Besides which, mamma has really been harrowed to think you might never get your handkerchief," said Dorothy, demurely.

"Why, the handkerchief was, of course, an important memento to me, for it brought me out of a swoon, and afterwards furnished me your name; but, do not let me lose the opportunity, now that it has come, to express my thanks, our thanks, Mr. Dexter, for your very generous services to us that dreadful night; in fact, for saving our lives, for though the building did not burn down, we should have been stifled to death by the smoke, I am sure, if we had stayed inside."

Mr. Dexter merely bowed his acknowledgments, while Dorothy, with a glance at her uncle and at the agent, who were talking at the other end of the piazza, said :—

"And now, mamma, perhaps it may be as well to tell Mr. Dexter that this visit is on business."

"Precisely my idea, Miss Dighton, business first and then whatever you like," said the agent, bustling up. "I've brought the party down to see the place; glad you're here, Mr. Dexter, you can go around with us and answer any questions that I can't. I guess we'll go over the house first — but look here, just look here, ma'am, at the view from this end of the piazza! Now, I call this unparalleled; don't b'lieve it can be beat in the country ; then you see you're sheltered from the north east; them woods cut off the winds. Why, you could live here the year round if you took the notion."

The agent now led the way into the house, followed by Mr. Curley. Dorothy remained leaning on the balustrade.

"Aren't you going with us?" asked her mother.

"No; I can trust your judgment; I will stay and enjoy the sea."

Mr. Dexter, upon hearing this, politely brought
a large willow chair and placed it for her convenience, and was proceeding to point out various interesting features in the view, when he
was summoned to give some information by the
busy agent.

Dorothy settled herself in the chair, and gave
herself up to the enjoyment of the scene. She
had been sitting thus but a few minutes when a
crunching sound was heard upon the gravel, and
looking up she saw a large Irish deer-hound
come slowly up the steps of the piazza, and,
after inspecting her a moment, lay himself down
on the rug at the top. After a passing glance at
the dog, Dorothy turned again to the beautiful
panorama before her, and was soon lost in rev-
erie, watching the white-winged ships glide
hither and thither in the distance, until at length,
as one passed out of her field of vision behind
the opposite corner of the house, a sudden fancy
prompted her to go to the other end of the
piazza and follow its course. Rising, she was
proceeding lazily to carry out her intent, when
she was stopped by a low growl from the apparently sleeping dog. Hesitating a moment, she
bestowed upon him a few flattering and reassuring words as an earnest of the innocence of her

intent, and again attempted to proceed, when another deeper and more significant growl brought her to a stand-still.

Accustomed to have her own way, Dorothy did not at all relish this interruption. She regarded the Cerberus a minute with an air of vexation, as if measuring his firmness of purpose. He lay motionless, his eyes half closed, so secure of his strength and position that he did not even deign to cast a sidelong look upon his prisoner.

The lazy impulse which had moved Dorothy at first to change her position, had now, under this unexpected obstacle, grown to an irresistible desire. She chafed at the temporary constraint all the more that it was quite unreasonable, and that remonstrance was unavailing. Recognizing the futility of wrath, however, she controlled her temper and resorted to cajolery. She approached her canine keeper with honeyed words, she flattered him, petted him, and tendered him coaxing endearments — all, however, at a respectful distance. It is doubtful if it be in human power to exhibit a more superb disdain of a weak artifice than did this majestic brute.

Casting about now for some new resource, Dorothy's eye fell upon her mother's lunch-basket, and she immediately resolved to try the more insidious overture of bribery. Taking some sandwiches from the basket she abstracted the meat, and offered it with a confident air to the dog. Again she had counted without her host. To her chagrin he only looked contempt-uously at her offering, which she had cast down before his very nose. She next produced some delicate bits of cake, but all in vain ; her various offerings lay strewn unnoticed about the floor, while he kept his steadfast eyes fixed on the distant sea.

Once more trusting to her combined blandish-ments or his forgetfulness, Dorothy tried to pass, when again a positive and threatening growl de-tained her. Her respect for the dog evidently rose with her indignation ; she now condescend-ed to employ remonstrance and satire.

"Go away, you horrid dog ! Go away, I say !" she cried, stamping imperiously upon the floor. "Shame, shame on you to growl at a woman ! Clear out ! Shoo !"

The April wind that lightly stirred the loose hairs on his shaggy coat did not less affect her canine keeper than these unsanctioned words. Indeed, if canine dignity were not far superior to human, he would have laughed in derision.

"This is too absurd — to be kept prisoner by

a dog!" exclaimed Dorothy, in exasperation, as she walked up and down in the limited space allowed her, bestowing futile abuse upon her imperturbable keeper as she passed.

"We will see," she at length exclaimed, as a sudden thought struck her, "if my wits are not a match for brute force!" and quickly approaching the end of the piazza on her own side, she climbed over the balustrade, with the intention of escaping into the garden, but she found herself at the height of seven or eight feet from the ground — a jump which she hesitated to take. It was well she did; the dog looked up, and, seeing her escaping over the fence, came bounding forward, and with one leap cleared the balustrade and landed below in the garden. Dorothy had evaded his onset by darting behind one of the pillars by which the piazza was supported. She instantly sprang back over the balustrade, and now, terribly frightened, ran, with all speed, for the hall door, which she reached just as the furious hound — having run around by the garden path — came tearing up the front steps, growling savagely. At that very moment the door opened and Dorothy flung herself into the arms of Ralph Dexter, who was coming to look for her.

"What!" cried Ralph, in a voice of thunder, as he faced the maddened animal.

The dog stopped as though transfixed. In an instant Dorothy, who, even in her fright, had not forgotten her wrath, recovered herself, seized a small cane from a stand in the hall, boldly turned about, and laid it smartly across the back and head of the now infuriated brute. The dog could not so far restrain himself as not to growl defiantly at this treatment; whereupon Ralph, in a towering temper, seized the cane, and was about to chastise him into submission, when Dorothy quickly threw herself between them, crying :—

"No, no, Mr. Dexter, do not!"

The ringing urgent tone stayed Ralph's uplifted arm.

"I beg it as a special favor, Mr. Dexter!"

Ralph dropped the cane and contented himself with uttering an expression of withering contempt which, strange to say, had more effect upon the dog than the blows; he crouched and crawled on the floor, fawned upon his master, and licked his feet in abject submission.

"Go!" cried Ralph in the same tone.

The dog turned with drooped tail and ears and was slinking away, when Dorothy again interfered.

"Oh, do forgive him!—After all, he thought he was doing his duty. Come, come here!" she cried, running to the disgraced animal, seizing him by the collar and dragging him towards his master.

"Please forgive him!" repeated Dorothy, impetuously; "he didn't molest me until I tried to run away. How did he know but I was a thief? Speak to him!"

"Well, sir," said Ralph, smiling in spite of himself at Dorothy's unconscious enthusiasm, "you must learn the difference between thieves and lady visitors!"

The dog pricked up somewhat at this change of tone, but still looked doubtfully at his master.

"Give him your hand," continued Dorothy, "see, he is still in doubt!"

Ralph put out his hand to caress the dog's head, when the latter jumped all over and about him with the most extravagant expressions of delight.

"Stay, sir; you have still a piece of humble pie to eat!" cried Dorothy, as she ran and gathered up her contemned fragments of meat, which the now subjugated beast obligingly ate from her hand.

"And what have you been doing all this time?" asked Mrs. Dighton, now appearing.

"Playing with the dog!" answered Dorothy, with a warning look at Ralph. "Have you been over the house already?"

"Oh no; only the lower floors."

"Very well, I will go up stairs with you and pick out my own room."

The whole party now went up stairs together, where Ralph led the way first to his own rooms to point out a favorite view from one of the windows. As he was busily engaged showing it to Dorothy and Mr. Curley, they were all startled by a cry of horror from Mrs. Dighton, which was presently explained by the fact that the busy agent, in opening a closet door, had suddenly disclosed a complete human skeleton dangling from a peg. Ralph hastened to explain that having at one time intended to study medicine, his father had procured for him this skeleton.

"It is the only specimen of the kind we have, Mrs. Dighton, and I recommend it to you as a preventive to hang a real skeleton in your closet, it keeps away all the ugly imaginary ones."

Dorothy turned from the window in time to catch his expression — so proud and happy and confident — as he uttered these words, and the scene often recurred to her in the light of after events.

After luncheon, as there was still time to spare, Mr. Dexter proposed a little sail in his yacht. Mrs. Dighton and Dorothy gladly accepted the offer, and the agent highly commended what he thought a fine stroke of policy on the part of Ralph. They accordingly all presently embarked save Mr. Curley, who declined on the ground that he was no sailor, and should very likely be seasick.

"Seasick," repeated the agent, looking compassionately back at Mr. Curley, who was waving them off from the landing, "there ain't any more danger of seasickness here than in a duck-pond!"

Fortified by a hearty luncheon, and by the prospect of making a commission, the agent was in the best of moods. "Now," he continued, "if there's one thing more than another I particularly like, it's a taste of the sea. To be able to step right down from your own piazza aboard your yacht, seems to me the finest thing in life."

"But why do you sell such a beautiful place, Mr. Dexter?" asked Dorothy.

"Why, because the sea air does not agree with my mother; it is too far from the city for my father, and it is too large to be used simply as my shooting box."

Ralph now crowded on all sail, and they were

soon flying before a stiff breeze. Indeed, the breeze soon proved fresher than they expected, and the sea became decidedly choppy. The agent was observed to throw away his cigar, and gradually become very silent.

He presently dropped one or two hints about "not going out too far," and being "careful not to lose that train;" but Ralph and Mrs. Dighton were talking, Dorothy was singing, so nobody took any notice of what he said until he suddenly recollected there were several points he wanted to talk over with Mr. Curley, and insisted upon being put ashore at once.

Ralph accordingly had no alternative but to put about, run in, and send him ashore in a dory.

"Never enjoyed anything so much in my life," he exclaimed as he rose to go. His face, however, when he turned to bid them good-by did not bear out this statement, being almost livid in hue, and contorted with a look of nausea mingled with a vanishing expression of fear. In his hurry to reach the boat he jumped too soon, a big wave intervened, and the unfortunate man went souse into the water. He came instantly to the surface, and with a look of frenzy seized the edge of the boat, into which he was presently hoisted by a stout serving man, to whom Ralph ered.

shouted directions to take him ashore and give him dry clothes.

They watched him anxiously until he landed, when Dorothy, turning her head, happened to catch Ralph's eye, and with one accord they burst into irresistible laughter, in which Mrs. Dighton presently joined.

" Our acquaintance has gone through its tragedy and comedy period, Mr. Dexter," said Dorothy, wiping her eyes, " what comes next ? "

An hour afterwards, on taking leave, Mrs. Dighton's satisfaction equaled Ralph's perplexity at Dorothy's parting remark as she stepped into the carriage : —

" I have become almost reconciled to you to-day, Mr. Dexter."

CHAPTER V.

REBECCA.

UNCONSCIOUS Mr. Dexter was walking on the brink of a precipice. And so perhaps are some whose firm hands now hold these pages, and whose secure hearts seem fortified in peace. "Whom do we mean?" We mean you who are to be crushed and mangled in the next railway collision! You who are to be blown up by the next steamboat disaster! You who are to be cut down by the next midnight assassin! You who are to be drowned in your next seaside vacation!

We mean you — honest, upright young man — who are going, next week, to yield to a diabolical temptation! You, sleek, hoary trustee, whose name on the back of a note makes it as good as gold ; who sit in the best pew in church, yet who are going to be exposed, to-morrow, for years of peculation and embezzlement! We mean you, public officer, who are soon to be

5

found guilty of venality and corruption! You are all walking on the brinks of precipices!

And which of us is not? Do not our daily walks lead us along the crumbling verge of frightful abysses? In what has a merciful Providence been more merciful than in withholding the prescience which would make cowards and madmen of us all; which would make the expected pin-prick of to-morrow offset the best joy of to-day!

Mr. Dexter left his stately home, stepped into his carriage, and drove away to his office, the same well-gloved, well-shod, well-appareled person we have been lately introduced to, so little dreaming of any harm that, as he crossed his strong hands upon his gold-headed cane and leaned back in his seat, he presented as fair a picture as could well be found of human confidence and satisfaction.

And well it was for Mr. Dexter's peace of mind that he could not see a certain other carriage stop at his own door, an hour after he had left it; that he could not see a pale, sick woman get out of that carriage and painfully climb the broad stone steps — for not for all the money to be made that day; not for any earthly consideration save the loss of power and fortune, would he have had her enter the door that opened to her.

Nevertheless she does enter ; enters and asks for Mrs. Dexter, to whom she sends up a card bearing the name : " Rebecca Hoyt."

The servant presently returns and says Mrs. Dexter begs to be excused, and asks Mrs. Hoyt to please state her business.

" Say I *must* see her ! " said Rebecca to the servant, " but stay ! "

Taking a card from her case she hurriedly wrote these few words : —

" My business is of a private nature and important. I cannot state it on paper ; I must see you. If necessary I will wait."

The servant returned directly and conducted her up-stairs into the drawing-room, where presently Mrs. Dexter appeared — a large, middle-aged woman, severely-dressed, with a cold formal manner. She bowed and seated herself with an expectant air.

Rebecca regarded her rival so long and curiously without speaking, that the latter at length said : —

" You wish to see me ? "

" Yes."

" ' On business of a private nature ? ' " repeated Mrs. Dexter, consulting the card in her hand.

"Yes."

"Your name is strange to me ; have you not made a mistake? I am Mrs. *Sydney* Dexter."

"It is with Mrs. *Sydney* Dexter I would speak," returned Rebecca, calmly.

"I am at your service," said Mrs. Dexter, after waiting another long interval.

"Yes — yes — excuse me, I am ill; I am weary with my ride, and " —

"Take your time, Madam."

"Mrs. Dexter," began Rebecca, in a tired and broken voice, but with her eyes fixed steadily upon that lady's face, "the revelation I am about to make to you is of a very painful nature; you may possibly not believe it; you may possibly be angry; you certainly will be pained and shocked!"

"I may be pained and shocked, but I can scarcely be angry at anything an entire stranger can have to communicate."

"Would to Heaven I might have remained an entire stranger to you! Would to Heaven I had never been driven to take this step — driven to it by the cruelty and perfidy of one who is only too well known to you!" exclaimed Rebecca, with sudden vehemence.

"'Known to me?'" repeated Mrs. Dexter, in surprise.

A bright hectic spot burned in the sick woman's cheeks, and her hands trembled with excitement as she leaned back in her chair and shut her eyes, as if gathering strength to go on.

"I behold you here, Madam," she continued presently, in a gentler tone, "surrounded by luxury, strong in health, secure—as you fondly suppose yourself—from dishonor or disgrace. Secure in the love of your friends, in the fidelity of your husband; happy in your home—home," she repeated with a bitter emphasis, "I too used to know the meaning of that word,—years and years ago—as a place where there is safety and innocence, and purity and love, but what can it matter? That word and all other human words and things will soon lose significance to me!"

"Your strange talks and still stranger manner, Madam, convince me"—

"Patience, patience; I will be brief; I will not detain you long. What I have to say, Mrs. Dexter, concerns a person very near and very dear to you, a person once — alas for my peace and happiness!—very near and dear to me; but whom I now"— she paused and quelled the growing vehemence of look and tone — "NOW," she repeated, leaning forward in her chair and speaking in a tone of repression that was more terrible than the wildest outburst, "I hate with all the strength of heart and will I have left; whom God may forgive, but whom I never can!"

"Again I say," began Mrs. Dexter, "you are mistaken! It is impossible"—

"He has blighted my life," pursued Rebecca, unheeding the interruption, "he has ruined my peace; he has robbed me of all worth loving or living for; he has deceived and betrayed, and now scorns and contemns me!"

"You are wandering; you are not in your right mind, my good woman! No one near to me can have so injured you!"

"*Can* have," repeated Rebecca, bitterly, "Your life is half spent, Madam, and are you still so confident?"

"I am."

"*I* was once, — *when I was a child.*"

"But"—

"Yes, yes, I know what you would say, but if I pause, it is that I grieve to afflict you; if I hesitate, it is that I would not disturb your peace."

"I will relieve you of all responsibility on that score," said Mrs. Dexter, proudly.

"But why should I hesitate!" exclaimed Rebecca, impetuously. "Why should I spare your feelings! Why should you not know something of the misery that has desolated my life! Proud woman, the person whom I mean is — is " —

Looking beyond Mrs. Dexter, and immediately over her head, Rebecca's eye fell upon a portrait on the wall. Breathless she gazed at it — that well-known face ; that face as she remembered it in years gone by, now looking down upon her with reproachful eyes.

" Speak ! "

The sick woman's pale lips trembled, her purpose faltered, her voice sank to an almost inaudible pitch as she replied : —

" A member of your household."

" It is false ! "

" You do not believe *me*, Madam," returned Rebecca, quickly, stung by this haughty answer, " but *here*," she cried, drawing from her pocket a package of letters, " is something that you *must* believe ! "

" I will not condescend to listen to any proof in support of such an accusation ! " said Mrs. Dexter, rising and advancing towards the bell.

" Stay ! " cried Rebecca, anticipating her purpose. " What I have to say must be said to you alone ! "

" I choose to have a witness," returned Mrs.

Dexter, ringing the bell vigorously, "the only person of my family to whom you can possibly refer is now, fortunately, in the house, to refute this odious charge."

The shock of this unexpected intelligence seemed for a moment to overcome Rebecca, but directly recovering her presence of mind, she said: "I beseech you, Madam, not to summon him. I have already appealed to him; appealed to him in vain. I come now to appeal to you, to throw myself upon your mercy, to beg of your charity and magnanimity a boon which he has refused."

"I can only listen to such an appeal when I have satisfied myself that you have any claims upon me."

"Then I have come in vain, for I have none!"

A servant here appeared in the doorway.

"Ask Mr. Dexter to come to the drawing-room for a moment!" said Mrs. Dexter.

"Be it so," continued Rebecca, firmly, "I will confront that false man; I will overcome him with the evidences of his guilt in your presence — in the presence of one whom, next to me, he has most injured in the world. He shall see that I cannot be contemned with impunity."

At this moment a firm, quick step was heard

in the hall, and directly after Ralph entered the room.

Rebecca turned deadly pale and half rose from her seat at sight of him, then slowly sinking back she seized the arms of her chair with convulsive clutch and regarded him with breathless suspense.

A silence fell upon the whole circle at Ralph's entrance, each waiting for the other to speak. Mrs. Dexter, turning suspiciously from the painful, breathless intensity of the mother's face to the innocent inquiry of the son's, asked in a hard, cold tone : — "

" Do you know this person ? "

Ralph shook his head without speaking, as he gazed composedly but curiously at the stranger.

" Did you ever see her before ? "

" Never to my knowledge ! "

At these words the agonized mother rose suddenly to her feet, her lips moved convulsively without emitting a sound, she stretched her hand out with an imploring gesture, took a step or two forward towards her wondering son, and, staggering, fell heavily to the floor before he could interpose.

Ralph sprang instantly and lifted her to a sofa, but fortunately she did not lose consciousness, and soon recovered strength to rise and put on her bonnet and cloak, which had been removed.

Turning to Mrs. Dexter, who now regarded her with the greatest curiosity and interest, puzzled to reconcile her genuine agitation with the unembarrassed innocence of Ralph's demeanor, she said calmly : —

"He is right; he does not know me ; I have made a mistake. Forgive me! I have caused you much anxiety and alarm, but I am ill, and, as you suspect, not quite in my right mind. I will go now. I will not trouble you longer, my carriage is waiting."

Ralph stepped forward and offered his arm. She leaned upon him for a moment, but trembled so violently that, putting him gently away, she cried : —

"No, no. I cannot bear it. — I beg your pardon. I can walk by myself. Good morning. Good — good-bye!" Turning as she reached the door, she stretched forth her hand towards Ralph with a gesture of inexpressible tenderness, and cried : —

"May God bless you — both," she added, with a sudden look at Mrs. Dexter, as she passed out of the room.

CHAPTER VI.

A LOST child, with disheveled curls and a scared look in his big brown eyes, went wandering down University Place. The bleak north-east wind had blown away his hat; some rough boys had stolen his hoop, of which he still held the stick clenched fast in his dimpled hand; the hurly-burly of the street and the passing crowd increased his bewilderment as he went straying on, farther and farther from home at every step, striving manfully to choke down the sobs with which his little throat was big.

Day was waning fast; with the approach of night his hope and courage at length gave way, and he began to cry piteously.

A lost child is a pathetic, but, in a great city, by no means an unusual spectacle. Such a picture of innocence, helplessness, and grief should, however, one would think, move the coldest heart. Unfortunately, the average citizen does not wear his heart upon his sleeve for daws to peck at; indeed, in the adult, that susceptible organ becomes so indurated by the constant contemplation of misery in every guise, that the ordinary, busy, well-to-do citizen is about as compassionate as a marble image or a tiger in a jungle. Not but that at home, before the blaze of his own hearth fire, when he has eaten his dinner and got on his slippers, he may blossom out into an exemplary Christian, a really humane man, an excellent neighbor, and a very good sort of fellow. The point we make is, that there seems really no time for emotional distractions between nine o'clock A. M. and six o'clock P. M.

All of which we offer for what it is worth to explain the fact that our stray little waif went crying along, block after block, amidst a street full of homeward-hurrying men, without receiving so much as a passing word. Half of those who saw him knew that the twenty minutes spent in taking him to the nearest station-house would make the difference between a hot and a cold dinner, and the other half comforted themselves, doubtless, with the thought that he would infallibly be found sooner or later by the police.

At length, obstructed by the crowd, the child stopped on a corner close to a street-vender's stand, where the brightly-lighted booth, with its attractive wares, for a moment diverted his thoughts from his own 'misery. The vendor, busily engaged in his traffic, did not notice his little neighbor until the latter, realizing his situation, burst again into tears, when turning about at once, the noisy chapman cried in astonishment : —

" Heigho, young one, where did *you* rain down from ? "

The peddler, who was a large fat man, had something the matter with his legs and stood supported upon crutches, which misfortune, however, seemed not in the least to affect his spirits, as was evidenced by a face fairly brimming over with good nature and the humorous effrontery belonging to his craft. Moreover, such seemed his insatiable thirst for melody that he framed most of his cries into jingling rhymes, with a dexterity due as much, doubtless, to long practice as to native aptitude. This being one of his busiest hours of the day, he interrupted his hawking cries only long enough to throw a chance word of comfort to the child, in a way at once comical and bewildering : —

" Hello, there, what 's to pay ? Cheer up, my little man !

"Evening papers, evening papers,
    Good to read and good for tapers;
    Herald, *Tribune*, *Times*, and *Sun*,
    Here's your papers, every one!

"What, crying still, Commodore! Lost your
way, eh? Oh, never mind; we'll fix you; just
wait!

"Want a paper — *Post*, you say?
        Here you are, sir, right away!

    "What, youngster, crying still?—tut, tut,
        Come, sit up here and have a nut!"

Finding the child inconsolable, the peddler
stopped a moment, lifted him up to a seat in a
little cubby hole beneath an awning, dried his
swollen eyes, and gave him a handful of warm
peanuts.

Here, eating his nuts, astonished and interested by the variety of catch-penny wares about
him, comforted, moreover, by the assurance that
he had, at length, found a friend, the little wan-
derer forgot his grief, while the busy peddler
ran on :—

"Here you are now, gents and ladies,
    Here's where your chance to make a trade is;
    He who always would be seen
    Wise and wealthy, sweet and clean,
        Must hither rush
        And buy a brush.

"There's a man for you; eat your nuts! —

Fresh peanuts, ladies and gentlemen! fresh roasted every minute, upon the faith and honor of a gentleman and a soldier."

"What you got here, True?" asked a policeman, coming up and regarding with idle curiosity the fair child stowed away at the back of the booth.

"Ah, Leftenant, how d'ye do? That?—why, that's a youngster I'm taking care of for his mother.

> "Oh, sweet and mild
> Is lovely child!

"Eh, Leftenant? Try them!" exclaimed the peddler, holding out a handful of peanuts.

"What's the little chap been crying about?" asked the policeman, taking the nuts.

"Pretty hard to say, I guess, Leftenant. Young ones cry as ducks swim, 'cos it's natural, you know—

> "You may break, you may ruin
> The child as you will,
> The scent of the cradle
> Will hang round him still.

"Anything doin' down to the City Hall?

> "Here's your papers, ladies, gents;
> The latest news for just five cents!

"Cold night, Leftenant,—help yourself!

"Here 's your patent coal-ash sifter,
Here 's your combination lifter !"

"No shenanigan about that boy, True, I hope?" said the policeman, as he turned to move off, munching his nuts.

"Shenanigan, Leftenant? What do you take me for?—

"Keep on the square,
Do all things fair.

"That 's me, Leftenant; good night; call again!

"Papers, papers! here you are,
Latest from the seat of war.
Fall in stocks an' rise in gold,
Peanuts hot and papers cold!

"Hello, youngster, at it again? There, I wouldn't, for we 're going home to the old hearthstone, *we* are, we 're going straight home to mamma — but where does mamma live, my covey?"

"I do-o-o-n't know," sobbed the child. "Oh I *do* want to go home."

"And so you shall ; one, two, three, and away we go. But now, let me see ; what 's your name?"

"It 's Baby."

"Baby? Baby what?"

"Baby Hoyt."

"Is that all? Isn't it Billie Hoyt, or Georgie Hoyt, or Tommy Hoyt?"

" No-o-o, it's Baby!"

"Of course, of course, it's Baby, but think now, isn't it Sammy, too?"

" No-o-o!"

"Or Jimmie, or Johnnie, or Freddie?"

As the child still shook his head, the peddler forbore teasing him with further questions, but wiping his eyes and wrapping him in a spare coat, put him down upon the walk. Then, after packing up for the night, the peddler proceeded to the nearest drug-shop, where he got a directory and repeated the addresses of the various Hoyts, to the anxious Baby : —

" Louis — Lemuel — Lorenzo " —

Baby shook his head.

" Marcus, Melvin, Orville, Peter, Patrick, Reuben, Rebecca " —

" Oh, that's it!"

" Rebecca, — Putney Place?"

" Yes, *that's* where I live!"

" Oh, it is, eh? Then lightly row, away we go! Come along, my hearty ; we'll get some supper and then —

> " Turn our face
> Toward Putney Place.

" Can't take hands. I'm all legs — four legs, You see! Take a grip o' my coat tail!

6

"So mamma's name is Rebecca; but where is papa?"

Baby shook his head.

"Gone up in a balloon?" asked the pertinacious True.

"He lives way off behind a great big high wall, and he can never come to us."

"Ha, ha! you don't say? Lives behind a high wall, does he? And who told you that?"

"Mamma told us that, for she has seen him!"

"Has she, indeed? Now, who would have thought it. So she has seen him —

> "And he lives behind a wall,
> A most tremendous wall!
> And never comes to call,
> Oh fol-de-riddle-dol,
> On his darling little boy-oy-oy!

"Behind a wall, ha, ha! Yes, that now is delicious! Wait till the Lady Pamela sees you, my chick-a-biddy, she of the dulcet note and lily hand. Here we are now, toot-si-cum! Look alive now; the Lady Pamela is at hand."

They stopped at the entrance to an area which led between a large gloomy block of store-houses and a smaller brick building, the character of which the peddler thus explained to the wondering Baby:—

"This is the Triton, my dear; 'Steamer, —

No. 10,' that's her last name; she is the boss machine of *this* island, and you oughter just see the animals that pull her — 'Wild George' and 'Jumping Jacob!' And the boys that run her, ah, they're the boys! Lady Pamela and I, we live in the rear, in the rear of the Triton; so we're Tritons, too. Wouldn't you like to come an' live here now, an' be a little Triton?"

"No," said the child emphatically.

"What, eh! you wouldn't? how very remarkable. 'Tention, company; forward, march!" continued the peddler, unlocking the gate with a latch-key, and gently pushing the child before him.

" Home at last; a kettle singing on the hearth, a table laid for three. Here we go now, there she is yonder; d'ye see that light? there's the Lady Pamela!"

Hobbling along the area, half-leading, half-propelling the astonished child through a deserted-looking back yard, the peddler came at length to a small structure, whose original character was sufficiently indicated by a faded sign bearing the words " Beals & Bilgo, House Carpenters." Climbing some rather rough-looking stairs at one end of the building, talking all the time in his rollicking way to his little guest, True opened a door and ushered Baby into a neat little passage, where an oil lamp was burning on a bracket.

"What, ho, Lady Pamela! up with the portcullis!" cried True.

Nobody appearing in answer to his call, the peddler hung his hat on a peg in the passage, and opening another door, pushed Baby before him into a bright, cheerful room, where an open fire was blazing in a small grate, a very large arm chair was drawn up before it, a centre-table stood near, covered with books and small ornaments, while a sofa and some chairs were disposed around the wall. The room almost outshone the rainbow; the carpet was a combination of the brightest colors; the wall-paper was covered with large bunches of flowers, while the curtains and furniture covering were of the gayest chintz. Altogether it was a most cheering contrast to the darkness outside, and the peddler's spirits rose accordingly to a still higher pitch.

An open door disclosed a little passage-way which — as well from the savory odors that came from it as from certain rattlings of pans and dishes — it was at once evident led to the kitchen.

> " My Lady P.,
> Oh where can she be ?

Sit down there, my man of wax, and put out
your feet to the fire !

> " Tarry not, fair one, come hither ; oh come,
> To greet your own true love, to welcome him home ! "

bellowed the hilarious peddler as he settled himself in the easy-chair.   Laying aside his crutches
he poked the fire vigorously, all the time roaring
out whimsical reproaches to the invisible and
obdurate Lady Pamela.

Meantime the odors from the kitchen grew
more and more fragrant, and the music of pots
and pans more constant, until at length steps
were heard in the passage.

> " Here she comes, make room, make room !
> Enveloped in a sweet perfume ;
> Like Venus rising from the sea,
> Behold my fairest Lady P. ! "

At these words a grim, bony little woman
appeared in the doorway, and walking straight
up to the peddler in a business-like way, submitted to the rapturous embrace which he
bestowed upon her.   Then having freed herself
from her spouse's arms, she smoothed her hair
and looked down upon Baby with an expression
as devoid of surprise or curiosity as though he

had sat in that chair, in that very place, from the
day he was born.

"Sweet Lady P.,
Pray smile on me!
I didn't run away,
But only lost my way.
My mamma lives in Putney Place,
— And she must have a pretty face, —
My papa never comes to call,
'Cos he resides behind a wall,
Which is not my affair, but his 'n;
Perhaps he lives in a — hem — palace.
But after tea we'll take a car,
And all go home to see mamma."

The Lady Pamela, who seemed perfectly to
understand this little epic, asked no other explanation, but nodded and said bluntly : —

"Been crying! wants his face washed!" and
without another word she led Baby into the
kitchen, carefully washed his face, and set him
up to the table, on top of a pile of big books,
arranged in a stout chair.

The peddler speedily followed, and placed himself at the head of the board, which was bounti-
fully set forth with a smoking oyster stew, cold
ham, hot muffins and buttered toast. Lady
Pamela poured the tea in an uncompromising
manner. She ate very sparingly herself, but
heaped Baby's plate with delicate morsels, and
kent the while a sharp eye on her husband.

"Ain't the stew good?" she asked shortly, when her husband, after two generous helpings of oysters, ventured to address himself to the ham.

"Good?—'tis superb, my connubial lamb;
But I thought for a change I'd just sample the ham."

"What's the matter with the muffins?" again asked the mistress of the house as she detected her busy spouse taking a piece of 'toast.

"Matter?—what's the matter with the sun and moon? What's the matter with the starry sky? What's the matter with the rolling universe?—Perfection! That's the matter with *them*. My love, I'm only sharpening my appetite on a bit of toast, as a canary sharpens his bill on a cuttle-fish. Cuttle-fish and toast, my dear, are very much alike,—both wholesome and both sharpening."

Baby, meantime, in the enjoyment of his good cheer forgot his absent mamma, and waited quite contentedly until the cheery peddler had smoked his after-supper pipe by the parlor fire, nursing the while, a big purring tabby-cat. Presently, however, it was time to go, and the peddler put on his hat and coat, and adjusted his crutches, while Lady Pamela bundled and wrapt Baby up so that he could hardly stir, and they set forth.

Baby went fast asleep in the car, and was so bewildered when he awoke and found himself out in the street, in the cold night air, that he came very near crying again; but the good-natured peddler told him that they were close to his home now; that mamma was waiting, and he would soon see her, and so at length they reached Putney Place.

Hardly had they turned the corner, however, when they were pounced upon by a brisk little figure in a shawl, who seized hold of Baby, and turned sharply upon his conductor with : —

"What're you doing with this child, that's what *I* want to know?"

"Why, my sweet-spoken young lady, I found the Commodore upon the street, crying as though his little bosom would burst."

"Yes; but where have you had him hid away all this time? Just tell me that!"

"Why, if this is the witness-box, an' I am up for cross-ex, I just took him home, an' the Lady Pamela gave him some supper" —

"The Lady Fiddlestick! What business had you to go taking him home when his ma is in fits, an' the police turnin' heavins an' earth to find him? A pretty kind of a person you be!"

" Why, my precious honey bee,
  Who 'd think *you* had a sting ?
  Jest stop a moment an' you 'll see
  The reason of the thing ! "

"Oh, fudge! Clear out, with you; you needn't trouble to come any further, Mr. Hobblesticks ! *I* can take him to his mother now."

" No trouble, my dear; nothing but a pleasure. It will delight my heart to see that fond mother embrace her lost darling."

" His mother won't want to see you; you wouldn't strike anybody blind with beauty ! "

" Wait, my honeypot, wait till you see me in the light, and perhaps you 'll change your mind. The Lady Pamela, now — and she has excellent taste — thinks I 'm a perfect Apollo."

" Bah ! " exclaimed the little hunchback, catching Baby up in her arms and hurrying away as if in hopes to outstrip the peddler. But if this were her purpose, it was of no avail, for the latter developed a rapidity of locomotion that would have astonished anybody not acquainted with the possibilities of crutches, so that when she at length reached Madame Velasco's door the alert cripple was close by her side.

Close by her side, too, he entered the house; close by her side stumped up the stairs, and

close upon her heels followed into the chamber,
where the anxious mother folded her restored
darling to her breast in a transport of gratitude.

Rebecca's delight at recovering her child rendered her deaf to the slurring introduction which
the skeptical Zilp awarded to the peddler, as well
as to the subsequent deprecating remarks with
which she commented on his account of the discovery of Baby, of the tender care Lady Pamela
had taken of him, and of the extraordinary fond-
ness of that estimable lady for children.

To Zilp's great disappointment, Rebecca
seemed much interested in the peddler's story.

" And so your wife is very fond of children?"
she asked.

" Fond, ma'am? I should hesitate to leave
her alone with a good plump one for fear she'd
eat it."

" And have you no children of your own?"

" Not a chick to scratch gravel for, ma'am."

" And the Lady Pamela, as you call her, is, I
suppose, your wife?"

" She's —

> My wife, my life,
> My dove, my love,
> My darling and my all,

if I may be permitted so to express myself. One

of the most wonderful women, ma'am, that ever lived on this terrestial ball."

"And where do you live? Is it far from here?"

"At the Triton, ma'am — the Triton in the rear!"

"The Triton?" repeated Rebecca, curiously.

"Yes, that 's the name of the old tub in the good old days when I run with the machine. I can't run with her now, ma'am, 'count of this, you see," said the peddler, glancing down ruefully at his crippled legs; "but there was a time when I could, an' then I was cap'n of the Triton, an' that 's the way this all came, you see, gettin' drenched at a fire — then rheumatism an' so forth. But I had my reward, ma'am — a testimonial in hard silver, with all the boys' names cut in — 'To True Blue, in acknowledgment, &c.' The new 'un, they call her 'Steamer No. 10,' and she 's *the* boss machine of the city, but nothin' to the Triton."

"'To True Blue?' Does that mean you?"

"Yes, there 's our card, ma'am — picture of Triton, you see at the top — had a few struck off for particular calls: —

"*Mr. and Mrs. Truman Ballou — At the Triton in the Rear.*'

"Boys will have their joke, clipped my name to Tru' B'lou, you see, an' then it got to be True Blue, an' they pretended there was a meanin' in it, an' so they had it cut on the Testimonial, an' there it is in the hard silver—'T-R-U-E B-L-U-E' —and the Lady Pamela, that's the apple of her eye, and so you see we're Tritons still,—

> "We're both Tritons still
> An' Tritons will be,
> While rivers run down
> To the murmuring sea.

Excuse me — or words to that effect, ma'am."

"And have you any employment?"

"In the variety business, ma'am. City set me up after my sickness, an' now everything is lovely, an' we bask, so to speak, in Fortune's glitterin' beams!" said True, rising to go.

"Accept my warmest thanks for your kindness to my dear child, Mr. True, or Mr. Blue, whichever you would prefer to be called, and also please accept this to buy some little thing for your wife as an expression of my gratitude. You will know what to get better than I," said Rebecca, handing to the cheerful cripple a bank note, which that thrifty individual accepted without demur.

"And now good-night, my friend; perhaps we may come and see you and your good wife one of these days."

"Do; that's right, ma'am, an' the Lady Pamela will show you the Testimonial."

CHAPTER VII.

CONFESSION.

THAT dull woman, the unfilial daughter of James Stuart, otherwise known as Anne Queen of England, has much to answer for besides political stupidity and obstinacy, if to her patronage be due the introduction of certain modes of household furniture and decoration — much of it tasteless in the extreme — the contemplation of which has begotten in many idle and fanciful folks a disorder not to be distinguished from divers manias for which worthy people have been shut up in mad-houses.

But the world runs to livery; every man's house must be ordered, and his wife dressed, like his neighbor's; and it may, perhaps, as well be in Queen Anne's style as another's; only we are driven to this little explosion of impatience out of pure sympathy for Mrs. Dighton and Dorothy, who, since Mr. Curley had bought the Dexter house, had found no peace in life.

Unfortunately, Mr. Curley's new purchase was

a large house, and, as the architects say, "it had possibilities," which its new owner straightway put to the test by setting about fitting it up in the "Queen Anne style." Queen Anne presided over their meals ; Queen Anne possessed their bed-rooms ; Queen Anne haunted their dreams ; indeed, Dorothy declared, in a fit of impatience, that the very food tasted of Queen Anne, and in fact their only escape from that royal and purblind matron was to rush out under the broad free heavens and gasp out their grievances to the great tranquilizing sea.

"But your uncle is happy, and after all, what does it matter?" said Mrs. Dighton, philosophically, as she stood upon the front steps waiting for the carriage one bright afternoon. "Men have to do something, and he might do so many worse things; suppose he were to take to drink, for instance."

"Oh, yes," returned Dorothy, adjusting her mother's wrap, "he might be crazy in many more disagreeable ways."

"Dorothy, Dorothy, you disrespectful child!"

"That's not disrespectful ; I should care just as much for Uncle Curl if he were stark mad. Besides, we're all more or less crazy ; I'm crazy for a boat, but there's no chance of my getting it unless it could be made in the Queen Anne style. I wonder if there is such a thing ;— here comes Uncle. I'll sound him upon it at once !"

"Not now, Dorothy ; the carriage will be here in a minute ; if you start that subject we shall not get away for an hour."

Not being in the mood for a drive, Dorothy waved her mother and uncle off, and then settled herself with her easel and colors on the piazza overlooking the sea, to make a sketch.

She had scarcely got to work when she was startled by the loud report of a gun, and looking up saw a yacht in full sail just entering their little cove, with the smoke of her salute still hovering upon the water.

Busied with her work, Dorothy took no further notice of the circumstance until she was aroused by a strange step on the piazza behind her; and turning about saw Ralph Dexter approaching.

"Good afternoon, Mr. Dexter! Oh, 'twas you who came in the yacht ; dear me, I fear I didn't properly notice your salute. I *did* give a whisk of my paint brush, but I dare say you didn't see it !"

"Why, no ; the distance is considerable, and a paint brush not being a very conspicuous object " —

"Oh, very well, the next time I 'll fly the flag. Pray find a seat."

"Thank you, I fear I shall not have time to sit ; I came down after my wherry ; it is locked up in the boat-house, and your uncle, I believe, has the key. I thought if I made haste I might run up to the city with the wind."

"How unfortunate! My uncle and mamma have gone for a drive, so you must either wait or come again."

"Oh, very well," said Ralph, taking a seat and casting a side-long look at the easel ; "in making a virtue of necessity, I shall only be indulging myself in an unexpected pleasure."

"I was just scolding about you, Mr. Dexter, when you appeared. See, I had begun to sketch your yacht! She looked so pretty as she rounded the point, with her sails spread ; but before I could get her sketched in every sail was furled, and there she lies now nothing but a skeleton !"

"I will have them hoist sail again directly," said Ralph, rising to go and give the order.

"No, no ; not for the world !"

"Yes, I insist ; 'tis but a minute's work."

"But see, I shall prevent you," exclaimed Dorothy, erasing with one stroke of her brush the half-sketched yacht from her picture.

7

"And why? Because you are unwilling to pay me such a compliment?"

"It wouldn't be a compliment. I began to paint the yacht for my own amusement, merely as a pretty feature in the scene, not because it was yours."

"But I should consider it a compliment, nevertheless."

"And I, I suppose, have no right to refuse even an implied request from one to whom we are under so great an obligation."

"That sounds a very little bit ironic, or satiric, or tartaric, Miss Dighton," said Ralph, smiling.

"Does it? Then I take it back; but it's only the truth."

"But I shall not allow you to say that; and I hope you do not feel so."

"I cannot help feeling so; you feel so yourself!"

"I?" exclaimed Ralph, with a very natural astonishment at this *naïve* charge. "Indeed I do not!"

"You have changed your mind since I saw you last, then."

"How so?"

"You thought differently then."

"Pray, may I ask what reason you have for saying that?"

"Your manner showed it."

"What, did I give myself creditor-airs?"

"No; but you received our acknowledgments in a sort of well-deserving way that told the story."

"Why, I suppose the small service I was so happy as to be able to render you—though as the event proved, it was quite superfluous—was at least worth a 'thank you,' if only for the intention. Would you have been better pleased if I had offered a polite but hypocritical disclaimer?"

"No," exclaimed Dorothy, emphatically, "I should have despised you then, as I expected to!"

"'Expected to?'" repeated Ralph, with a highly amused look at this very unusual candor.

"Yes; you would then have confirmed your reputation."

"Indeed! What evil report of me can have traveled so far as to have reached you?" asked Ralph, looking a little blank.

"You might not consider it an evil report."

"But you do."

"Oh no, not evil; only not enviable."

"I am curious to hear it, for I have a similar confession to make to you."

"With regard to myself?"

"Yes," replied Ralph, laughing at Dorothy's tone of consternation.

"I do not blame you for jesting," she said, reddening, "for the conversation is, certainly, in the highest degree absurd, between comparative strangers as we are; the mistake was mine, and I beg your pardon for giving it such a turn. Let us now change the subject and say something about Time or Space, or some other safe and unembarrassing topic!"

"By no means; we should neither of us, I am sure, be satisfied to leave the subject in this state; we owe mutual explanations, we must have it out!" said Ralph, with a whimsical air.

"Perhaps you are right; I dare say you would make yourself wretched imagining I meant something a thousand times worse than I do, whereas it will prove only a tea-pot tempest," returned Dorothy, laughing; "but if we pursue the conversation it' must only be with entire frankness."

"Certainly; I am prepared for that, and I ought to have no doubts of you upon that score."

"Your great readiness in acceding leads me to suspect you of anticipating the pleasure of saying something unpalatable to punish me for scaring you so." .

"Your suspicions are correct; I revel in the disclosure I am about to make and your expected discomfiture."

"I deserve it," said Dorothy, stoutly, "but I may disappoint you in the matter of the discomfiture."

"Now for it," said Ralph, with a delighted air; "shall I unbosom myself first?"

"No; it is only fair for me to begin, and I hope, Mr. Dexter, that you will follow my example of perfect candor. In the first place, then," continued Dorothy, picking up her brush and going on with her sketch as she talked, "I must acknowledge that with regard to you I began with a prejudice; I was very much vexed at being placed under such an extreme obligation to an entire stranger" —

"But I have already assured you that" —

"I must stipulate not to be interrupted," continued Dorothy. "I have such a native love of independence that I do not like to be put at such a disadvantage, and so I began by cherishing an indefinite grudge towards you, which I am aware is somewhat unreasonable, and which you are welcome to laugh at if you choose."

"Not at all; it is what I expected; you are only justifying your. reputation," said Ralph, demurely. "I beg your pardon," he continued, as Dorothy turned about with a little stare of vexation and remonstrance. "I was only using your own expression, Miss Dighton!"

"True; it is quite fair. But, owing you this grudge, as I say, when mamma came home with an account of you from one of your enthusiastic friends, which your appearance, your — your"— Dorothy hesitated a moment, "well, your dress, in short, certainly justified"—

"Eh, 'dress?'" repeated Ralph, running his eye quickly over his well-fitting habilaments.

"Yes, your clothes, Mr. Dexter. I could not help feeling a gratification in finding that you were not going — that is, I mean that you were not likely to turn out the hero, after all, that mamma had so persistently represented you."

"I have then one friend in camp. I trust I shall be found to deserve Mrs. Dighton's good opinion. But"—

"I haven't yet told what your reputation is, you would say. No; I am coming to that. We were told, then, first, as soon as your name was mentioned, that you were"—

Dorothy interrupted herself to correct an outline.

"What?" asked Ralph, unable to control his eagerness.

"A — very — fine — *dancer!*" said Dorothy, slowly, with a little half-suppressed satirical emphasis on the last word.

"Yes," said Ralph, composedly, "I believe I am ; that is, I dance well, and I am rather proud of it. Was that all, Miss Dighton?"

"Not quite," answered Dorothy, plainly disappointed in the effect of her communication thus far. "Your friend went on to say that you were one of the beaux of the town."

"Indeed!" exclaimed Ralph, with a smile, "anything further, Miss Dighton?"

"No ; I wish for your sake there had been."

"And do you consider that so very damaging?"

"Why, when it is the first, and in fact, principal thing that one admiring friend has to say of another, it is — to my mind at least — it is" —

"Pray do not hesitate, Miss Dighton!"

"Disappointing," concluded Dorothy.

"Is that the word you were going to use?" asked Ralph, his eyes gleaming with merriment.

"No," returned Dorothy, dryly, as she painted away busily; "I was going to say *annihilating!*"

Ralph restrained himself no longer, but burst into a hearty laugh.

"I am glad you find it amusing, Mr. Dexter," said Dorothy, in a tone of pique, "though I hardly see how you can."

"I trust that with regard to a part of this report, Miss Dighton, your own reputation may prove as little deserved as mine. It is not, of course, for me to claim that I am worthy of any better estimation at the hands of my friends, nor shall I attempt to defend myself from an imputation which my own actions may, perhaps, have justified to a greater degree than I am prepared to admit; but I would ask if, in receiving such reports of another, even of a stranger, you ought not to make some small allowance for the source from which they come? I mean, may not an injudicious friend, and much more a shallow acquaintance, damage—I beg pardon, the phrase is *damn*—one with faint praise, and with the very best of intentions entirely misrepresent one?"

"Undoubtedly;" and it is partly from an uncomfortable feeling that I have been too ready in accepting these reports, that I am now induced to make this very frank statement."

"Which then I shall venture to take as an

indication that you have changed your mind with regard to them?"

"That is hardly fair, if it is meant for a question."

"True; please regard it only as a surmise!"

"And now, Mr. Dexter," said Dorothy, laying down her brush, turning and looking her caller full in the face, "for *your* confession!"

"Which is so far from formidable that, as you suggest, I should certainly be disappointed if I expected to detect you in any discomfiture on account of it. I am tempted to believe, however, that, like my own, it is partly true and partly false."

"Whatever it be, it can hardly astonish me, for, according to mamma, I am constantly shocking somebody; at any rate, you are not responsible for it, even if you *do* believe it."

"Whether I believe it or not — as to which I think I have not yet given any intimation — the experience of this interview has shown me how easily it may be believed by one who has not the penetration which" —

"Which you have — thank you!" interrupted Dorothy, smiling, "I shall take that to be your meaning unless you disavow it; but suspense is becoming painful; do let us hear it, good or bad!" .

"I was told, then, that I should find Miss Dighton *very disconcerting and very hard to understand.*"

"Heigho, is that all?" asked Dorothy with a great sigh of relief. "I was prepared for homicide or heresy, or something worse. That must be entirely true, mamma has said it so many times — and here she comes to confirm it!"

Supposing, naturally, that Ralph had come to make a call, Mrs. Dighton was duly pleased and complimented. Had she known that he only came on an errand, she would scarcely have given him, on parting, such a cordial invitation to dine with them the following week.

It was a trifle, — Ralph's forgetting to say anything more about the wherry. But trifles are often momentous ; on this one hung an acquaintanceship — and all that came of it.

CHAPTER VIII.

"WILD GEORGE" and "Jumping Jacob" are so well trained in their duties that at the first stroke of the alarm they start from their stalls — where night and day they stand caparisoned in burnished, brass-mounted trappings — and, rushing forth, put themselves in proper place on either side the pole, ready to be harnessed by their alert and eager masters.

Tugs and braces are soon adjusted, men jump to their seats, the stern old driver seizes the reins, the warning-gong sounds, and Steamer No. 10 rushes forth into the street before the first alarm has fairly stopped ringing.

A public hack stands in the way — crash! — one of its wheels is broken in a twinkling and the whole vehicle nearly capsized. But Steamer No. 10 does not stop for such a bagatelle; the law gives it the right of way; it is a servant of the public; the public safety, of which it is the appointed guardian, is threatened, and so without thought or care for the damage done it thunders off to the distant fire.

The driver of the damaged hack stormed and swore; its lady passenger was sadly frightened and shocked by the collision; but the former was obliged to swallow his wrath as best he could, and the latter had just let down the glass slide to inquire about the extent of the injury and quiet the irate hackman, when the area-gate burst open and, like a huge frog, out hopped True Blue upon his flying crutches, fast followed by his faithful spouse, only to behold their beloved Triton, which they had come to see off, disappearing in the distance.

The lady in the carriage instantly recognized True, and beckoned to him.

"Mr. Ballou," she said as he came hobbling up, "I am very glad to find you; I was hunting for your house when we met with this accident. Can I — will you let me go in for a few minutes?"

"*Let* you, Ma'am? Will the earth let the sun shine upon it? This is the happiest hour of my life. 'Beals and Bilgo' will be honored. Let me present my wife. Come here, my dear, and pay your respects to the mother of the Commodore! — Putney Place, you know."

"Better come in ?" said Lady Pamela, advancing stiffly and extending a horny hand.

Rebecca stepped out of the carriage, and, bidding the driver get it repaired and return for her as soon as possible, followed True and his wife into the house.

"Look sick," exclaimed Lady Pamela, noticing the feeble step and exhausted breath of her guest as they entered the little parlor, "better lay down!"

"Thank you, I will," said Rebecca, "I fear I am somewhat shaken up by the collision."

The Lady Pamela arranged the pillow and brought a glass of cordial, which seemed to revive her visitor greatly.

"Your husband tells me you are fond of children," said the latter, handing back the glass.

"Yes, kind er."

Rebecca looked curiously and anxiously at the stony face hovering over her, evidently making little of her reply.

"The Lady Pamela, Ma'am, is a philosopher ; she's no waster of words, an' when she says 'kind er,' that's all she'd say if you asked her if she was fond of me or the Triton. There are some folks that talk, an' some folks that *mean ;* *my* wife, I'm proud to say, ain't one of the first."

"You have a pleasant home here in this out-of-the-way spot, where you can do as you like, where there is nobody to molest or criticise you. This is a home indeed — you must be very happy!"

"Nothin' to complain of!" said Lady Pamela.

"Happy, Ma'am," said True; "the Lady Pamela is a regular hummin'-bird for happiness; she buzzes about improvin' the shinin' hour, gatherin' honey from every openin' pot an' porringer."

"You have other rooms than these, I suppose?"

"Certainly, Ma'am; a banquetin'-hall yonder," pointing to the kitchen, "and sleeping boudoirs beyond; all finished in the finest style of the late B. & B."

"Rooms enough to take care of!" added Lady Pamela, pulling the dead leaves from her window plants.

"Tell me, my good friends," said Rebecca, after musing a long time and attentively studying the faces of the pair before her, "what if a poor, wretched creature, who has no home nor friends, should come to you for shelter; what if an unhappy mother, whom the world has outlawed and outcast, should come to you with her

tender, innocent babes, begging for a refuge —
would you dare receive her ; would you dare
brave the world's opinion ; would you dare take
such an one into your bright, happy little home,
shield her from persecution, and hide her from
the sight of men ? "

Quite unprepared for this strange address,
True and his worthy wife looked at each other
uncomfortably and made no answer.

" You do not speak ; well, I do not blame you !
Why should *you* take in one whom the world
casts out ! Who are you to dare do what the
world forbids ! Why should you be different
from other men and women ! But perhaps you
do not understand me," she continued, glancing
at the perplexed faces of her hearers. " I came
here for a purpose ; I came to ask a favor of you ;
a favor so great that I dare ask it of no one else
on earth. I came to ask you to let *me* come here
to *die !* To ask you, after my death, to take my
dear, helpless children as your own ; to be kind
to them and bring them up the best you can, as
honest men and women, teaching them to work
with their *hands* at some useful occupation ;
teaching them to fear God, to love truth, and —
to forget me."

True hitched uneasily in his chair, played with
his crutch, and again glanced at his wife.

" I have some means ; a small sum of money which will do something towards paying for their board and education for a few years, until they get better able to take care of themselves."

True nervously cleared his throat as if about to speak, but the words would not come.

" It is a great thing I ask of you," continued Rebecca, her voice growing huskier, "a great thing to ask of a friend, much more of a stranger. But my time is short ; I cannot stop to study proprieties. I come to you because God tells me to come. I come as one fellow-being in distress comes to another, because I see something in your faces, and I feel that there is something in your hearts to which I shall not appeal in vain. I can say no more — my breath and strength are all gone ! "

" Why, we hardly know, Ma'am," began True, after considerable hemming and hawing, " what to say, right off, to such a what-you-may-call side-winder. It a little knocks the breath out of us, you see, at first go-off. We are highly honored " —

" No, no," interrupted Rebecca impetuously, " do not say that ; do not make any mistake on that point ! It is I who would be honored by your society and friendship. Association with *me* can bring honor to no one."

" *We* think you are a little hard on yourself, Ma'am ; we think you are a little down-in-the-mouth, you see, now, 'count of bein' sick. But we know you are the mother of the Commodore, an' his father, he says, lives behind a wall. We know there are a good many kinds of walls, an' we don't care what kind of a wall this is ; we don't want to know anybody's secrets, an' we don't ask no questions, Lady Pamela and I."

The Lady Pamela sat with her eyes fixed intently upon her husband, following closely what he said, and now and then showing her approval by an emphatic nod.

"We 're poor folks an' we have our own way of bein' proud," continued True ; "p'r'aps we h'aint much to be proud of, but there 's some that live in big houses an' make a splurge that we wouldn't swap places with. We 've got a good home, an' we have enough to eat and drink, an' we 've got a little penny laid up against a rainy day, an' we 're thankful for it all."

True paused and Lady Pamela nodded vigorously.

" And now," continued True, presently, "when you come to us an' say you 're in trouble, we say we 're sorry for you, an' wish we could do something to help you, an' what we can, we will, you

8

may be sure of that; but when you ask to come
here with your children, to make a home, we say
we don't know, it's very sudden, we must take a
little time to think about it,—don't we, my dear?"
he concluded, looking doubtfully at his wife.

"*I* say — don't care who ye be, 'f you're sick,
no home; little children; goin' to die; no one
to take care of ye — come along! that's what I
say!"

And Lady Pamela got up and swept out, like
a gust of wind, into the kitchen, where she
relieved herself by making a prodigious clatter
among the pots and kettles.

"Hooray, my dear, there you go! Never was
such a woman! What a matron of an orphan
asylum you'd make!" cried True, looking admiringly after his wife. "That settles the question, Ma'am," he continued, addressing Rebecca,
"if *she* consents I consent. If I hesitated 'twas
on her account; I thought if she an' you shouldn't
happen to hitch; if the children didn't take to
her or she didn't take to the children, 'twould be
a muss all 'round, and we'd better talk it over a
little. But she's settled the question, and so,
ma'am, here we are as you see us, Tritons an'
nothin' more, an' if you an' your babies want to
come an' be Tritons too, why, I say welcome!

The palatial halls of 'Beals and Bilgo' are open to you, —

"From Paris to Rome,
O'er dry land or salt foam,
Wherever you will-go,
My dear 'Beals and Bilgo,'
There 's no place like home."

As Rebecca rose, with streaming eyes and choking voice, to express her thanks for this generous offer, the driver came thundering at the door and announced the carriage.

True made such a thumping with his crutches, and hopped to the window to look out so many times while Rebecca was speaking, that, what with the pounding of the driver it would have been extremely doubtful, but for certain furtive resorts to his coat-sleeves, if he had heard a word she said.

The Lady Pamela, too, behaved in quite as inexplicable a manner when Rebecca took her hand at the door to say a word of thanks at parting, for she suddenly turned about upon the astonished hackman with — "What are *you* standin' there starin' like a stuck pig for, you goggle-eyed thing!" and then darted into the house, muttering something about "taking cold in her head." ·

"Good bye!" cried True from the doorway,

in his cheeriest tone. "Take care of the steps! Give my compliments to the Commodore! Expect to see you soon; 'Beals and Bilgo' always ready. We shall all be happy as clams when we get settled;—when we are all—all"—

"Tritons!" said Rebecca, waving her hand and smiling through her tears.

CHAPTER IX.

"WHO'S that coming up the avenue, Dorothy?"

"It's Mr. Dexter, poor wretch, coming to make his dinner-call. What an abuse of good nature it is to require one to come thirty miles to make a call of mere ceremony. We ought to have absolved him from it."

"He might not have thanked us," said Mrs. Dighton, casting an anxious glance at Dorothy's toilet.

"Which means"—

"Which means, my dear, that it is not out of the bounds of probability he may enjoy coming."

"Considering that he talked to you most of the time when he was here last, the modesty of that speech is not conspicuous."

"Why, my dear," returned Mrs. Dighton with a sly twinkle in her eye, "this is Mr. Dexter's old home, and your uncle is a very entertaining man; but even if it should turn out that I am one of the attractions, I see nothing strange in it; I hope I am not yet so uninteresting that it would not repay one taking an hour's ride to see me."

"Bravo, Rhody," cried Dorothy, clapping her hands with a delighted laugh; "you are certainly the staunchest old lady, and the most comical little bunch of conceit that ever was! Why," she continued, wiping her eyes, "you are getting so puffed up with vanity that you will sail off before our eyes one of these fine days, to some place over the sea, where your unrivaled charms will be appreciated."

"Sh—tut—tut;—there, Mr. Dexter has seen us, and is raising his hat."

"Throw him a kiss, Rhody, do!"

"For shame, you saucy girl!" said Mrs. Dighton, with an air of dignity.

There was just time for the spoiled daughter to make peace with her offended mamma by falling upon her, covering her with kisses, and leaving her almost out of breath, before the approaching visitor emerged from a little clump of shrubbery which, for a moment, screened him from view.

"Good afternoon, Mr. Dexter," exclaimed Mrs. Dighton, advancing hospitably; "you have the distinction of being our only caller thus far to-day."

"A distinction which I hope I shall retain,"
returned Ralph, bowing to Dorothy.

"Fie, how selfish," exclaimed the latter, rising
and placing a chair; "and how rash, too; think,
what if we should prove mutually stupid! See
now what an opportunity I have given you to
say something fine!"

"Which, if I were to avail myself of, I should
probably be repaid by some cutting sarcasm."

"To be sure, and you would deserve it."

"And have you then no compunctions against
artfully leading a man into a snare and then
making a guy of him?"

"Oh, not the slightest; but now, to avoid all
snares and man-traps, pray sit down here and
teach us the names of all those vessels that go
sailing yonder. Mamma calls them all ships. I
know better than that, but can't tell the whys
and the wherefores."

"I shall be most honored to have two such
pupils," said Ralph, taking the proffered seat.

"Very well, then; first class in navigation,"
cried Dorothy, drawing her chair up alongside
her mother's.

"Attention, young lady at the head," said
Ralph. "What is a ship?"

"You're the young lady at the head, Rhody,"

whispered Dorothy. "Speak up;—any sort of thing with a sail."

"Why, I may as well say that as any thing else," said Mrs. Dighton, smiling. "I know no better."

"A ship, then," began Ralph, raising an impressive forefinger, "is"—

"I beg pardon, Mr. Dexter," interrupted Dorothy, "there comes Uncle Curl up the avenue. I have a bone to pick with him; you must excuse me."

And away she ran, without noticing the little flush of mortification that crept over Ralph's face at the light indifference of her manner; Mrs. Dighton was more observing.

Dorothy ran across the lawn to meet her uncle, and walked slowly back with him. Nearing the house, they sat down upon a rustic seat and continued their talk;—meantime the fact that Dorothy pelted her uncle with flowers, showed the importance of the interruption. It was Mr. Curley moreover who first rose and made the move to go.

Whether or not all this was remarked from the piazza may be inferred from the fact that Ralph evidently had to constrain himself to control a filmy little frostiness in his tone and manner as Dorothy came laughing back, with,—

"How comes on the navigation? I expect by this time mamma is quite versed in maritime affairs."

"The lesson was postponed until you came back," said Mrs. Dighton, quickly, coming to the relief of Ralph, who had evidently forgotten all about it from the moment Dorothy withdrew.

"Indeed!" cried Dorothy, "how very kind of you."

"Yes," said Mrs. Dighton significantly, "it was certainly very polite in Mr. Dexter."

"Which means, Mr. Dexter," remarked Dorothy, turning to Ralph, "that *I* was *not* polite; and that it was very rude in me to run away and leave you. But what do *you* think? Which was the more important, to observe the proprieties or maintain discipline over my uncle?"

"Whichever was your duty," returned Ralph, not quite thawed out.

"Oh dear, dear, that would take such a lot of hard thinking to settle, that I must give it up. Is inclination any guide to duty?"

"None at all," said Ralph, smiling, but none the less evidently in earnest, "else I fear you would easily be absolved."

"There," cried Dorothy, laughing merrily, "mamma was horrified at my remark, but what will she say to yours?"

"What was the matter with mine?" asked Ralph, with a discomfited air. "I meant"—

"You meant to be truthful, and so did I; what a pity one cannot always be truthful without sometimes being impolite."

"I beg your pardon if I have said anything amiss."

"Done," cried Dorothy, throwing some flowers into her mother's lap and extending her hand, "let's shake hands on it as men do after — or is it before a duel?"

This captivating frankness quite subjugated Ralph, and he shook hands cordially.

"Uncle Curl met one of the neighbors below on the road, who said the surf was rolling in magnificently around the point on the rocks. Wouldn't you like to take a canter around there, Mr. Dexter? You can have my uncle's horse."

Ralph was evidently much pleased at the invitation, but hesitated. "I fear,"—he began, pulling out his watch.

"Oh, you must stay to tea and take the late train," interrupted Dorothy. "I am surprised that you and mamma have not got that arranged before this."

"Mamma took it for granted," interrupted Mrs. Dighton, adroitly; "but now, my dear, run

away and order your horses directly; there's no
time to be lost if you expect to get back to tea!"

Ralph made no further objection. In ten
minutes Dorothy returned in her riding habit;
in ten minutes more they were off. The road
led at first through the open country, and, at
length, turned into some pine woods as they
approached the sea.

Dorothy was in riotous spirits, challenged
Ralph to little races, urged her horse up steep
banks after inaccessible flowers, and made the
woods ring with snatches of song.

" What a relief to get away where you can be
as crazy as you like — eh, Mr. Dexter? Fancy
behaving like that on Fifth Avenue?"

" Why not?" asked Ralph, absently, with the
possible intent of keeping his companion talking.

" For no reason that I know save that you'd
be shut up in a mad-house."

" But you would have the consolation of knowing that you were not mad," languidly urged
Ralph.

" Rather poor consolation to one in a straight
jacket."

" Why, it strikes me as the only consolation
the case admits of."

" Which does not prevent it being very poor

all the same ; but don't you suppose all the mad
folks think they're oppressed ; that they're the
victims of prejudice and ignorance and so
forth ? "

" Not a doubt of it."

" How horrible ! And I dare say many of them
are no crazier than we are — that is, I beg
pardon, than *I* am. But here we are at last ;
let's tie our horses and sit on the rocks ! "

They dismounted accordingly, and Dorothy
recklessly scrambled down the steep rocks in her
long riding-habit, and seated herself where the
waves dashed up to her very feet.

" I like this, partly, I suppose, because I 'm
afraid of it," she said, after a long silence, during
which Ralph had sat quietly studying her absorbed face ; " because it is so mighty and I am
so weak ; because it can catch me up and toss
me into nothingness in a minute ; because it
drowns my voice, overwhelms my strength, and
dwarfs me to insignificance."

" That feeling is the result merely of the com-
parison of mass with mass, — your person with
the sea. No doubt it can wash your body
about like a rag, but with all its power it cannot touch the real *you*. For me," continued
Ralph, half-proudly, " I feel a kind of superiority

to it. I know that I shall endure after this bulk
of water, big as it is, shall have been vaporized
in the Universal Fire. I think of it but as a sub-
ject-power, a giant slave that *is*, already, and can
be made still more enormously useful when it
shall have been thoroughly taught the lesson of
subjection."

"Oh," cried Dorothy, a little appalled by the
boldness of the thought, "I never dared think
there was anything in me that could withstand
or outlive the awful power of the sea. It seems,
in some way, a part of God to me."

"And so is this," said Ralph, holding out a
drop of spray upon his hand, "and the sea is
nothing but a countless host of these particles.
But I was thinking something very different,"
he continued, "something more practical and not
so fine. I was wondering, with such a medium,
free as the air to them all, why men do not utilize
the sea more. Why, when they get rich, instead
of building a house to be planted down in one
little narrow spot of earth, each man does not
build himself a ship to live in, to make a home
of ; a ship in which he can get away from his
little circle of friends and neighbors, and go
about all over the world. It wouldn't cost any
more than a house, and the difference between

the two in the matter of pleasure and independence is immeasurable."

"I should not like it," said Dorothy, emphatically, "I think such a life would be little and
selfish, would be running away from duty; would
be shirking responsibility. I want to live among
men. I want to do something to help them. It
seems to me that the world is suffering for great
helpers. There is so much to be done and so
little time and strength to do it, I wonder how
anybody can be content to sit still and be happy.
I despise myself for my own indifference, for
my own frivolity and idleness, without being
able to cure it. Oh!" she cried, starting to her
feet and flinging out her arms impetuously,
"why was I born so weak! Why am I so insig-
nificant and puerile, with such work to be done
all about me, and such constant irrepressible
longings to do it!"

Ralph looked at her with astonishment. It
seemed as if in a moment she had passed from
girlhood to womanhood. A noble enthusiasm
dignified her features, her figure swelled to stat-
uesque proportions, and there was a grand freedom in her gesture as, possessed with her subject, and unconscious of the admiration of her
companion, she continued : —

"I long, I yearn to be able to break free at one throe from all these hampering customs and conventionalities that keep me down, and take hold with brain and hand to help on some of the great movements towards uplifting my own kind. I pray for the strength and courage to do it, but they do not come — and why do they not? I fret at the narrowness and paltriness of my life, and I wait and wait in vain for some outside force to lift me up out of it, but all my efforts amount only to this," she concluded, in a tone of dejection — "mere futile bursts of impatience."

"Mr. Dexter," she continued, after a few minutes' silence, and still evidently full of her subject, "did you ever think of the glorious fullness and richness of life of one of those great workers and leaders of men? How trivial to them the little individual cares and ills of everyday living must become, how narrow and contemptible the paltry aims and ambitions of common men, as they go scrambling after their golden baubles and buzzing about their sensual pleasures!"

As Ralph was about to reply, a little gust of wind lifted Dorothy's hat, and carried it over the rock in front of them; it fell a distance of twelve or fifteen feet and lodged where the next considerable wave would wash it out.

Despite her remonstrance, Ralph immediately climbed down after it ; the getting down was sufficiently difficult, but the getting back up the steep wet rock almost impracticable. By dint of hard scrambling, however, he at length succeeded at the expense of an ugly flesh wound produced by tearing his hand on the jagged rocks.

As it was his right hand, Dorothy made him sit down and let her bind it up. Stripping up her soft cambric handkerchief, she stanched the blood, replaced the skin nicely, and proceeded to dress the wound, lecturing Ralph meantime on his recklessness.

He watched her with more than a passing interest as her face, intent on her task, was brought close to his. Did he detect any particular concern or interest in those tranquil eyes, any flutter in that firm, cool touch? Tenderly and sympathetically as she performed her task, did it make any difference to her that it was *his* hand? Was it anything but a commonplace service she was rendering? Evidently Ralph did not at once conclude ; perhaps her next remark misled him.

"This is not the first time, Mr. Dexter, you have shed blood for me — how can I ever repay you ? "

"In many ways!" said Ralph, significantly.

"I hope I shall not fail when the occasion offers," she returned, in a cordial, unembarrassed tone. "But, dear me," she added immediately, preventing the rejoinder that trembled on Ralph's lips, "how wet your coat is from this spray! We must go at once!"

"Your own is just as wet," returned Ralph, touching her sleeve.

"Oh, that is of no account, if only I can keep my mother at a safe distance till it is changed."

Mrs. Dighton was all ready to meet them with the announcement that tea was waiting. Dorothy left Ralph in her charge with directions that he should have a dry coat, and ran away to change her dress. At the tea-table she was full of spirits and gayety, and rallied Ralph successfully about his scheme of floating homes upon the sea, but after tea she deserted the party on the piazza, and went away by herself to play the piano in the dark parlor. When, however, Ralph ventured in to join her, she suddenly stopped, said she was merely thrumming nothings, begged to be excused from playing in earnest, and led him back upon the piazza, where she again left

9

him to her mother and devoted herself to teasing
her uncle.

Ralph soon rose to go, and took his leave a
little moodily despite Dorothy's giving him her
hand very cordially at parting, and saying : —

"You must come again soon, and give us the
lesson in navigation."

"What is young Dexter doing here so much?"
asked Mr. Curley, after Dorothy had gone to bed.

"Why, he has been here to call several times,"
said Mrs. Dighton, indifferently, "but this is his
old home, and there's nothing surprising in it."

"To be sure, that didn't occur to me; I
thought perhaps he was making up to Dorothy."

"Well, between ourselves, Samuel, I think he
is ; but she is the strangest girl ; I don't know
what he could have thought of her to-day.
There were but two constructions to put upon
her conduct, and he will be likely to choose the
most obvious and make a sad mistake."

"What has she done that is so peculiar ?"

"She has been behaving like a consummate
coquette, when all the time she was quite indifferent and half unconscious of him."

"Yes, yes ; she don't care a button for *him*,"
said Mr. Curley, lighting a fresh cigar. "He

had better not come around here with his love-making, or she will send him to the right-a-bout."

"That's just what I fear."

"Fear, sister? What are you talking about?" asked Mr. Curley, taking alarm. "You wouldn't have the child married?"

"'Married?' — Hm-m-m, no; but it wouldn't hurt her to be engaged."

"Pooh, pooh; she's a chit, a mere baby yet!"

"She is eighteen."

"Impossible; Dorothy eighteen? You must be mistaken."

"I am not very likely to be mistaken about the age of my only child; she may be a chit and a baby to you, Samuel, but to the rest of the world she's a young woman."

"Well, if she were as old as Methuselah, who is this young Dexter that he should presume"—

"He is one of the most estimable young men I have ever met," interrupted Mrs. Dighton, warmly, "and the more I see of him, the better I like him."

"On the other hand, he strikes me as a very commonplace young popinjay."

"That's simply because you never give a thought to anything outside your pottery, and

have never taken the trouble to talk with him.
He is a young man of education, character, and
fortune, and I should be very sorry indeed to see
Dorothy slight him."

"Well, if he were Crœsus himself, and came
of undoubted archangelic lineage, he's not good
enough for our Dorothy."

"That's the trouble ; nobody will ever be good
enough for her in your eyes.   You have spoiled
her with indulgence and turned her head with
vanity, as far as it can be turned — poor child,
her natural unconsciousness has been her only
protection."

"The truth is, sister, this country life is too
dull for you ; you are pining for something to
do, and so you go to scheming and match-
making.   But I give you warning !   Marry off
your servant-women ; try your hand at the vil-
lagers ; but hands off Dorothy, or I'll run away
to Europe with her !"

"Good night ; I shall waste no more breath
upon the subject ; you are quite as absurd as
Dorothy !"

CHAPTER X.

COSSETS.

WHEN a man sits down to make his own will he straightway forgets all the humor of the situation ; forgets all the good things that have been said about moribund ancestors and waiting heirs, about gouty legators and starving legatees ; remembers the stock witticisms upon the subject only to find them quite pointless, if not a little ghastly, and, indeed, it is ten to one that he makes it a very solemn and heavy occasion.

To every prudent man who has spent a lifetime in getting together a hoard of things of esteemed sublunary value, and who has a very natural interest in deciding what is to become of it, the hour for settling that question — so far as in him lies — sooner or later arrives.

It arrived to Mr. Sydney Dexter one morning on his way down town ; that is, the thought then occurred to him, and suddenly assumed such an unusual and pressing importance that, before going to business, he stepped in and broached the matter to his lawyer. His lawyer was very glad to see him, was, in fact, in a very cheerful and jocular mood, and proceeded to indulge in various light pleasantries about his client's hale appearance, the object of his call, and what not, until he was checked by the portentous solemnity of his client's manner, which, to the experienced practitioner, must have seemed a little ludicrous if he ever allowed anything to appear in that light which concerned so profitable a client as Mr. Sydney Dexter.

Mr. Dexter had acquired a large estate, and was naturally very cautious and careful in disposing of it; he showed a purpose of informing himself fully of the exact legal effect of every clause in the proposed will to such an extent that when, after a long interview, his counsel was called away by a court engagement, Mr. Dexter found, to his great vexation, that the whole time had been spent in talk, and that not even the caption of the will had been written. But as the lawyer, rubbing his hands with a little comforting air, very truly said : —

"We've got the ground cleared at any rate, and the rest of it is plain sailing."

The lawyer's metaphor was a little mixed, but

the lawyer's meaning was as clear as the lawyer's head ; and apparently true enough too, for
nothing remained but to put into legal "quips
and quirks " the substance of the minutes he had
taken.

" Plain sailing." With those reassuring words
the cheering attorney shut the carriage door on
his client, and went smiling away on his own
errand. But a lawyer, however clear-headed, is
not a prophet. Divination is no part of his craft.
Neither are words always facts, nor, alas, even
necessarily truths ; nor indeed anything at all
but specious vibrations of the air.

" Plain sailing ? " Why, yes, the seas are
smooth, the sky is bright, the winds are fair
to-day ; — but who knows of to-morrow ?

Contenting himself with making an appoint-
ment to execute the will the next day, Mr. Dexter drove to his own banking-house, passed
through the busy hall where busy clerks bent
obsequious heads before him, and proceeded to
his private room.

Mr. Dexter, seated at his own desk, impresses
us as a power ; he has long impressed the world
as such, for here, in his own stronghold, he sits
intrenched behind the most impregnable of
material bulwarks — money.

Mr. Dexter, too, has the confident air of one
conscious of power and accustomed to exercise
it. He has seen the world too long time bowing
at his feet, to have a very exalted respect for it.
He knows too well that the old story of the
golden calf is typical of a principle as enduring
as humanity ; knows too well that, to-day, as
aforetime in the wilderness, the molten beast
claims the first homage of mankind, and that its
brutish and insensate image is still set up in
every mart and on every 'change as a rival to the
everlasting Jehovah.

But Mr. Dexter, meanwhile, opens his morning's
letters ; dictates answers to a nimble amanuensis ;
makes orders, sends telegrams, pronounces judgments whose influence reaches to the ends of the
earth. We marvel at the swiftness of decision,
at the executive vigor, which come of native
powers ripened by long experience. We attend
Mr. Dexter as he goes out upon the street ; we
note the deference with which the street doffs its
hat and says civil things. But Mr. Dexter pays
little heed to all this deference, for Mr. Dexter's
busy head is full of schemes. He goes scheming
up and down into numerous little cells and coops
where sit other men as full of schemes as he ;
men who smile mechanical smiles, and watch

each other with lynx-like eyes, and lie to each other in every look and gesture save only with the literal tongue. ·

And Mr. Dexter attends meetings of this board of trustees and that board of directors, where are other men much like himself, assembled to discuss and direct the affairs of great corporations ; and what with it all Mr. Dexter returns to his own office with a weary air and rather a jaded look, and passing into his private room shuts the door as an intimation that he wishes not to be disturbed. He rings his bell presently and despatches a note to his lawyer, directing the messenger to shut the door as he goes out. A half hour, an hour, two hours pass and the door remains shut. It is unusual. The cashier is a little anxious ; he has something that needs attention ; he goes to the door, hesitates, turns away, then goes back and knocks gently. No answer. Mr. Dexter is evidently asleep—an unprecedented thing in the history of the office.

The cashier retires ; another half hour passes ; time presses ; business is imperative ; the anxious cashier goes to the door and knocks again, and all the clerks up and down the hall, with one strange accord, stop in their work and fix their eyes on the unopening door. No sound from

within ; the cashier can wait no longer ; he turns
the latch and enters, passes through the little
ante-room, peeps into the inner office, and sees
his lethargic chief sitting fast asleep at his desk.
He speaks to him, — calls his name, — calls it
louder, — goes up and touches him upon the
shoulder, — shakes him by the arm, then ——

Yes ; feel his head, Mr. Cashier ! It will never
beat again.   Try his pulse ! It will throb no
more.   These important matters of credit and
discount must still wait.   Mr. Dexter has gone
to settle an account of longer standing.

Yes ; gather around, you underlings ! The lion
is dead ; you need not fear the lightning of his
eye nor dread the thunder of his voice !

Yes ; come, you breathless men of medicine ;
shake your grave heads and go through your
harmless pow-wow, — the case is already beyond
your reach !

Big as it may be, busy as it may be, irreverent,
unbelieving, cynical, hard, wicked as it may be,
there is one thing that never fails to affect a
great commercial town : the death of one of its
money kings.   The utilitarian spirit receives a
check ; the wide realm of matter feels a pang,
for Mammon is struck to earth by a blow from

an·unseen and terrible Hand. The whole community stops and stares and rubs its eyes, and then, the bolt having passed, and the air cleared, they stolidly set up their dumb, fallen god again upon its pedestal, and prostrate themselves anew before its doltish form.

Society, too, pauses for a moment and composes her face to a decent gravity at sight of the crape on the door knob. She looks to see that the great house is duly darkened, and that the servants move about with bated breath. She hears with approval that the bereaved widow, shut up in her room, is struggling with all the force of a strong nature, fortified by a zealous religious faith, to bear up under the appalling suddenness of the blow ; that the son, pale and shocked, sits alone by the smouldering fire in the library, from morning till night, and can scarcely be induced to eat a morsel or speak a word. She looks about with sharp eye to see that all the arrangements are as they should be, as, with her practiced mourning face, she utters a nicely-worded condolence and hurries away to make ready for the wedding of one of her favorite votaries in the next street.

In due turn come the worshipful corporations, societies, clubs, organizations to which the dead

man had belonged, and hold commemorative
meetings and pass sounding resolutions as to the
virtue, intelligence, purity, and worth of his
character. Away, Truth, you shameless vixen !
Back, Candor, you noisy termagant ! *De mortuis
nil nisi bonum !*

"Dust to dust — ashes to ashes," and all was
over. As the funeral procession was returning
from the grave, it was stopped for one of those
inscrutable reasons known only to undertakers.
Ralph, looking idly from the window, saw close
beside him a small and singular group of
mourners gathered about an open grave — two
small children, a cripple hobbling about on
crutches, who seemed giving directions, and a
lean, severe-looking little woman, who held the
smallest child by the hand, and occasionally
caught it spasmodically in her arms. The coffin
stood by the grave, ready to be lowered ; the
elder child, a girl of about nine, stood looking at
it in mute, tearless agony. A drizzling rain fell
upon the exposed coffin and added to the indescribable desolation of the scene. Diverted, for
a moment, from his own misery, Ralph seized a
neglected bouquet of choice flowers that lay on
the cushion before him, and, opening the carriage
door, stepped out and placed it upon the strange

coffin, reading as he did so, with careless eye, the name upon the plate :—

"REBECCA HOYT."

The little girl looked for a moment at the offering, then at the strange donor, and with a heart-rending cry of "my mother," threw herself upon the coffin in a paroxysm of grief. Ralph gently lifted her, spoke to her tenderly, and gave her to the grim little woman, who, clasping both children in her bony arms, muttered hoarsely :—

"Poor Cossets."

CHAPTER XI.

A NAMELESS NOBODY.

THE cheerful attorney composed his face to a fitting gravity when he waited upon Mrs. Dexter, about a week after the funeral, and asked her attention to a few business details.

"I dare say you will be surprised to hear, Mrs. Dexter, that your husband left no will."

"I am not surprised; I have never given the subject a moment's thought," returned that lady, coldly; "is it necessary for me to discuss it so soon?"

"I regret to say it is. It is advisable that some definite arrangements should be made with regard to the business; large interests are at stake and Mr. Dexter's personal representative ought immediately to be decided upon."

"And do I necessarily have a part in this?"

"You are the person chiefly interested; you ought at once to apply for administration upon your husband's estate."

" That, I should think, would more properly belong to my son — to Mr. Ralph Dexter."

" On the contrary, Mr. Ralph Dexter has nothing to do with it."

" Indeed ! "

" Mr. Ralph Dexter was, I believe, not your own son ? "

" He was not."

" Nor any kin to either you or your husband ? "

" No."

" Then he has no rights in the matter ; he is entirely dependent upon your *charity* for anything he may get out of the estate."

Mrs. Dexter was so astonished at this statement that she failed to notice the rather singular term and emphasis her legal adviser had used.

" You surprise me extremely," she said, " but of course it must be so — and yet, his father, I am sure, designed " —

" To make some provision for him — yes ! "

" You knew then of Mr. Dexter's purpose ? "

" Mr. Dexter called and consulted me about making a will the very day he died."

" Did he give you any intimation of the purport of it ? "

" Ye-e-s — that is " —

" What was it ? " asked Mrs. Dexter, eagerly.

" Excuse me. Mr. Dexter's verbally expressed wishes are not of the least validity now, they were communicated to me confidentially, and — they might prove an embarrassment rather than " —

" Whatever they may have been, I wish to hear them."

" As you please, Madam, but I beg you to understand that I repeat them only as a personal favor to you and in the strictest confidence, warning you, as your legal adviser, that they are not binding now, and that you are not called upon to regard them in the slightest."

Mrs. Dexter bowed coldly, with an expectant air.

" After the usual provision for the payment of debts," began the lawyer, with an uncomfortable look, " Mr. Dexter made several bequests to public charitable institutions."

" Do you remember the names of the charities and the amounts he wished to give ? "

" I have a memorandum of them."

" And then ? "

" Then followed private legacies of small amounts to various relatives."

" Have you the particulars of those ? "

" I have."

" Pray proceed ! "

" Then there was a provision for his widow."

" And do you remember the particulars of that ? "

" Not with precision," returned the cautious attorney.

" But generally ? "

" Why, generally, there was the house and furniture, carriages, pictures, plate, etc., a policy of life insurance, some shares of bank stock, and a legacy in money."

" Of what amount ? "

" I will not be sure."

" But about what ? "

" Something like twenty-five thousand dollars, I should say."

Whatever emotion of surprise or disappointment Mrs. Dexter may have felt at mention of this small sum, her cold, inflexible face gave no indication of it ; her first aversion to the discussion of business had, however, already given way to an unmistakable interest in it.

" But the bulk of his property," she continued ; " what was to be done with that ? "

The lawyer hesitated again under his client's severe eye and very direct questions.

10

"It was to be left to his adopted son — to Mr. Ralph Dexter."

"Was any reason assigned by Mr. Dexter," continued his widow, after a few minutes' silence, "for leaving me so small a sum?"

"Yes; it was to have been stated in the will — 'on account of your ample private fortune.'"

"With regard to Ralph," pursued Mrs. Dexter after another pause; "he knows nothing about himself; he is still ignorant of the facts of his birth; he has every reason to think that he is our own son; it will be necessary now, I suppose, to undeceive him?"

"Certainly."

"If so, I wish — I prefer that he should hear the truth from you; you can then inform him fully of his exact legal relations to his father's — that is, to my husband's estate!"

The lawyer bowed.

"You will confer a great favor upon me by acquainting him with these facts; and — at — the — same — time," continued Mrs. Dexter, hesitating, "you might say that the annual allowance given him by Mr. Dexter will still be deposited with my banker to his order, and that any further reasonable sums he may need, in a business way, I shall be most happy to advance him."

"But, about the facts of his birth, his real name, &c., — he will naturally be curious as to that, and all motive of secresy is now, of course " —

"I know nothing about it at all. I took him solely to please my husband, who, if *he* knew anything of his antecedents, never told me ; he was brought to the house by a respectable elderly person, who said that she was not at liberty to answer any questions about the child, save that his mother was a lady and a person of a very noble character, who had been unfortunate."

The next day Ralph received a note from the family lawyer, asking him to call at his office on important business. Ralph went at the appointed hour. The smiling attorney received him with respectful courtesy and ushered him into his private room. But even that experienced man of affairs was a little at a loss how to introduce his business, as he regarded the young man sitting so unsuspectingly before him, with his calm proud eyes, his air of high breeding, of generous living, of freedom from care, of unbounded hope and uncurbed ambition.

The lawyer threw himself back in his leather chair, crossed his legs, and assumed a business air : —

"Mr. Dexter," he began, "I want to have a little talk with you about your father's affairs. It is only due to you that you should be informed at the earliest possible moment of the exact state in which things have been left. Of course his dying intestate in this unexpected way leaves matters in rather a perplexing condition ; and his estate must now be settled in a manner very different from what he designed or would have wished. The law now takes everything out of our hands, and we have nothing to do but submit."

Ralph nodded in unconcerned acquiescence.

" I regret to say," resumed the lawyer, hitching uneasily in his chair, "that you are the person most concerned by this failure of your father's to make a will, and that in fact it very materially affects your interests."

"Indeed ! " said Ralph, with a look of interest.

"Yes," continued the man of law with increasing hesitation, "and I regret to say, Mr. Dexter, that I cannot make this clear without at the same time disclosing to you facts of which I have reason to believe you are now entirely ignorant, and the announcement of which will, I fear, greatly surprise and shock you."

After such an introduction, Ralph not unnat-

urally awaited the revelation with a look of strong
curiosity ; but the absence of any anxiety or embarrassment in his face showed how little he was
prepared for what was coming.

" Mr. Dexter, may I ask, before proceeding
further, if you have any remembrances of your
early childhood in which your surroundings were
different from those of late years ? "

" None whatever."

" Have you ever heard a whisper or intimation
to the effect that your relations to the family
of the late Mr. Dexter were other than they
seemed ? "

" I do not think I quite understand you,"
answered Ralph with a puzzled air.

" Have you ever had any cause to suspect that
you were not in reality the son of Mr. and Mrs.
Dexter ? "

" Never ! " exclaimed Ralph, while a little wave
of color crept slowly over his face.

" Has nothing in your own feelings, your own
impressions, told you that they might not be
your own father and mother ? "

" Nothing ! " cried Ralph, starting forward in-
stinctively in his seat and casting a look of indignation upon his questioner. " It is impossible ;
my father could not have so deceived me ; he

could not have talked to me, treated me as he
did if I had not been his own child. My
mother " —

He stopped ; a strange, quick, indescribable
expression of intelligence, of discovery, as though
the veil of some old mystery had been suddenly
rent, as though an unexpected light had been let
in upon some dark crypt of memory, swept across
his face. Impulse brought a quick exclamation
to his lips which Prudence only half repressed,
as he confronted his companion with a look of
dumb amazement, and his face gradually paled
till only two round spots of intense color glowed
in his cheeks.

" I sincerely regret if I have pained you ; I
feared this intelligence would be shocking, and
nothing but the actual necessity could have induced me to tell you."

" You have told me nothing, sir ! I repel
your insinuations as false and impossible. I will
accept only the most direct statements and the
most certain proofs in such a matter."

" You are right ; I hesitated to tell you the
blunt facts at once, but it is necessary you
should know them. Be assured I shall tell you
nothing that I cannot substantiate. It is my
duty, then, to inform you that you are not, as
you suppose, the son of Mr. and Mrs. Dexter."

"I have but your word for that."

"Here is something better; here is evidence that you cannot doubt!" said the lawyer, opening a drawer and taking out a slip of paper.

"You know this handwriting; it is a note Mr. Dexter sent me only an hour or two before he was found dead in his room. I have reason to believe that these were the last words he ever wrote."

Ralph took the note and read the few lines with visible emotion : —

"DEAR SIR : — I omitted to tell you this morning what perhaps you ought to know, that Ralph is not the child of Mrs. Dexter and myself, but an adopted son. If necessary, so state it in the will; let there be no possible ground for misconstruction in that instrument!

"Yours respectfully,

"SYDNEY DEXTER."

Ralph rose and paced the room in silence, the letter in his hand.

"But my mother, — that is, Mrs. Dexter," — he said at length, "why did she not tell me of this?"

"She wished, I suppose, to spare both you and herself the pain of such an interview."

"But it is at her request that "—

"Yes; she desired me to make the announce-ment, that I might at the same time acquaint you with the legal aspects of the case."

"Ah!"

"You are now, of course, prepared to hear, Mr. Dexter, that, in the absence of any testa-mentary provision, there is — I would say you are "—

"A beggar!" said Ralph, calmly.

"Why, not quite so bad as that, I am happy to say, for, by the generosity of Mrs. Dexter, the annual allowance given you by your father will be continued. Also Mrs. Dexter was good enough to say that any reasonable sums which may be necessary to start you in any business or profession, she will cheerfully furnish."

"Indeed!" exclaimed Ralph, with a bitter emphasis; then suddenly changing his tone, he continued: "She is very kind. I have no claim upon her. I have no reason to expect such gen-erous treatment at her hands. But pray may I ask, sir," he continued, turning suddenly towards the lawyer, "if my father, that is, I mean the late Mr. Dexter, gave you any information about my family or the circumstances of my birth?"

"That is all he said," returned the attorney, pointing to the note.

"But Mrs. Dexter, I suppose, knows about it?"

"On the contrary, she knows nothing."

"Not even my name?"

"Not even that, I regret to say."

"Have you anything else to say to me?"

"Nothing,—save that I shall be very happy to serve you in any way."

Ralph merely bowed his thanks at this complimentary phrase, and taking his hat bade the lawyer a formal good-day and withdrew.

He went straight to his club, sought a quiet corner near one of the windows, and sat for two hours almost motionless, looking out upon the street. With what indomitable will he held himself hard down to the task of realizing his position, with what fortitude he accepted the situation, may be conceived, for in those two hours he had evidently fought his battle and taken his resolve. He rose with a calm, decided air, rang for writing materials, and wrote the following letter:—

"DEAR MADAM,—I have just come from a long interview with your lawyer. He has made known to me—he says at your desire—that I am neither child nor kinsman of yours or the late Mr. Dexter's; that the facts concerning my birth are not known; that Mr. Dexter's death, without a will, has left me with no legal right or title to any part of his estate, to a shelter in his house, or even to the name I bear. He has also made known to me your benevolent purpose in my behalf. I thank you cordially for your kind offer, for your good wishes, and for the interest which I am assured you take in my welfare; and while I must henceforth decline to avail myself of your assistance, I none the less acknowledge all your goodness in the past; I thank you for all the care and trouble I must have cost you, and hope that I may sometime be able to render you a more fitting return.

"If your charity, in taking and bringing up as your own the child of poor and perhaps obscure origin, shall prove in the end mistaken — shall even result in a great injustice to the unfortunate object of your bounty, I will strive only to remember the generous impulse that prompted you, — I will strive only to recall with gratitude your care and benevolence.

"Having nothing better to which I am entitled I can only subscribe myself,

"Yours with the greatest respect and esteem.

"A NAMELESS NOBODY."

CHAPTER XII.

"THE fair side! The fair side; always put the fair side out, my dear; the big ones on the top — so!"

True Blue with practiced eye and busy hands was arranging a fresh store of fruit, nuts, and confectionery in the tiniest, snuggest, and brightest of booths, built into a nook in the wall directly opposite his own well-known stand on the street corner. Little Rachel stood by, watching his movements with absorbed interest.

> "Keep a fair outside
> And a stiff upper lip,
> If ever of fortune's
> Sweet favor you 'd sip.

Bear that in mind, my dear Titania!" continued True, putting the finishing touches to his work, and regarding the whole with a critical eye.

"But isn't it naughty, Mr. Blue, to put all the bad spots out of sight?"

"Naughty! Ho, ho, ho, naughty is *very*

good! Why, there is no such word in business! Naughty! Ha, ha, ha — how *de*licious!" exclaimed True, leaning back upon his crutches and laughing until his fat sides shook again.

"My dear Titania, you're in business now, you know, don't you?"

Rachel nodded rather doubtfully.

"Well then, my chick-a-biddy, don't ever use that word again. Now you've got into business, you want to be business-*like*, you know; you must learn to keep your eyes peeled and know what you're about. Now, my dear, in the first place what's the objective pint of all business?"

"I guess I don't know."

"Of course you don't know, an' so I'm goin' to tell you — it's grub an' raiment!"

"What is that?"

"Why, bread an' butter for you an' Baby to eat; an' shoes an' stockin's an' clothes for you to wear, and a bed for you to sleep in — don't you want to earn money to buy all them things?"

"Oh, yes, and I want to get a little house like yours and Lady Pamela's, and a nurse for Baby, to take him out walking."

"Whoa — wh-o-a! Hold on, my Queen of the Fairies, let Fancy droop her wing!

"Don't pick up stray kittens,
Lest you git scratched;
Or enumerate chickens
Before they are hatched.

Which means, my dear, that you must first learn, before you can earn; an' I am goin' to teach you; I am goin' to instill into you business principles; without business principles, Titania, my dear, you would go — you would go," repeated True, polishing an apple, "straight to smash!"

Rachel looked alarmed at this possible result of her business efforts, until True Blue resumed:

"But I shall take care that you *do* have business principles, and that you do *not* go to smash!"

The child with sharp eyes and eager ears stood watching and listening to her instructor, making no nice moral distinctions, and accepting all his teachings as infallible.

"Oh there, there, Mr. Blue, that's a specked one you're putting on the top!"

"Why, so it is, my dear!" exclaimed the peddler, beaming on his apt pupil. "So it is, and we will tuck it under there — so; — that's more business like. — That's right; look sharp and keep your eyes open; none of your specked things in sight. Do you see all them big, tall marble stores over there?"

Rachel nodded.

"Well, my dear, all the men that own them stores, they're rich; an' they live in grand houses finer than Putney Place, — oh, a great deal finer than Putney Place; an' they have grand carriages, an' grand clothes, an' gold and silver an' gems to bind their hair, an' all that; an' how d'ye spose they got it?"

"I can't think!" exclaimed Rachel, almost breathless at the coming revelation.

"*By keepin' the specked side down!*" said True in a solemn and rather awful voice. "That's how they got it; an' that's how anybody gits anything. That's how folks git married. Oh, don't *they* keep the specked side down till after the minister's said: 'Let no man put asunder.' *I* guess so! An' how do the lawyers win their cases? By keeping the specked side out of sight of the judge and jury! An' all these great men you read of in the papers, that rule the country and sit in high places, — how do they ever git up so high in the favor of the people? By keepin' their specked side down! Now everything human and everything nateral has a specked side; it's in the necessity of the case; an' the man that keeps that down an' puts it out of sight, *he's* the man that understands

business; *he's* the man that gits on, and the
sooner he does understand it, the sooner he does
git on. Now, my dear Titania," concluded True,
as he noticed that Rachel's attention wandered,
"what have I been talking to you about?"

" Keeping the specked side down."

" An' what does the specked side mean?"

" I don't know."

" It means the poor side, the weak side, the
bad side, the unattractive, dirty, unpleasant,
dull, mouldy, rotten side; it means the side that
ain't up to the scratch," said True, shifting the
apples and bringing the oranges to the front.

"Oh, isn't it pretty," cried Rachel, clapping
her hands with delight, as she stepped down by
True's side upon the walk, and surveyed the
carefully-arranged stall, the little counter with
its new glass jars and bright tin pans filled with
confectionery; with its baskets of nuts, rosy
apples, and golden oranges; with the little chair
tucked in behind the counter out of sight, where
she was to sit and read or sew when there was
no customer.

"Yes, my dear Titania, an' this is all yours;
your dear mamma, she said to me — now don't
go an' cry, but listen to what I say — when your
dear mamma was just about breathin' her last,

she said to me: 'Mr. Blue,' says she, 'I leave my children in your care, because I think you're honest an' have a good heart. Take the little money I've got and use it so as to do them the most good, an' if you can fix it anyways so that they can get an eddication, that is what I want, but I leave it all to you.'"

Big tears gathered in Rachel's eyes, and her little lips quivered at this mention of her mother, but she controlled her emotion and listened intently as True proceeded : —

"An' so, my dear, I took some of that money an' fixed up this little stall for you, an' now I'm going to give you an eddication, as your mamma wished — a business eddication, Titania, which is the only sort of an eddication that is of any account. I'm goin' to begin to-day ; I'm goin' to begin here an' now," continued True, hobbling to the end of the little counter, where he unlocked and opened a drawer and produced two small, neat account-books.

"There, my dear, I'm goin' to give you the first rule an' don't you ever forgit it! Rule One, say !"

"Rule One !"

"Set everything down in black an' white !"

"Set everything down in black and white," repeated Rachel.

"That means, my dear, put it down in ink an'
paper; set down in this blue book everything
you buy, an' in this red book everything you
sell, to the last peanut an' peppermint! Name
of thing on the right an' figgers on the left ; an'
now," he continued, producing from the drawer
a pen and a bottle of ink, "write your name on
the outside of them books !"

At this moment a boy stopped before the little
booth and began inspecting the fruit.

" How much for them apples ?"

" Go an' wait on your first customer, Titania !"

The child advanced timidly, handed the boy
the largest apple from the top of the heap, received the penny payment, and came joyfully
running to put it in the drawer...

" What did you go an' give that little beggar
your biggest apple for ?"

" He pointed to it !" said the child apologet-
ically.

" Ho, ho, ho !" roared True, "pointed to it,
did he ? Ho, ho, ho, your eddication has been
neglected, my Queen of the Fairies. But slow
an' easy 's the word ; we 'll come to that by-an'-
by ; one rule a day ; that 's my motto ;—now
what 's Rule One ?"

" Set everything down in black and white !"

11

"Very good; now look sharp an' do it :—
O-n-e ap-ple — 1. Don't let anybody steal your
goods, now, for I must go across to that old gentleman, who is the very picture of a man that
wants to buy a patent stove-lifter to carry home
to his wife." And True hobbled away to his
own stand to catch a customer.

Rachel's bright, pretty face attracted a good
many curious eyes during the day, and she sold
several dozen apples and oranges, so that at
night she found the bottom of her little drawer
quite covered with pennies, which True turned
into a stout little leather bag and gave to her to
carry. While Rachel put on her cloak and
gloves, True made his preparations to go home.
He first packed away all his own goods in a
heavy oaken chest, which he locked with a massive padlock and left on the sidewalk for the
night ; he then put up a great wooden shutter in
front of the little booth, fastened it by a thick
cross-bar of iron, and secured that with another
big padlock, of which he gave Rachel the key,
saying :—

"There, Titania, that's yourn, an' I want to
teach you to take care of it !"

Rachel drew a deep sigh of relief at the happy
completion of her first day of business, and then

with a joyous skip turned her face towards home.
As they drew near the little area door, she fairly
trembled with eagerness; she could scarcely
wait for True's slow movements; as soon as the
door was unlocked, she bounded away up the
yard, and there sure enough was the light shining in the window, and there, better still, was
Baby, with his nose flattened against the pane,
looking out for them. She swung her arm and
cried out, but Baby could not see her in the
dark yard, and it was only when he heard the
noise of True's crutches on the stairs that he
came scampering to the door, flung his arms
about Rachel's neck, and laughed aloud with
delight.

And so they went in to the cosy little parlor,
True hobbling after them, shouting in his cheeriest tones :—

"What ho, there, Lady Pamela, advance and
give the countersign !"

Whereupon, after a little, Lady Pamela appeared in the door-way, with her look of chronic
woe and, putting her wet hands behind her, came
forward to receive her usual embrace, and then
withdrew without speaking a word.

Very soon supper was ready, and Rachel and
Baby went skipping out to Lady Pamela, who

lifted the latter up and perched him upon a pile
of big books which she had put in his chair, and
there just in front of his place was a litttle cake
with his name baked in raised letters on the top.
And then the way that Baby laughed,.and Rachel
laughed, and True laughed, quite upset Lady
Pamela's own gravity, and she was betrayed into
one little spasmodic grin herself, which however
looked so much like a grimace that they were
all glad when she resumed her old grim look and
rattled the tea cups and spoons as usual.

True, with the carving knife and the steel,
clashed and fenced away in imitation of a stage
duel as he cried : —

> " B-a Ba : b-y by :
> Oh what a dainty cake,
> The beauteous Lady Pamela
> For Baby she did make."

" An' now send up your plates, my dears, let
us eat and be merry ! Eh, what has the Lady
P. got there ? What, milk ? A cup of milk for
each ?

> " Oh, would that we were boys again,
> The Lady P. and I,
> We too would have a cup of milk
> To drink when we were dry ! "

" Ha, ha, ha ! " laughed Rachel, " she couldn't
be a boy ! "

" She couldn't be a boy," reiterated Baby taking a huge bite of his cake.

" Ho, ho, couldn't she — so she couldn't ; now think of that, my dear ; you couldn't be a boy ! Now don't go and make up your mind to be a boy, my charmer, for a boy, a boy you cannot be ! "

And True ended with a little cadenza which he directly apologized for : —

" I beg your pardon, ladies and gentlemen, please lay it to the joyful nature of this occasion ! "

" What's the matter with the kidney stew ? " asked the Lady Pamela, watching her husband with jealous eye as he helped himself to a slice of cold ham.

" The kidney stew, my dear Lady P., may be said to be perfection ; it may be doubted if there were ever finer kidneys, and there certainly was never better stew, but when I cast my eye upon that ham I said : ' her lily hand hath done it ; —

'The Lady Pam
She boiled that ham;
It looks so nice
I'll take a slice.'"

The Lady Pamela, as usual, ate little herself, but waited upon the others assiduously ; every

refusal to be helped even a third or fourth time
she immediately suspected of being grounded
upon a distaste for the viand.

"If the tea ain't good, don't drink it!" she
cried sharply, as True ventured to play a moment with his spoon.

"Good!" repeated True melodramatically, "it
is in the immediate neighborhood, if not the
very next door, to ambrosial nectar.

> · "Such a fine cup of T,
> My dear Lady P.,
> Ne'er came o'er the C,
> And I doubt if there B—

Such another in the whole Celestial Emperor's
teetotal territory—a half a cup clear, my love!"

Having satisfied his thirst and by the same act
his spouse, True rose from the table and they all
adjourned to the litle parlor, where True produced his pipe, settled himself in his easy-chair,
and calling about him the children told them the
story of "Rupert the Rider; or, The Fiend of
the Black Forest," a thrilling melodrama once
played at the Bowery Theatre.

The children listened with big eyes and bated
breath to the wonderful story, and thought the
Bowery must be altogether the finest place in the
world—an opinion in which True evidently ac-
quiesced.

"And now, Titania my dear, if you pay attention to business an' don't go into bankruptcy,
we will all go to the Bowery some night when
there's a good play — you and I and Lady Pamela and the Baby. But here comes the fair
Lady P. to speak for herself! And now are you
ready, my dear," continued True, knocking the
ashes from his pipe, "are you ready, I ask, to
touch the murmuring lyre?"

Lady Pamela made no reply, but drying her
hands on her apron she went to a corner of the
room and, opening a battered-looking seraphine,
played a simple prelude, when True, without
moving from his seat, poured forth in stentorian
tones the woful ballad of: "My Willie's on the
Dark Blue Sea." He followed this by "Lilly
Dale" and "Massa's in the Cold, Cold Ground,"
all being pieces of a pathetic turn, which, however, would never have been guessed from True's
interpretation. The poor little seraphine in the
matter of tune and indeed richness of tone had
evidently seen better days, but it was so drowned
and lost in the rushing tide of True's vigorous
baritone, that it could not be thought offensive.

The music over, True consulted his big silver
chronometer and cried, as he saw Baby preparing
to settle himself upon the rug : —

"Heigho! the dustman's coming. Tell me, Lady P., what rhymes with sleepy heads?"

"Beds!" returned Lady Pamela, shortly, shutting the seraphine.

"Hurray! you are a born poet, my dear, a nymph of what-do-you-call-it. 'Beds' you say rhymes with 'heads,' and Shakespeare himself couldn't have made a better rhyme."

Lady Pamela produced a candle, and taking the drowsy Baby by the hand led him and Rachel away to bed, while True, having replenished the fire and filled his pipe, settled himself to the enjoyment of a " Beadle Dime Novel."

Bright and early the next morning, and every morning during the week, Rachel was at her post, so that by Saturday night she had quite a store of pennies. These True directed her to do up in rolls, which he exchanged for silver. And Lady Pamela brought down from the top shelf of the cupboard a cracked, blue-and-white china teapot which was assigned to Rachel for her bank, and in it every night she deposited her daily earnings, keeping out a little to make change for the following day.

Meantime, as True said, "her eddication" had not been neglected. Every day she learned one new principle and reviewed those learned before, and Saturday night, when they had gathered around the fire after supper, they had a grand review.

" What's Rule One ? " asked True, stretching his crippled leg and poking the tobacco down in his pipe.

" Set everything down in black and white."

" An' what does that mean ? "

" It means to write down everything in your books."

" Rule Two ? "

" Keep your place *clean !* "

" And what does that mean ? "

" It means sweep the floor and the walk, dust the counter, and rub up your stock."

" Rule Three ? "

" Always make a trade !"

" And that "—

" That means, don't let anybody go away without buying something !"   —

" Yes, even if you have to sell at cost," added True. " And now what's Rule Four ? "

" Never loaf in your shop."

" Expound."

" It means, always keep busy, and if you haven't got anything to do, make believe you have !"

" Rule Five ! "

" Sell the poorest first ! "

"Yes, git red of your worst things first ; don't let anybody paw over your goods if you can help it."

" Rule Six ? "

"Make folks remember you !"

"Yes, be smart and polite ; be up an' a-comin' ; take some pains to suit customers, an' pass a word with them ! Now then for Rule Seven. This is the Saturday-night rule when you bring home your week's earnin's : — Save your money !"

" Save your money," repeated Rachel.

" Yes, a penny saved is a penny earned : remember that ! Now, my dear, them are all fundamental principles, an' you've got to learn 'em to succeed ; but what's the fundamentalest of all ? "

" Keep the specked side down ! "

"Good, my dear ; git out your bank now an' count your money ; you'll be a female Rothschild if you stick to your eddication an' mind your P's an' Q's ! "

CHAPTER XIII.

RIDDLES FOR THE SPHINX.

A "VOICE and nothing more" — impersonal, intangible and irresponsible, Rumor might fitly be symbolized by a wingèd tongue. Coming now in insidious whisper, now in blatant cry that fills the echoing air, it still finds eager ears, still raises vain hopes and works needless misery !

Of late Rumor had been very busy with Ralph Dexter's name. Scarcely three months had elapsed since his father's death, when it began to be bruited about that he had disappeared from society ; that he was seen no more at the club, at his old haunts, or with his former intimates ; and hints were darkly added that he had taken to evil courses.

"Evil courses" — saints and sinners ! — how his friends bandied the phrase about and wagged their exemplary heads ! With what a melancholy delight, good souls, they listened to the sad account, and discussed its latest details as

the prattling barber trimmed their heads or
shaved their chins of a morning. But which of
them all stretched forth a helping hand to Ralph,
or put about him a brotherly protecting arm?
Never a man! They thought it much that they
were still willing to bestow condescending smiles
and patronizing bows upon one who had " hay on
his horn." Serene pygmies, — how secure they
were in their own good estate, as if the crape
were not, to-morrow, to be tied to their own
door-knobs, and some ghastly grinning skeleton
stalk forth out of their own closets.

As for Ralph, what he thought or cared about
it may be gathered from his talk to his dog:
" Fortune frowns on your master, Dick; the
world is down on him. And you wag your tail
and lick his hand all the same? Why, then you
are a fool, Dick; a poor dumb fool that deserves
to lose his bone for not knowing better than to
be faithful when society raises her eyebrows
and shrugs her respectable shoulders. Fie, fie;
give us your paw, sir! What, love and respect?
Why, the rest of them, good Christian men and
college graduates, only pity and criticise. Poor,
shaggy, foolish brute, how they would all stare if
the truth were printed in the morning paper, —
that for available sympathy, for real solace and

comfort when one is down in the mouth, a dog is
worth a dozen human friends. Ha, ha ! and yet
those human snobs beat, bully, and abuse you.
No matter, Dick, the devil is dead, and the dog's
day is coming. There's a bone for you ! "

In due time, of course, one of those wagging
wingèd Tongues flew in at Mrs. Dighton's window, and she, warm-hearted, indignant little
woman, cast it quickly out. But to what purpose? The very next open window let in a
whole troop of the noisy, croaking ravens, that
nearly deafened the good dame with their
clamor ; and day after day they came fluttering
in on the four winds, and buzzed and hummed
until she was forced to pay some heed. But she
still continued to defend Ralph stoutly in her
own family circle, while Dorothy yawned and
Uncle Curl said, oracularly, that he had "never
expected anything better of that young sprig."

Perhaps it was the maternal instinct that was
stirred in the good lady's heart. Perhaps she
would fain have been Ralph's mother, to inter-
fere actively in his behalf. But then, she was the
mother of somebody else, and her eyes wandered
fondly to Dorothy, and while she marveled how
the latter could be so indifferent in the matter,
she nevertheless rejoiced at it, and trembled to

think how different it might all have been if
some of her own busy schemes in the past had
been more successful.

But when is it ever safe to congratulate ourselves? Is it not better at the moment of our
fullest content, like the wise heathen, to pray for
some slight misfortune?

One evening, after they had come back to
town, Dorothy and her mother sat alone in the
parlor, stowed away in a nook at one end of the
room, formed by a large bay window—their
favorite resort when alone. Dorothy, in a low
chair close by a small table holding a moderator
lamp, had a book in her lap, while her mother
sat opposite, knitting charity stockings, with a
face unusually grave and absorbed.

"A penny for your thoughts, Rhody!"

"It would prove a very bad speculation for
you, my dear."

"Why?"

"I was thinking of poor Mr. Dexter."

"Why will you waste so much time on that
wretched scapegrace?"

"It is so sad to think of such a promising
young man going to ruin."

"He may not be going to ruin after all—you
only know what the gossips say."

"I know what everybody says, and I fear there is no doubt about it. I think he is that kind of a man ; if he once took the wrong course he would go on boldly and recklessly to the end. I tremble to think of it."

" Pooh ; all young men are pretty much alike ; if things don't go to suit them they sow wild oats, or whatever you call it. I presume it's a great relief ; I've often thought I'd like to sow a few myself."

" You poor, silly child ; young men are very far from being all alike, and sowing wild oats is a very different thing from open, reckless, and continued dissipation. With regard to Mr. Dexter, it only shows how much he needed his father's influence ; the moment that was removed he plunged at once into every form of vice."

" Oh, well, he'll get tired by and by and re-form ; don't fret, Rhody, dear. Attention now ; I'm going to read !"

And Dorothy, spreading her map on an easel for reference, opened her book and began, while Mrs. Dighton, happy in her daughter's uncon-cern, cleared her own brow and settled herself to listen.

But before they had finished a chapter, a ser-vant entered the room with a card. Mrs. Digh-

ton, taking it carelessly from the proffered tray,
received as perceptible a shock as if she had
touched a Leyden jar. She exclaimed, hurriedly : —

"Why, dear me, I — who would have thought
of " —

"What's the matter?"

"'Tis he!"

"Mr. Dexter?"

"Yes; and — and I think you had better go
up stairs, my dear."

"'Up stairs'" repeated Dorothy in round-
eyed astonishment.

"Yes, yes; you ought not — that is — I do
not want you to see him."

"How very queer you are!" exclaimed Dorothy, quite puzzled at her mother's words.

The next moment Ralph entered the room,
scarcely recognizable with his haggard face, half-
grown beard, and ill-ordered dress; it required
all Mrs. Dighton's address to master her surprise at his changed appearance. As for Dorothy, she made no secret of her astonishment.
With a grave, shocked look she rose to shake
hands, and could scarcely falter out, "How do
you do?"

Evidently at a loss how to open the conversation, Mrs. Dighton followed her own instincts and conventional rules, and made nevertheless a sad mistake.

"We were very very sorry to hear of your affliction, Mr. Dexter ; we have thought of you much, and I was several times on the point of writing to assure you of our sympathy ; but I thought you would receive so much written condolence from your more immediate friends that it might only trouble you."

"Thank you !" Ralph's face instantly clouded, and he spoke almost coldly. Looking up, a moment after, he asked abruptly : —

" Have you been to the opera, Mrs. Dighton ?"

Mrs. Dighton changed color, and was very much disconcerted, but Ralph's perfectly respectful tone and look precluded the thought of intentional rudeness.

" Yes — no — that is, my daughter and brother have been," she answered, somewhat incoherently.

At this moment a servant entered with more cards — visitors for Mrs. Dighton.

The latter rose and looked from.the servant to Dorothy with evident embarrassment.

" I must see them, I suppose."

" Certainly ; why do you hesitate ?"

"I did not wish to leave you to — that is, I — you must then excuse me."

"Pray do not consider me," said Ralph, "I will talk with Miss Dorothy."

Mrs. Dighton did not seem very much reassured by this arrangement, but uttered a feeble "thank you" and withdrew.

"See what a distance we came back to meet you, Mr. Dexter! Mamma and I were on a trip up the Nile when you came," said Dorothy, pointing to her map and book.

"The Nile?" repeated Ralph, absently.

"Yes; this scrawling black mark is the course of the river. This pin with the head of red sealing-wax is our dahabeah. We have just completed one day's journey, and are now hauled up for the night, finding out where we are, while the dragoman gets supper."

"Good notion," said Ralph, with a faint smile, "better than the real thing; saves so much bother — that is, if you could only escape from home, from friends, from the past and present, from the memory of everything that had ever been, as well."

"'Home and friends?' It's just because we cannot make up our minds to leave them that we do not really go."

"What do you mean by home, Miss Dorothy?"

"That sounds like a catechism question," said Dorothy, "I never was good at a definition, and perhaps I cannot tell you in a breath what I do mean, but I will try. I mean first this place itself and all its belongings ; this house where I was born, and all the things in it ; then I mean the people — my mother and uncle and one or two old servants ; then all the dear old associations and tender memories connected with every spot in the neighborhood, where I have had so many joys, sorrows, hopes, and dreams : I mean all this, with much, very much more that I cannot express, but which seems a part of myself, a part of my own heart and life."

Ralph remained silent for several minutes, evidently pondering Dorothy's answer. When he at length spoke, it was with folded arms, knitted brows, and eyes fixed on the floor, as though following out his own thoughts rather than addressing his companion.

"What if there were no such place, Miss Dighton," he began, "no place where you belonged, no place where you were sure of a welcome ! What if all these things that you treasure were suddenly destroyed, withered to ashes

before your eyes! What if all these dear associations proved false, and all these tender memories a mockery!"

"I cannot conceive such a case," said Dorothy,
with a puzzled look.

"What if all this happened in a moment!
What if, without any fault of your own, you
awoke to the fact that every relation in life was
altered, that the nearest earthly bonds were sev-
ered, that your dearest friend had proved your
worst enemy, that a stigma was affixed to your
very birth!"

"Why imagine such things; let us think of
something pleasanter!" said Dorothy, uneasily.

"Nay," pursued Ralph, oblivious of the interruption, "suppose that with every earthly belonging, that with every hope of the future, that with
every remembrance of the past, your very name
also were stripped from you, and you were left a
creature of circumstances, a pariah, a mere thing
with limbs and blood-vessels!"

"There can be no such thing," returned
Dorothy, wondering at her visitor's vehemence.
"Fortune may prove fickle, trouble and change
may come, but your name and your honor and
your individuality are your own. Nothing can
take them away! The past too is secure; the
past with all its tender and sweet recollections."

"Hm-m-m, to be sure; you must be right; there can be no such thing! But suppose, Miss Dighton, as a mere matter of imagination, it were true — what would be left in the way of duty?"

"Much; if you have left a clear conscience, a good intelligence, and sound bodily health, you have, after all, the best gifts of fortune still! Let the past go if it must; live for the present, for the future! Resolve to make yourself a position, independent of what is or has been!"

Dorothy did not stop to study her words; she did not know how much the conversation might signify, but she spoke with the force of conviction.

"But suppose," continued Ralph, "I do not care for all this; suppose I laugh at the pomp and circumstance of worldly 'position' as you call it!"

"Do you not think the esteem of good men worth having?"

"No, they may be fools; I would as soon have the esteem of bad men. But who are the good men and who are the bad men? A man is called bad if he breaks a law made by a set of dunces who haven't half his own intelligence."

"But is it not best to conform to what the

largest part of mankind have agreed in thinking
right or wrong?"

"Ha, ha, ha!" laughed Ralph, "I beg your
pardon, Miss Dighton, but that question is very
funny.   No, no, and again no, I say; and
imagine, if you please, a string of noes from here
to Patagonia.   Did not the largest part of mankind once think the world was flat?   Suppose
Kepler, Galileo, and Columbus had followed
your rule!"

"Oh, that was in science.   I mean in the
matter of right and wrong, of virtue and morals."

Ralph smiled sardonically.   "Didn't the Catholics slash and burn the heretics, and the Protest-
ants the Catholics?   Did not the Puritans torture
and slay innocent old women for witches?   Is it
not held laudable in India to burn the widow on
her husband's funeral pyre?   Where is the rule,
where is the example?   Who is wise and good
— he who lived yesterday, who lives to-day, or
who will live to-morrow?"

"Very well," said Dorothy, a little discomfited,
"yielding the matter of opinion, there is left the
duty of doing; it is necessary to have some occupation in life, to busy your hands and thoughts
with."

"To what end?   To wear out your soul and

body that somebody else may get the benefit of
it? To earn a wretched pittance, barely enough
to pay for your beggarly crust and shabby
lodging?"

"But you can eat that crust in sweet content,
knowing that you earned it by the labor of your
own hands."

"So if you have more intelligence and do not
care what other men no wiser than yourself may
think, you can eat a very much better dinner, and
sleep in a very much better bed, from your earnings made in a very easy and gentlemanly way,
where you need not bend your back nor soil your
hands."

"Oh, Mr. Dexter," exclaimed Dorothy, in a
tone of horror, "you do not mean"—

"Yes; I mean the gaming-table! Why do
you look so shocked, Miss Dighton?" he continued, with a light laugh. "Are you a slave to
the old teachings and the old prejudices? Tell
me now, out of your own mind, what is the
objection to gaming?"

"Why, first, it brings you into the company of
low people."

"Nothing of the sort, I assure you; that is
what I expected. These notions are repeated
about society from one old lady to another, and

they all believe them, when, as a matter of fact, they are all wrong. The men whom I meet to play with are polite, cultivated men ; yes, men with wit and intelligence enough to furnish out half a dozen drawing-room creatures."

" Yes, but they are not moral ! "

" Are they not ? That 's because we are not agreed in what morality consists, If it is necessary to spend one's days selling lumber and wool, —yes, and cheating our customer the best we can in doing it, — and one's evenings by the fireside prating gossip or talking interior decorations, — I beg your uncle's pardon, — then these men are not moral. But who defines morality thus ? These gentlemen do not steal or rob ; moreover, they pay their honest debts, which your honest tradesmen get out of if they can, even if they have to go through bankruptcy to do it."

" Oh, Mr. Dexter, you pervert everything so, you talk with such a terrible levity."

" Levity, Miss Dighton ? I never was more serious in my life. I am answering your objections against gaming, but yet you have made none that will stand."

" But gaming is wrong in itself."

" Who or what makes it so ? "

" Why, it is against the law."

"Who made the law?" asked Ralph, with a little scoffing laugh; "a set of corrupt politicians, venal rascals who sold their votes where they could get the most money, or else a set of prejudiced blockheads who blindly follow in the footsteps of their fathers, without thinking that their fathers were one degree more stupid and wooden than they."

"But would you then disregard other laws — every law that you disagree with?"

"Certainly; if it stands in my way!"

"But this would be the end of society — society couldn't get along without laws."

"Let it give way to something else then; if it cannot exist without the bonds forged for it by ignorance and prejudice, the sooner it is done away with, the better."

At this moment Mrs. Dighton returned to the room and took her old seat.

"Don't let me interrupt; — pray what is the subject?"

"Why, Miss Dorothy says she is just starting out on a tour up the Nile and I have been propounding a few riddles for the Sphinx."

"You are a great stranger, Mr. Dexter," continued Mrs. Dighton, with a quick look of curiosity at the grave faces before her.

"I hope not," returned Ralph, in his old easy way. "I thought we were getting to be friends."

"Friends are not made nor kept by absence and neglect," replied Mrs. Dighton, in a society tone. Then, as if suddenly conscious of her words and fearful of encouraging a cordiality she might have cause to regret, she added immediately : —

"But you have given up your summer plan of going abroad to study your profession, Mr. Dexter." ·

"'My profession?'" echoed Ralph, with a quizzical air, "let me see, what was my profession then?"

"Excuse me," said Mrs. Dighton, coloring, "I thought you were to be an architect."

"Ah, to be sure, I was subject to that delusion for a time, but that flew away with the summer swallows."

"It is a rather difficult matter, I suppose, to settle upon a profession," said Mrs. Dighton, evidently a little uncertain how to proceed.

"Yes, yes ; there's a great deal of good brain force and lots of valuable time wasted in settling that foolish question."

Mrs. Dighton looked puzzled, but was relieved from further embarrassment by the irruption from the library of Mr. Curley and several equally enthusiastic gentlemen who had been appointed to decorate their unfortunate pastor's library.

"I appeal to you, sister, and to you, Dorothy; we have come to a dead-lock, as they say in Congress, and we want your judgments. The question is this; the floor being a marquetry of Norway spruce and sandal wood, whether the book cases should be ebonized cherry or stained ash? I am for the latter; the *portière* between the study and the ante-room, which comes close to the case, being *écru* plush, or a Morris stamped velvet, — we haven't quite decided which, — with Turkey red bands, and the ornaments Limoges vases and brass sconces, I contend that the tone of the whole will be much better with the ash."

"It theemeth to me, the ebonithed wood will be much more thtriking," lisped a young man with eye-glasses and ladylike manners, — a great authority in interior decorations.

"That's the precise question," retorted Mr. Curley; "do we want contrast or harmony? I'm for the latter."

"Oh, if three such doctors disagree, it will never do to take us in," said Mrs. Dighton, answering for the others and cleverly keeping out of the dispute.

"And what do you say, Mr. Dexter?" asked Mr. Curley, eager for support from some quarter.

"Oh, I'm but a barbarian; I should say bare walls and pine shelves would answer every purpose."

Perhaps Mr. Curley detected the carefully concealed contempt in this reply, for he withdrew discomfited, with his committee, and Ralph rose to go.

"Dorothy, my dear, how could you ask him to come again?" asked Mrs. Dighton, as the door closed.

"Because," returned Dorothy, with a look of profound astonishment at the question, "he needs to go somewhere to get clear of the fatal atmosphere he lives in; because he needs friends now more than ever before in his life; and lastly because I supposed I should be particularly obliging you."

"I am very much interested in Mr. Dexter, and I would do anything I consistently could to help him; but I hope you will not encourage him to come here."

"I certainly shall not *dis*courage him," said Dorothy, decidedly, as she started her dahabeah up the Nile.

CHAPTER XIV.

YES OR NO.

DOROTHY'S dahabeah went on up the Nile; night after night the sealing-wax pin shifted from place to place along the black line upon the map, but busy Mrs. Dighton, knitting away at her charity stockings, presently discovered that the reader's voice was singularly wanting in inflection; that she did the author but small justice in making sense of some of his long periods; that, in spite of the sealing-wax pin, she showed herself decidedly mixed in her geography when they stopped for any discussion of the text, and that, in fine, her mind was evidently roaming far enough away from the land of the Sphinx and the Pyramids.

Perhaps the following letter, received by Ralph Dexter about a week after his call at the Dightons', may in a measure explain Dorothy's abstraction : —

"MY DEAR MR. DEXTER : — The *propriety* of my writing this letter to you may be questiona-

ble ; I am content that it should be. My only
thought has been,—' Is it my duty?' The letter
itself is sufficient evidence of my decision upon
that point.

" The thought that you may have no friend ;
that there might be nobody in the world who
would dare, or, daring, have interest enough, to
write you such a letter has decided me. You
may think it presumption in me ; you may even
laugh or sneer,—for your own sake I should be
very sorry if you did,—but let me begin by
assuring you of my perfect indifference to any
such reception of my proffered advice, for advice
it is that I am so bold as to offer you.

"And first I will confess that I had great difficulty in freeing my mind of the impression that
much of your talk the other evening was due to
affectation or a passing depression of spirits. I
do not think so now ; I believe you are in a very
deplorable state mentally and morally.

" It is true I have not had much experience of
the world ; it is true I have not given much
thought to the subjects upon which we talked ;
it is possible that I may be narrow and immature
in my views upon those subjects : but making
all such allowances, my unaided reason tells me
that you are wrong. Reason and Conscience

alike tell me that society, the world, human life
cannot all be so false, so shallow, such an utter
sham and monstrous lie as you think. It is
neither self-delusion nor self-conceit to say that
I know I have moments of noble impulse ; I will
go further and say I know you have, and I don't
believe there is a man or a woman living who
has not.

"In trying to account for your present state
of mind I can attribute it only—at the risk of
affronting you, Mr. Dexter, I must speak the
truth ; I promised myself when I sat down to
write this letter that I would hesitate at no
plainness of speech, however obnoxious, confident that you can never suffer the pain in
reading that I do in writing it—I repeat, then,
that I attribute your present mood entirely to
weakness, inexcusable weakness ; and I am surprised to find you a person of much more of a
not very worthy sort of pride, and much less
strength of will, than I had supposed.

"Mr. Dexter, I would ask you, with reference
to cherishing this mood of feeling and thought,
these simple questions : Is it manly? Is it
generous ? Is it attended with one moment's
peace, with one feeling of honest pride, with one
hope for the future ? Is it not, on the contrary,

selfish, demoralizing, unnatural, untrue, and pro-
ductive of unrest and misery?

"I know you have been heavily afflicted, and
you have my heart-felt sympathy; you further
hinted at things that confirm some floating
rumors that have come to our ears; I cannot
intrude upon the sanctity of your grief; I cannot
touch upon misfortunes of which I know nothing.
I do not invite, I do not wish your confidence,
but I can and do say that even if fortune, family,
name itself be gone; even if everything be gone
but innocence and self-respect, there is still the
best part left, and everything is still possible to
constancy of purpose.

"I call upon you, Mr. Dexter, to redeem yourself from this abject thraldom to circumstances;
to win for yourself a higher place in the esteem
of good men than Fortune has taken away; to
hold fast to your own self-respect, to maintain
your honor, to propose to yourself some enno-
bling aim in life! Consider the hordes of poor,
weak, unfriended, wretched creatures in the
world, to be lifted up and cared for! Think of
the ignorance and sin to be cured, and resolve to
live for something beside yourself! Then you
will know a fuller happiness than you have lost;
then you will feel how unworthy of your better
self is your present way of life.'

"And now, my dear sir, I shall make no apology for my frankness. If you cannot, if you do not understand my motive, the hesitation and scruples I have been obliged to overcome to bring myself to say what I have said to you, it would be idle for me to apologize for it. But however you receive this appeal, whether you thank or blame me for it, you shall still have my best wishes, prayers, hopes, — yes, and I will add, — *faith*, that you will one day see the light and walk in it.

"Very Truly Your Friend,

"DOROTHY DIGHTON."

Ralph received the above letter one morning as he sat at breakfast, and it will not surprise any masculine reader to hear that instead of seeking his usual companions and pursuits that evening, he found himself shortly after dinner at the door of Mr. Samuel Curley's house.

He was admitted and shown into the library, where Dorothy and her uncle were seated. The former colored deeply at sight of him, and Ralph was so intent in noting her face that he failed to return her uncle's greeting. But Mr. Curley was in a social mood and would not be ignored; he demanded the attention of both to some

13

additions he had been making to his cabinet of China.

"Ah, these Doultons are delicious! Now aren't they? Reach me that vase, Dorothy dear! Notice the detail in this plaque, Mr. Dexter; this now was done by Miss Barlow, — Here is her signature 'F. C. B.' on the bottom, — and see what good vigorous work it is. There now is a vocation for a woman; talk about woman's rights? Faugh! Let her go to work and try to do something and she'll find she has rights enough! Notice, please, that I have massed the Doultons in the back-ground as a foil to this brilliant Gien Faience; while over here, amongst this severe Worcester ware, I have put my gorgeous Palissy — Ah-h-h what a glaze — look at that lizard!" exclaimed Mr. Curley rubbing his hands and drawing in the air through his parched lips with a caressing sound.

"Oh, you are looking at the lower shelf. Yes, yes; there — there now I have put my Limoges and Sèvres and Bisquet. I delight in contrasts you see. You may object that the one is so broad and the other so finical in treatment that the Sèvres is spoiled; but I think not; the distinctive features of each are emphasized, that is all. Here again, for the same reason I put my Wedgewood and blue Meissen together, — other styles of Dresden are on this shelf. Ah — you are looking at those tiles ; yes, those are by Battam — the elder Battam, pretty and dainty, but nothing to compare in color and design with these Doulton tiles, every one hand-wrought, every one a picture."

"Where's all your Majolica ?" asked Dorothy, observing Ralph's attention wander.

" Majolica ? do you like Majolica ? Then you are mine, body and soul ! Look at this plaque, and this jug, and this, and this !" exclaimed the enthusiastic collector, handing out piece after piece. " And now," he cried, turning about with gleaming eyes and hands held behind him, " I'm going to overpower you ! And I beg you not to look at this with your modern irreverent eyes ; look at it with your imagination ! This," he cried, producing a battered-looking plate, "this is a genuine antique ; I picked it up in Italy for a song, right out of the clutches of half a dozen English collectors. No, no," he continued, as Ralph attempted to take it, "I never let *this* go out of my hands ; this must be four hundred years old at least ! "

Just as the ecstatic Mr. Curley was proceeding to open his Oriental cabinet, the clock struck

nine, and he was reminded that he must go for
Mrs. Dighton, who was out spending the evening.

"I received your letter, Miss Dighton," said
Ralph, taking a seat near Dorothy, as soon as
the door closed upon her uncle, "and I came to
thank you for it."

Dorothy sat looking into the open fire and
made no answer.

"Whether you are right or wrong, whether I
am right or wrong, it was very generous and
very friendly in you to write the letter. I suppose a bad man may derive as much comfort
from a little sympathy and friendliness as a good
man."

"I didn't say you were a bad man, Mr. Dexter," said Dorothy, quietly.

"You didn't say it, but you meant it."

"No," returned Dorothy, weighing her words,
"I did not!"

"Why, then, did you urge me so hard to become a good man?" asked Ralph, repressing a
smile.

Dorothy detected the smile in the tone, and
raising her eyes quickly caught the quizzical
look in his face.

"Because I thought, as I still think, Mr. Dexter, that you are in great danger of becoming a bad man, surrounded by such associations as you are, leading a life of ease, self-indulgence, mere physical gratification, and, worse than all, continued unhealthful excitement," answered Dorothy, warmly.

"How long continuance in such a life makes a man bad?" asked Ralph.

"That depends upon how much character he has!"

"But if he has a great deal of a 'not very worthy sort of pride' and very little 'strength of will?'"

"Mr. Dexter, you must excuse me from discussing this matter further," said Dorothy, rising with an air of offended dignity, "I already repent having written the letter; I thought it was my duty. I thought if you were blindly going on in such a course, merely because there was nobody to warn you, to recall you to your senses, that I would rather take the risk, that I would rather subject myself to such a misconstruction, that I would rather lay myself open to such a sneer as it is only too plain" —

"Miss Dighton, now you are not only discrediting your own generous purpose, but doing me also a great injustice," interposed Ralph, seriously, "I am far from misconstruing, I am incapable of sneering at one of the most generous acts of sympathy and friendship I have ever known in my life. If I had felt otherwise I should not have been here to-night. I thought that I should never know enthusiasm again; that such emotion had been frozen up in me for ever; but I declare to you, Miss Dighton, I can find no words in which to express the warmth of my gratitude and the sense of obligation which I shall ever feel under to you for your noble appeal. I come here to-night to thank you in person for your interest in one so unworthy your regard, and to beg you, if you can shut your eyes to my faults, to still keep that interest, to still continue to hold me in such respect as you may. It is my misfortune that I find it impossible sometimes to be serious, even upon the most serious subjects; but I beg you will not always judge me by what appears, but believe that there may sometimes underlie my light looks and light speech something better worth your respect."

Ralph, betrayed into earnestness, spoke eloquently and with fervor. Rising from his seat he strode towards Dorothy, and extended his hand as he continued : —

"Say, I beg, Miss Dighton, that you forgive;

that you are not offended with me! Say that we still are friends!"

Dorothy took his proffered hand, as she replied : —

"I have nothing to forgive, Mr. Dexter, and whether we continue to be friends must depend upon you."

"Does that mean that I must follow your advice before I can hope for your friendship?"

"It means that I shall be your friend so long as you wish it; so long as you show that you prize my friendship."

• "And what must I do to show that?"

"Be true to yourself!"

"That is the hardest task you could set me; to be true to myself is to be true to a most inconstant, irrational, and unworthy standard."

"To be true to yourself, you must be true to your best self! One cannot be mistaken as to the best side of his nature."

"What if there be no best side; what if all are equally bad, or at least equally dreary and sterile?"

"Let us be serious, Mr. Dexter!" said Dorothy, rather impatiently.

Ralph gazed at her inquiringly, without speaking.

"It is one of my complaints against you that you persist in making such speeches as that."

"And shall I not say what comes into my mind,—what your words naturally suggest?"

"Not when it is affectation!" said Dorothy, sharply.

"The trouble is, Miss Dighton," said Ralph, laughing, "you assume that I was once a very commendable sort of person, what you might call, in fact, a model young man, and that I have alarmingly degenerated; whereas the fact is I never was either particularly virtuous or particularly vicious, and but for your vigorous attempts at reform I should never have known that I had become so horribly depraved."

"It is scarcely worth while to disavow the vigorous attempts at reform, or deny the depravity, as you seem so well content with yourself."

"I dare say I have deserved that thunderbolt," said Ralph, resignedly.

"It is not a thunderbolt, Mr. Dexter; it is simply the expression of my hopelessness in attempting to turn this discussion to any good purpose, and I think we had better drop it at once."

"I am very sorry to weary or displease you, but I beg you to have still a moment's patience

with me. You speak of the hordes of poor,
unfriended creatures whom I ought to lift up
and care for. What can I do for them? I have
no longer any means, and as for good advice,
they might profit by that as little as I have."

"You can do what other benevolent people do
—give your time and your talents to help on the
work of reform."

"Missionaries, you mean? Hm—m—m—
perhaps? I hadn't thought of that! I suppose
I might go for a missionary. I might, perhaps,
impose on the untutored savage."

"There are other charities and reforms beside
foreign missions," replied Dorothy, half smiling
in spite of herself.

"But these reforms, these charities are, I suppose, rather elevating than remunerative. What
about the question of bread and butter? Rather
a vulgar question, I know, but it will obtrude
itself."

"You must, of course, make all this work
subsidiary to your regular occupation."

"But," said Ralph, after a few minutes' consideration, "these benevolent pursuits might,
perhaps, be thought a little inconsistent with my
present profession."

"Oh, don't speak so lightly," cried Dorothy, starting from her seat; "it is horrible to hear you! Do not be so—so—shameless as to call it your profession!"

"Would you rather I should amuse myself and you by a polite fiction?"

Dorothy sank back in her chair and gazed at the dying fire some moments in silence.

"No," she said at length, and emphatically, "no, I would rather you should acknowledge it, dreadful as it is; much rather you should look the whole situation squarely in the face without concealment or equivocation;—but oh, it only makes the need of some change, some escape, the more crying! I call upon you, then, again; I appeal to you once more to break loose from it all; to lift yourself up out of it while there is still time, while you yet may!"

"It must indeed be dreadful when you can feel so about it. It is almost a compensation for the evil to find one so truly interested in my safety. I begin to feel what you mean, Miss Dighton," continued Ralph, looking at her earnestly. "I may almost say I feel the longing for something better spring up in my heart in answer to your words, and if it were to any purpose, if there were any one to whom my life were of any value, I might almost hope to succeed; but to work for myself, on myself, — you are right, it is necessary to have some one else to work for, to please and to satisfy, or it is of no use trying."

"Fie, Mr. Dexter; every friend you have would be interested; we should be interested — I should " —

In a moment Ralph's eyes flamed with a new fire; his whole face glowed as he said : —

"Go on, go on, Miss Dighton! You wake in me a new hope. Do you mean that you would be interested in *me* more than in those thousand other creatures you have spoken of? Dare I hope that you would watch over me with a special interest? That you would condescend to guide, aid, inspire, and cheer me on the way up out of this darkness? That you would be that companion, that friend, for whom I might live instead of for myself; that if in time I should win your entire respect, deserve your entire esteem, you might some day become to me " —

"Oh, stop, stop, Mr. Dexter, I beg you!" cried Dorothy, rising in alarm.

"Something dearer to me than any earthly friend has ever been; something dearer than

ever life has been ? Do not answer rashly, but
let me hope, let me feel, that at some time, if not
now, you can be what I ask ; that at some time
you can say yes " —

The door opened, and Mrs. Dighton entered
the room.

CHAPTER XV

THE BRONZE IMAGE.

MRS. DIGHTON came into the room as gently as a snowflake and as inopportunely as a bomb-shell.

Neither Dorothy nor Ralph had enough of that very convenient but not very enviable kind of cleverness called tact, to assume in a moment the air of nothing in which a poorer sort of people might have found refuge from detection.

As it was, Ralph scarcely refrained from glowering at the intruder, who, taking in the situation with one swift glance from face to face, came forward in a flutter of alarm lest she had arrived too late. Drawing up a chair between the young people, she showed a neat bit of self-control by falling at once to telling a droll story which she had just heard from some member of the company she had left. Dorothy, almost hidden from sight in her huge easy-chair, sat gazing intently into the smouldering fire, where now but a single eye of flame looked out from a grotesque face formed

by the gray embers.   Ralph paid no heed to the
idle chatter of his hostess, but after one or two
absent remarks rose abruptly and went out.

Mrs. Dighton chose not to say anything to
Dorothy upon the subject of Ralph or his call,
and only remarked, when her daughter came for
a good-night kiss an hour before the usual
time : —

" Sleepy child, our dahabeah has been drawn
up at Philæ these past three days, waiting for a
start ! "

As for Ralph, he went home and paced his
chamber floor, smoked savagely, flung himself
into bed and flung himself out of bed, paced and
smoked, smoked and paced again.   And so the
long night wore away till the gray dawn came
creeping into his windows.   The morning was
passed in the same restless fashion, until noon
found him again upon the broad stone steps of
Mr. Curley's house.

Mrs. Dighton was sitting alone in the library
when his card was brought up, and Mrs. Dighton
told the exact truth when she said :—

" Miss Dorothy is engaged ; ask the gentleman
to please excuse her."

Miss Dorothy *was* engaged ; engaged at that

moment in her own little studio, listlessly sketching; but it may, perhaps, be doubted whether she would have asked to be excused from seeing a visitor on account of what she was doing, much more it may be doubted—whatever may have been her feelings towards Ralph Dexter—whether she would have sent him such a message. As it is, it must forever remain a matter of speculation what might have been the result of that prevented interview.

Without time to consider the consequences of what she did, Mrs. Dighton had acted upon the aroused maternal instinct of protection to her daughter. It was, no doubt, some misgiving as to the step she had taken, that led her to go up stairs shortly after Ralph's call, walk straight to Dorothy's door, and put her hand on the latch. —But what malign impulse then stayed her course, kept her hesitating till her resolution cooled, impelled her to walk slowly up and down the hall, and then to steal softly down the stairs! Foolish little woman, if you had but obeyed that first courageous impulse, and spoken out those few honest words that were in your heart, you might have spared yourself unspeakable misery, and spared the world this story of your weakness!

Meantime the fact that Dorothy chose to keep

her own counsel as to what had passed between her and Ralph alarmed and distressed her mother. Never before had complete confidence been wanting between them. Relying, however, upon the habits of a lifetime and a devoted filial affection, Mrs. Dighton waited for her daughter to speak.

Any determinate chain of events standing to each other in the logical relation of cause and effect may be said to form to us, reasoning creatures, a kind of moral tramway, upon which, once started, consistency compels us to proceed. And so it was with Mrs. Dighton; having switched off from the natural, straight-forward course, there was no getting back, and so she was obliged to keep guard on the door, to watch the daily letters, to be down before the rest of the family in the morning, to deprive herself of her regular walks and rides, and to mount guard on all occasions whenever Dorothy moved.

Coming down, one morning, on her detective errand, she stopped before the little table in a corner of the hall, close by the dining-room door, where the morning's mail-matter was always left, ready to be taken in to the breakfast-table by the first-comer of the family. A single letter lay in the centre of the small table, scarcely distinguishable in the uncertain light from its white marble background. Mrs. Dighton bent over and breathlessly examined the address. She knew all her daughter's correspondents. This was a strange hand; a bold masculine hand. She turned the letter quickly. On the back was a small engraved monogram. One look sufficed. A noise was heard in the upper hall. She dropped the letter, drew back and looked around with a startled air. All was still again. She put her hands behind her and again bent over the table; turned and walked up the hall; but only to return again to the table. Presently the sound of a coming step caused her to fly into the drawing-room and thrum upon the piano, — it was only one of the servants coming down-stairs.

Rising and pacing nervously back and forth in the drawing-room, she stopped suddenly before a large bronze statuette. Her eye fired with a sudden thought; noting carefully the dimensions of the image, she hurried back to the hall and inspected the little table, and then immediately rang the bell.

The servant that appeared was a man who had grown old in the family service; it was well for Mrs. Dighton's purpose that his sight was not what it had been.

14

"Thomas," said the lady, carelessly, as she sat thrumming upon the piano, "I wish you would take that bronze, yonder on the cabinet, and put it on the little table in the corner of the hall."

Without question or comment, the careful old man lifted the shining image with both hands, and it plainly taxed his strength to the utmost as he bore it extended before him, with short quick steps, across the room and down the hall.

In his eagerness to set down his load would he first glance at the table ? If he did, would he distinguish the white envelope upon the white marble in the obscure corner, with his failing sight ? Did these questions whirl through Mrs. Dighton's brain ? Did her heart almost cease to beat with suspense ? Whatever she thought and however her heart beat, her cheek was as cool and unchanged as her muslin breakfast cap, and she never for a moment stopped playing the simple melody she had begun ; and there she still sat at the piano when Dorothy and her uncle came in, arm-in-arm, to bid her good morning on their way to breakfast.

Rising and taking her brother's other arm, Mrs. Dighton returned the greeting of both quietly, and they proceeded together towards the dining-room.

"Hello, whose work is this?" cried Mr. Curley, regarding his displaced statue in amazement.

"Oh, that is a freak of mine; it occurred to me as I sat playing this morning, and I told Thomas to bring it out here. This corner is so dismal, I thought the bronze would light it up. And so it does; see, too, how well he has posed it — you couldn't have done better yourself, Samuel!"

Mrs. Dighton's excuse was good enough, her words, too, were plausible, and neither her brother nor her daughter seemed to remark the hurry of her utterance or the little note of nervousness in her voice.

"Sister, you certainly have a most remarkable head for crotchets; lighting up this dark, out-of-the-way corner with that magnificent bronze is truly a very original notion. It is simply hiding our brightest light under a bushel."

"Hiding! not at all; it never showed to half so much advantage before. It needed a bit of gloom to bring out its real value of tone and material. However," she continued, with an excellent understanding of her brother, "pray move it back if it displeases you! I thought, perhaps, we could in this way make room for the

Japanese bronze you have been so long coveting and could find no room for."

"To be sure," said Mr. Curley, falling at once into the little trap, "but the Japanese bronze will cost me a pretty penny, and I am surprised at your sanctioning such an extravagance. If I buy that I shall have to cut down on other things; we shall have to pinch for it."

"As well pinch for that as for anything," interposed Dorothy, unconsciously coming to her mother's assistance. "You are getting to be a veritable curmudgeon, Uncle Curl. I've been pinching for a new saddle till " —

"Take care, sauce box, or I'll curtail your allowance!" returned the fond uncle, making a favorite threat.

"Don't say that, for then it is sure to come out of my pocket," said Mrs. Dighton.

"I am not sure that I should not like to be pinched for once, just to make myself an object of interest. In novels it is only the poor people, the folks that make the tremendous sacrifices and pawn their jewels and what not, that are interesting."

Dorothy was talking the lightest nonsense, but it seemed to jar strangely upon her mother's nerves.

"Poverty doesn't make people any more interesting than idleness, or vice, or dissipation, and we must be pretty careful to limit our interest in either case," said the latter sharply.

Dorothy looked at her mother curiously, but made no reply.

The image in the hall deserved Mr. Curley's encomium. It was a statue of Hero in the finest silver-bronze, representing the figure, half the size of life, of an exquisitely beautiful woman leaning upon some draped support and holding in one hand the lamp, whose ray is to serve as a beacon to guide her daring lover across the darkened Hellespont, while her eyes, with wistful, anxious expectancy, are peering into the unanswering gloom.

The type of tender, early love, of constancy, of blighted hope, a strange chance made this lovely Hero the instrument of a tyranny like to that under which she had herself suffered ; that made her the guardian of Mrs. Dighton's secret ; that made her an avenging Nemesis to Mrs. Dighton herself. To the latter the very beauty, the metallic composure of the statue soon became frightful ; her wistful gaze became an accusing stare ; the silver gleam of her antique

lamp seemed to throw a disclosing ray downward upon the hidden secret. She could not
deal with this as with an ordinary skeleton, pop
it into a safe closet and turn a key upon it, but
here it must stand subject to a thousand chances
of discovery, in her very path, confronting her at
every turn, where her passing draperies must
brush it half a dozen times a day.

But Custom moulds us to any shape. Continued
fear begets insensibility. The blossom of secur-
ity unfolds in the very shadow of long-impending
danger. Reaction comes to over-strained nerves,
and the startled heart resumes anon its so-many
throbs a minute.

And so, after a time, Mrs. Dighton began to
breathe again in peace, to lay aside her fears, and
intermit her surveillance, until a trivial occur-
rence one day showed the insecurity of her re-
pose.

She was coming down to tea, when, as she
stepped from the last stair and turned towards
the dining-room, she beheld Dorothy standing
with her arms about the bronze Hero, leaning
upon it. Mrs. Dighton advanced, trembling like
an aspen, and was inexpressibly relieved to find
that Dorothy was talking with her uncle (who
sat opposite in a hall chair), and had taken this
lounging attitude to accommodate her indolence.

"Why, Rhody, what's the matter? You're white as a ghost?"

"I — I thought something was the matter with *you;* lolling in such a strange way in that dark corner."

"Ridiculous little woman," whispered Dorothy, clasping her mother and drawing her aside to allow Mr. Curley to pass into the dining-room. "And suppose something really dreadful was to happen to me?"

"Do not — Oh, do not, my darling; there is enough real misery in the world without imagining more; let us not speculate upon how we should act! We should act as God gives us strength."

"Why, what a peevish, whimsical little body it is getting to be," said Dorothy, caressing her mother fondly.

"Dorothy," said Mrs. Dighton, solemnly, "I have often thought, my child, and I feel sure from a thorough understanding of myself, that if you should ever change in your feelings to me, if that free, happy, and perfect confidence which ever since you were a tender child I have maintained between us were to be broken ; if anyone were ever suffered to come between us and mar this perfect companionship, I should lose my reason, as I certainly should my peace and happiness forever upon this earth."

Mrs. Dighton spoke with a fervor and an air of candor that showed a strange insensibility to the nature of the offense she had committed against her daughter. As she looked searchingly into that daughter's eyes, a little troubled look came and went in the latter's face.

" Promise me, Dorothy, promise me, my dear, dear child, that nothing *shall* ever come between us ; that you will have no secret from me ; that you will never give me cause for such a horrid fear ! "

" Why, Rhody, don't be a sentimental and absurd old lady. I shall never keep anything from you that you ought to know, nor allow anybody to come between us ; and I will swear as many dreadful oaths as you like, to be true and faithful. Come now, hold up your right hand and let us swear that we never have been wanting in faith and constancy and we never will be to the end of time ! "

In spite of her forty years and her excellent aplomb, Mrs. Dighton quailed before her daughter's frank, straightforward look, and flushed as she stammered evasively :—

" Let us rather pray God that we may do right

in the future, and let the past take care of itself!"

"Any way to suit you, Rhody. I have no
doubts nor forebodings, as you seem to have, you
dark, suspicious little creature! I *know* you
never did and never will deceive me!"

Mrs. Dighton made a movement as though
she were about to throw herself upon her daughter's neck and confess all, but Dorothy in moving
accidentally stirred the bronze, when straightway her mother, with a nervous look, disengaged
her arms and drew her away from the figure,
exclaiming with another prevarication : —

"God knows, my darling, I never will!"

The foregoing were the words spoken above
the bronze image. The following were the words
that lay written beneath it : —

" MY DEAR MISS DIGHTON :

" I am unwilling to construe your refusal to see
me to-day to mean anything more than that my
visit was ill-timed and inconvenient to you. I
will not hasten to assume that you meant
thereby to put an end to all intercourse between
us ; to indicate thereby your displeasure at my
last words with you. But do not, I beg, dismiss
me in this utter silence ! If you are displeased,

at least speak; I can bear that better than
silence. I do not, I cannot blame you for
refusing to link your fortunes to one who is a
bankrupt in all the world cares for; to one who
cannot even offer you a respectable name; to
one upon whom you already justly look down as
degraded.

" If I cannot have your love ; if you cannot
become to me that best of friends who I thought
might lift me up out of this depth into which I
have fallen ; that one for whom I could work,
fight, wait, no matter how long, so that I might
hope at last to win ; if you cannot become this —
my inspiration, my good genius, at least still
remain my friend ! Do not cast me off for loving
you too well ! Still let me think of you as the
only being left upon earth who has recognized
any good in me, who still thinks me worthy of
pity if not esteem !

"Very faithfully yours,
"RALPH DEXTER."

CHAPTER XVI.

DUTY.

IF the famous Greek myth of Io and the Gadfly be supposed to typify only guilty souls pursued by the condign stings of Conscience, proper justice has never been done to its significance; for it may easily be extended to include a large class of the innocent, — of those upright and worthy folk, so cold-blooded and wanting in the lusts of the flesh that they have never given Conscience any real, healthful work to do. But conscience is a restless faculty; it will be about something, and, left to itself, is only too apt to generate a morbid activity, in which it hunts and goads its hapless owner up and down this mortal life, buzzing the one word " Duty " everlastingly in his ears, and pricking him ever on to a barren and undesigned perfection. From which, if it be inferred that we think sanctity is not a normal and healthful product of this life, we can only say we do not hold ourselves responsible for inferences; we know the wisdom of reticence, and are not to be trapped into committing ourselves. ·

Clearly recognizing the fact that, between the *gadfly* and the *butterfly* conscience, there lies a whole moral world of difference, we fallible creatures that hold the comfortable middle ground between the sin and sanctity poles may, we trust, satisfy ourselves with some happy cross between those representative insects as a fitter guide for our present stage of development, without being obliged more particularly to define our position.

Now, whether Mrs. Dexter's conscience was or was not one of the gadfly order, we do not venture to state. Far be it from us to prejudge any man or woman whose story we tell, and so we leave it an open question, warning any hasty person against accepting the above general reflections as even a suggestion of our opinion.

With regard to Ralph, Mrs. Dexter had, as we have seen, learned from her lawyer precisely what were her rights and duties, and not only this, but had taken the precaution to have his opinion carefully committed to paper, to prevent all possibility of mistake. Acting upon this information, it was plainly her part to invest herself with her rights and responsibilities, and proceed to the discharge of her duties. If this disappointed any hopes unwarrantably cherished by Ralph, Mrs. Dexter certainly could not be held responsible; she had gone out of the way of strict duty, and constrained herself to offer him aid in any form he might indicate. No reasonable person could say that anything more was required of her. And yet she seems not to have felt quite satisfied that her own skirts were clear of responsibility in the matter of his future. Duty at any rate plainly required her to remonstrate against the wild course he was taking, and she did it unflinchingly in two or three letters, which were coldly received and briefly acknowledged. As time passed on, Mrs. Dexter became more uneasy; she took pains to inform herself about Ralph's habits and ways of life, she wrote him advice, she sent him polite invitations to visit her, and received as many polite regrets.

Pondering upon this subject one afternoon as she was driving along Fourteenth street, Mrs. Dexter suddenly saw Ralph some distance before her, going in the same direction. She instantly ordered the coachman to overtake him; the latter accordingly touched up his horses, but before they came within hailing distance, Ralph turned up the steps of a large, old-fashioned house, and entered.

Mrs. Dexter drove to the door, and, as the coachman could not leave his horses, she was obliged to get out and ring the bell for herself, evidently resolved not to let the occasion slip without having a word with her adopted son.

The black man, who opened the door, was so astonished at the unusual appearance of a lady, that he made poor work of his answer to Mrs. Dexter's inquiry for Ralph, and muttering something about "speakin' to de Curnel" withdrew, leaving Mrs. Dexter standing in the hall.

A keen-looking, elaborately-dressed man presently appeared, and, after scrutinizing Mrs. Dexter carefully, asked, in a tone in which suspicion was only thinly veiled by politeness, whom she wished to see.

" Mr. Dexter."

"What Mr. Dexter?"

" Mr. Ralph Dexter. You will oblige me by giving him this card!"

" Mr. Ralph Dexter does not live here," returned the Colonel evasively.

." I saw him enter this house three minutes ago."

"Indeed?" said the Colonel, evidently impressed by the austere presence of his visitor as well as by a chance glimpse of her equipage seen through the open door. "Then he must be calling upon some member of my family. — Thomas," he continued, turning to the servant, who stood hovering in the background, "see if Mr. Ralph Dexter is in the house, and if he is, hand him this card!"

The Colonel added something *sotto voce* to the servant as he approached, and turned just in time to greet a fashionable-looking young man, who came sauntering in through the door, regarding Mrs. Dexter with a puzzled look as he passed. The Colonel gave the new-comer a quick wink, and the two immediately greeted each other as society acquaintances.

Whether this by-play was observed by Mrs. Dexter could never have been told from her face. The servant returned immediately, and said Mr. Dexter was in, and would see the lady up-stairs. Following the man, Mrs. Dexter was led to a front room on the second floor, which was sumptuously furnished and bore signs of having been hastily vacated, for there was a lingering trace of cigar-smoke in the air, a stray glove upon the floor, and some half-emptied glasses of wine upon the table.

Mrs. Dexter had scarcely seated herself when Ralph appeared. Sauntering into the room with his habitual easy air, he greeted her politely, but manifested no surprise at her visit.

" Ralph," she began at once, " I discovered your presence here only by accident, and I visit you in such a place only because I have been unable to obtain an interview with you in any other way. I had hoped you would have deemed me worthy the small consideration of an occasional visit."

" Mrs. Dexter," said Ralph, calmly, " there is no reason why there should not be entire frankness between us ; there are no conditions of fear or favor that I know of to prevent. I do not come to see you for two quite sufficient reasons : You do not want to see *me*, and I do not want to see *you*."

" If anything were wanting to my grief and horror at finding you in a place whose character I dare not even guess at, and among associations I tremble to think of, it would be supplied by the strange and unwarrantable attitude of defiance you have assumed towards me ! "

" I have no cause to entertain such a feeling towards you, nor do I ; what you please to call defiance may be simply independence."

" The world calls it by another name."

" I do not care what the world calls it."

"If you will not acknowledge the world as a judge, God and your own conscience should teach you that a disregard of the opinion of your best friends, and of all worthy and respectable people ; a contempt and disrespect for those to whom you are under obligations for years of care and service are not to be lightly excused on the plea of independence."

" I recognize no obligations to anyone."

" If twenty years of care and superintendence of your health and education establish no obligation, then I have no clear idea of one."

" Am I to consider as an obligation what has proved the greatest curse of my life ? Are obligations to be forced upon an innocent and unconscious child only to be thrown in his teeth when he comes to maturity?" asked Ralph, with unruffled composure.

" You use extraordinary language ; do you call it the curse of your life that we took you from a home of poverty and, for aught I know, shame, tenderly cared for you, brought you up, and gave you every advantage that money could procure ?"

" I do !"

" It may and it must result in a curse if you

15

persist in your wicked and shameful course," said Mrs. Dexter, indignantly.

"You had no right to take me from my native condition, whatever that may have been; no more right than you have to take the bird from the forest and put it in your cage, and expect thereby to impose upon it an obligation."

"If I wished to argue the point, I might remind you of the husbandman and serpent of the fable."

"You might, if you are willing to do me a great injustice."

"Injustice?"

"Yes; I have never injured you in word or deed; I am incapable of a hostile purpose towards you."

"You injure me constantly by your perverse and reckless life; our relations are already the subject of public comment."

"Mrs. Dexter," returned Ralph, with a lurking irony in his voice, "if it is fear of public opinion that has led you here, be assured we shall both survive the trial! It is only the magpie element in society that talks; do not fear, it will not busy itself with us long; it will soon find a fresher subject!"

"Your sneer is undeserved; I have lived long

enough to disregard the opinion of the world in matters where I have the approval of my own conscience. I do not complain on that account. I can bear whatever misconstruction the world may put upon my acts, but I hoped for a different return from one whom I have watched over for so many years."

"Mrs. Dexter, let us be quite candid! I would not do you an injustice; it is possible that you believe all you say to be true ; it is possible that you now look back and think of me as an object of affectionate solicitude upon your part. I have not been so blind. Since I have been able to think and judge for myself, your actions and motives have been a daily study with me. You have done your duty by me as you conceived it ; you have been wanting in no outward observance, but otherwise you have manifested an indifference which only by a struggle with yourself was saved from aversion. You have never uttered to me one involuntary word of commendation or affection ; you have never, in all these years, bestowed upon me a single caress. I do not complain of this. I respect you for not assuming an interest you did not feel, but that this feeling and this treatment have insensibly built up between us a barrier impregnable to mere words and arguments, you cannot be surprised at, and should not now affect to deplore."

Mrs. Dexter raised her hand as if to speak, but Ralph continued : —

"Furthermore, I am convinced my departure from your house was a positive relief to you ; it removed a constraint ; a long-borne burden. Mrs. Dexter, you will not look me in the face and pretend that your visit here was prompted by any personal affection for me ; that my presence in your house would contribute anything to your happiness ; that you miss me as a companion ; that there was anything in our past association that you remember with pleasure or would seek to recall !"

When one is a little uncertain as to one's motives, the searching critical gaze of an intelligent eye is sometimes hard to meet. And so Mrs. Dexter, despite her confidence in the rectitude of her purposes, and the infallibility of her judgment, found something in the bold frankness of this charge before which she wavered.

"I hardly expected," she began, after a moment's hesitation, " to be cross-examined as to my interest in you at this late day. It is contrary to my habit and temperament to make professions ; my actions must speak for themselves.

At the same time I would remind you that in looking back upon any portion of our past lives, it is much to be able to say that we have conscientiously tried to do our duty."

" I agree with you, and I think you can conscientiously say it. Duty has been the god that you have worshiped ; it is in obedience to this god that you come here to-day. I am bound to respect your motive, even if I do not quite understand your purpose."

"My purpose is," returned Mrs. Dexter, severely, " to call upon you to leave this dreadful life, these low and degrading associations ; to return to an upright and honorable way of living ; to establish yourself in some respectable business. My purpose is to beg of you, before it is too late, to consider the consequences of persisting in your present course."

" What reasons you may have for stigmatizing as you do my present mode of life and my associations, are best known to yourself. I hope they are sufficient and satisfactory. If I do not take the same view of the matter as you and others of my former associates do, who assume to speak for what is called the world, I am, I suppose, entitled to my opinion, and have this advantage, that I, at least speak with some knowledge of the subject."

"I see the uselessness of arguing with you," said Mrs. Dexter, rising; "if you will not listen to the voice of reason or entreaty, to the counsel or warning of friends, the consequences must rest entirely with you. I have but one word more to say: I have before offered you a home whenever you choose to avail yourself of it, I now renew that offer; furthermore, I will engage to make a suitable provision for you whenever you are ready to assure me that it shall not be put to improper purposes. Again I beg you to think over what I have said, to consider the offer I make you; again I beg you to remember that in case you willfully persist in declining it, I shall not consider myself responsible in the least for what may result."

"Be assured I shall discharge you from all liability on my account. I thank you, as before, for your kind offers, which, as before, I must decline; I thank you for your visit, and I beg you to remember that if I can ever render you a service I am entirely at your command."

Mrs. Dexter pulled down her veil and turned to go. Ralph opened the door and conducted her down stairs to her carriage. They parted with a simple bow, and, however Ralph may have felt, Mrs. Dexter drove home a happier woman.

CHAPTER XVII.

WHETHER Dorothy made a mental reservation in the pact she concluded with her mother, or whether a sense of honor in the feeling that what had passed between her and Ralph was his secret as much as her own restrained her, she kept her lips shut upon that subject. The fact that she chose to withhold her confidence in this matter alone confirmed Mrs. Dighton in her suspicions that it was on account of its unusual interest and importance. This, of course, only increased the latter's anxiety and her fears as to the possible consequences of a discovery of her own interference in the matter.

Months rolled by, and Ralph's name had never passed Dorothy's lips. Aside from this reticence, however, she was as usual ; went the little round of her duties — charities, studies, riding, and walking — with unfailing fidelity and steady cheerfulness ; only her watchful mother missed

those old moods of badinage and boisterous
gayety which, though they had brought down
upon Dorothy nothing but reproof from her
elders, were sadly missed by them since she had
become graver.

In Mrs. Dighton herself, these months had
wrought a more marked change; grief, anxiety,
and fear had driven the bloom from her cheek,
the glow from her eye, and all the natural cheerfulness from her manner. In vain she strove to
dissemble the loss of health and spirits — the
change was too apparent.

It was on Mr. Curley's questioning her as to
the cause of this, one night after Dorothy had
retired, that Mrs. Dighton suddenly determined
to take him into her confidence. She accordingly told him of the scene in the library and
her own suspicions, carefully omitting all mention of Ralph's subsequent call, or of the intercepted letter.

"Pooh, pooh," said Mr. Curley, "it is only
another one of your imaginings, my dear! If
there had been any love-making it would have
been followed up before now, and we should
have heard about it, take my word for it!"

"I am not sure," returned Mrs. Dighton —
who had reasons of her own for not being very

much consoled by the last consideration —
"Dorothy knows how much I disapprove of his
coming here, and she may have hesitated to
tell me."

"Disapprove of his coming here? Why,
what else have you been plotting to bring
about?"

"That was before he became such a dreadful
rake."

"Well, I hope this will teach you to have
done with match-making; but for the matter of
any harm that's done, you needn't lose any more
flesh about that!"

"I wish I need not, but I'm horribly afraid
she's engaged to him."

"Fiddlestick! my dear, it's not Dorothy's
way at all to keep such a thing to herself; she
would out with it, whether you liked it or not, if
they were really promised to each other."

"Yes," returned Mrs. Dighton, "that's my
only hope; it seems to me, too, that she would
tell us if she were actually engaged; but I don't
know," she continued, with a little sigh, "girls
often turn right about when they get engaged,
and act in the strangest and most inconsistent
way. He may have wished her to keep silent."

"By far the most likely thing of all is — if

there were really any love-making — that she
gave him the cold shoulder and sent him packing. That's it," cried Mr. Curley, confidently,
"that's it, of course ; that covers the whole case ;
that explains why he hasn't been here, accounts
for her silence and all."

"But to think that she can keep anything
from me," said Mrs. Dighton, with a voice full of
tears, "and above all such a thing as this, which
may affect her whole future ! It is not like Dorothy ; it is his influence ; he has already come
between us !" exclaimed the wretched little
mother, suppressing a sob.

"There, sister, don't be weak about it. Dorothy isn't a fool ; depend upon it, she's all right,
and has some good reason for what she does !
keep quiet and this will all soon blow over.
Look yonder at that bit of Venetian glass on the
mantle piece, just as the light strikes it now —
Oo — o — o !" exclaimed Mr. Curley, with one
of his favorite expressions of delight.

That Mrs. Dighton was not much helped by
her brother's advice was her own fault, in that
she gave him only half the case ; but she was
plainly enough comforted by the talk, and rose
to retire with a sigh of relief.

Despairing now of Dorothy's confidence, she evidently hoped to take it by surprise, and to this end kept a constant watch upon her daughter's moods, studied her face in those little, off-guard moments, the between-whiles of occupation, as she sat idly playing at the piano, as she listlessly gazed from the window at twilight, or into the flickering hearth-fire at night. Dorothy's serene unconsciousness favored this observation, but, despite her opportunities and her penetration, Mrs. Dighton acknowledged to her brother that she was completely baffled in her object.

"She is a strange girl; how can she be so insensible after such an experience, whatever may have been the result of it!"

"Pooh, Dorothy isn't one of those shallow pools that every passing breath ruffles. Her turmoils, if she has any, go on down below the line and plummet of your eye. So now, sister, have done fretting about this! Get out your carriage and exercise your horses; go about your calls and charities, and let us have a change of worries! Come down town with me to a sale of Japanese goods this morning!"

But accident soon gave Mrs. Dighton her long-wished-for opportunity of testing Dorothy more nearly. One of her society friends and gossips, making a late morning call, one day, was kept to luncheon, and while they sat at table the lively lady electrified her hostess as she passed up her tea-cup, by saying :—

"Did you ever hear of anything like that stony Mrs. Dexter?"

"What about her?" asked Mrs. Dighton, pausing, almost breathless, with the cup in her hand.

"Why, my dear, think of her living alone in that great house, enjoying an immense fortune, while her son is going to the dogs."

"You mean her adopted son, or rather her husband's adopted son, — for, I understand, she makes that distinction," said Mrs. Dighton, with her eye nervously fixed upon Dorothy, and in her abstraction pouring the slops into the cream-jug.

"Whoever adopted him," continued the visitor, "her husband was devotedly fond of him, and, as is well known, meant to have left him the bulk of his estate."

"But," continued Mrs. Dighton, with her eyes still riveted on her daughter, "I hear she offered to provide for him liberally."

"'Provide for him!'" repeated her friend, with proper scorn. "But how? By directing her attorney to tell him that he was a beggar, that everything belonged to her, and then condescendingly adding that she would continue to support him."

" It must have been a great shock to him, but I do not see that he has anything to complain of, and there is certainly nothing to justify his present conduct," said Mrs. Dighton, trembling from head to foot with agitation, and never for a moment taking her eyes from Dorothy.

" He thinks differently; he is, I hear, really fierce in his resentment towards Mr. and Mrs. Dexter, that they dared to adopt him and bring him up in ignorance of his own name and origin."

" Well, I hope he'll see the folly of his present course, at any rate."

" I don't know," pursued the visitor, stirring her tea, " everybody thinks him ruined. He has lost all his ambition and is perfectly reckless : he has given up his profession, he drinks and gambles and is wild as a hawk. All his old friends have given him the cold shoulder, and there is a report that he was turned out of the club for intoxication."

" Mamma, shall I serve you a slice of tongue ?"

Dorothy raised her eyes and met her mother's searching gaze with steady tranquillity.

On relating this interview to her brother that evening, Mrs. Dighton confessed herself more perplexed than ever by Dorothy's conduct:—

" If her composure was only assumed, Samuel, how could she maintain it so; how *could* she look so indifferent ? "

" Oh, in matters of love, women can generally do anything ; but this case, as I told you before, is all in your imagination."

" If it is all my imagination, if she had been really indifferent, why did she not join in the conversation ? Why did she not show the passing interest one naturally would in an acquaintance ? "

" Because she preferred eating her dinner to gossiping."

" She talked on other subjects fast enough."

" Which only shows she wasn't interested in this."

" You may be right, Samuel ! " returned his sister, and she evidently began to persuade herself he was, for she presently plucked up a little more cheerfulness ; her brow cleared of some of its trouble ; her fears, if not dismissed, were laid to rest ; she ceased her surveillance of Dorothy, and once more busied herself about her own affairs with something of her old-time life and gayety.

What secure grounds Mrs. Dighton had for her new-found peace will presently be seen.

One night about a month after the luncheon scene they all went to a concert. On leaving the hall, the moon was so bright and the air so refreshing after the heated room, that Dorothy begged to walk home ; her mother and uncle consented, and they set forth.

Their way led for several blocks through Broadway, where, as they were walking along, quietly discussing the concert, they passed a brilliantly-lighted bar-room, the door of which, for the moment, stood open. A loud burst of laughter from within attracted their attention, and, unconsciously, they slackened their pace a little as they came opposite the door, when, suddenly, to the amazement of Mrs. Dighton and her brother, Dorothy left their side, darted into the lighted saloon, and advanced into the midst of a group of men that stood lounging about the counter.

Dorothy's entrance to the saloon electrified its inmates — who were for the most part fashionably-dressed and rather fast-looking young men — as much as it had her friends.

Oblivious of everything but her purpose, she confronted Ralph Dexter, who stood with a glass of wine in his hand, quite ·stupefied at her appearance. For a moment a smile and a wink went round the circle, but presently those young *roués*, as they looked again at the pure face and honest, reproachful eyes of this young woman, one after another took off their hats, and with an uneasy, half-embarrassed air, turned away. Not a word was said. Ralph tossed the crystal glass from his hand to the marble floor,· where it was shattered to a hundred pieces ; then offering his arm to Dorothy he led her from the hall.

Pale and trembling, Mrs. Dighton met them on the threshold. Ralph lifted his hat as they passed ; neither attempted to speak. Mr. Curley gave his sister his arm and slowly followed them.

" Mr. Dexter," said Dorothy, after they had proceeded for some distance in silence, "you saved my life once at the risk of your own. I have tried to-night to save you from a greater peril than death, at the risk of subjecting you to some mortification .and ridicule. My motive must be my excuse."

Ralph walked on in silence and attempted no

reply, while Dorothy began at length to feel the embarrassment natural to the situation.

"Excuse me," she said presently, stopping, "I need not take you out of your way; I will rejoin my mother and uncle!"

"I have no way; one way is the same as another to me," said Ralph moodily.

"But" —

"If you are ashamed to walk with me, we will wait."

Dorothy took his arm and walked on, saying:

"After what has just happened that speech, if not insulting, is very unkind."

"Perhaps it is. I beg your pardon; I was thinking of what has gone before. I thought I had long ago ceased to be an object of interest to you."

"I don't know why you should think so."

"Have I not had reason enough?"

"I don't know what you call reason enough; I have always felt, and I am sure I have always expressed, a strong interest in your — your" —

"Reform," suggested Ralph bitterly.

"Welfare," continued Dorothy, "and I have done all I could to help you. A young woman's ways of helping a man are necessarily limited."

16

"If you had always shown the interest you now profess — I " —

Ralph hesitated, and Dorothy interposed in a tone of extreme surprise : —

"I do not understand you ! "

"I will not pain you by referring to the circumstances of our last interview, but I am curious to know how Miss Dighton reconciles her present professions with what has since happened."

"I know of nothing which has since happened that I cannot quite easily reconcile with my present professions."

"Stay, Miss Dighton ! " returned Ralph in a haughty, almost an angry tone ; "I would rather think you contemptuous than disingenuous. There is no need of subterfuge. I am no longer of consequence enough to make it worth while. I am hardened to contempt ; I have had enough late experience of that ; but I trust I have still intelligence enough to despise prevarication."

Dorothy stopped short, dropped his arm and stood for a moment breathless with indignation.

"If I understand you, you mean that you do not believe what I have said. I have never been so insulted. I will do you the honor of assuming that you do not realize what you are saying. But whether you do or not, I demand that you instantly explain yourself in the plainest language at your command."

"I beg your pardon with all my heart if I have done you an injustice; I did not mean to anger, much less insult you, only your seeming inconsistency for a moment irritated me. I may be wrong. I have nothing to explain; it is all dark to me; you only can explain."

By this time Mrs. Dighton had recovered her presence of mind and came up to make the best of the situation.

"I hope you are not taking leave here; you must go home with us, Mr. Dexter," she exclaimed, cordially, "it's quite an age since we've seen you. How oddly things come about. I was thinking of you only this evening as we passed the theatre where we made your acquaintance. I looked up at the window-ledge and fairly grew dizzy at the thought of standing there."

As she talked, Mrs. Dighton had dexterously contrived to walk on with Mr. Dexter, and leave Dorothy behind with her uncle. The situation thus altered to her mind, she affected not to notice Ralph's moodiness, but went on briskly talking till they came to her own door.

They waited for the others to come up. Ralph lingered a moment and looked wistfully at Dorothy. Would she second her mother's invitation to him to go in? She did not speak. Exchanging empty commonplaces he went gradually down the steps; turned, lifted his hat, said, "Good night," and walked slowly away.

CHAPTER XVIII.

R ALPH made good his words that any way
was his way, by strolling off at random
after he had said good night to the Dightons.
His thoughts may be imagined. Looked at in
any light, Dorothy's behavior must have been to
him a riddle. Her refusal to see him when he
called, her failure to answer his letter, — how
reconcile these with her invasion of the saloon,
with her present professions of interest, or these
again with her refusal to join in her mother's
invitation. Was she silent through indignation?
If so, what right had she to be indignant at his
very just reproaches?

"'Disconcerting and hard to understand?'"
he muttered. "She is justifying her reputation
with a vengeance."

In the midst of these reflections he was startled
by the noise of an altercation, mingled with cries
for help, apparently close at hand. Turning a
corner he beheld a couple of half-grown children,

a boy and a girl, engaged in a hand-to-hand
fight. As he drew nearer he saw that the girl
was deformed, but seemingly no whit the less
vigorous on that account, for she held her own
staunchly till her opponent, taking advantage of
a breathing-spell when she was off-guard, suddenly tripped and threw her violently to the
ground, and then took to his heels.

Ralph hastened up, helped her to rise, and
inquired if she was hurt.

"Well, I guess I ain't made of cast-iron, an'
w'en I hit my head against a stone I feel it,"
she replied in a tone not quite unfamiliar to us.

On attempting to walk, however, it appeared
she had sprained her ankle, and was obliged to
accept Ralph's assistance, which she did with
manifest reluctance.

"Guess I ain't a cripple, if I am a hunchback," she muttered, trying to limp along alone.

"No; but you have hurt your foot and must
have some help."

"Drat that little gutter-pig! I'll give it to
him when I catch him, see if I don't ; he needn't
think he can come that again on me — jest you
wait ! "

"'That's right," said Ralph, humoring the
wrathful little creature, "but now we shall have
to see about getting home."

"Don't you b'lieve I can lick that boy?"

"Oh, I'm sure you can."

"You be?" she asked, regarding Ralph suspiciously; "most of 'em think 'cause I'm a hunchback I ain't good for anything, but they'll find out; I've stood enough of their sass, calling me names; I'll skin *him* alive when I catch him — jest you wait!"

"That's right," said Ralph again, "give him a good drubbing, but some other time; you must get home now. Can you walk?"

"Guess I can drag along somehow — you *would* lick that boy, wouldn't you?"

"Certainly; lick him to shoe-strings."

"He, he, he! So I will; I will now, jest you wait! Lick him to shoe-strings, that's what I'll do, an' then I'll tie the shoe-strings into a hard knot!"

Ralph hailed a passing hack, and when it came up he opened the door and lifted the irate child in without a word.

"Now, then, Miss Xantippe, where do you live?"

"Goin' to take *me* home in a carriage?"

"Yes."

"You goin' too?"

"Yes."

"I live in Putney Place — Number Five; guess *their* eyes 'll stick out w'en they see me comin' home in a hack. *You* 'll have to pay for it, you know," she continued, turning suddenly to Ralph, "*I* ain't got no money."

Reassured by Ralph's nod of acquiescence, she straightway gave herself up to the novel delight of riding in a carriage, now looking out of one window, now another, and again lolling back upon the cushions, interrupting her transports now and then by a groan over her wounded leg and an added malediction upon the boy.

"What's your name?" asked Ralph, by way of passing the time.

"Zilp; Zilpy Nudd w'en you write it."

"And how came you out on the street so late at night?"

"Run away to look at the store-winders; — don't you like to look in the store-winders?"

"Where do you live?"

"I live with Madame."

"And who is Madame?"

"Madame V'lasco; don't you know *her?*" asked the child with a stare of surprise.

"No; why should I?"

"'Cause *everybody* knows Madame; she's the great clairv'yant, don't you know? She knows

everything; you ought to jes' see all the fine
ladies that come in grand carriages to have their
fortunes told an' their in'ards looked at."

" Does Madame cure sick people ?"

" Guess she does ; she can see right through
you with her eyes shut, jes' if you was all glass,
an' see w'at 's the matter of you."

"Indeed !"

As they drew up before the door of Number
Five, a woman draped in a shawl was seen upon
the steps, looking out and anxiously scanning
the street.

" There she is ; that 's Madame; she 's lookin'
for me — won't she stare to see me git out of a
carriage ?"

And stare she certainly did, not only at Zilp,
but at the strange young man who came helping
her up the steps.

" Why, Zilp, is it you ? What is the matter ?"

" Oh, nothin' ; I 'm only a little hurt; I was
lickin' a boy, an' he tripped me when I wasn't
lookin', an' this gen'leman he see us an' brung
me home !"

" You naughty, disobedient child, have I not
told you never to fight upon the street, and to
take no notice of the boys ?"

" Yes ; an' so I did try not to, but that boy, —

that boy," she repeated between her clenched
teeth, "he sassed me till I couldn't stand it."

"I am very much obliged to you, sir, for
bringing her home," said Madame, turning for
the first time to Ralph, "you must allow me to
pay for the carriage."

"Thank you, no," said Ralph dryly; "that is
my own affair."

"I beg your pardon," returned the woman, "I
offered because I thought it was my duty; this
child is my servant and *protégée* — but," she continued, gazing earnestly at Ralph, "there is
something in your voice and manner familiar to
me; have I seen you before?"

"Never, I think."

"Excuse me; I never was mistaken in such
an impression — will you give me your name?"

"Dexter."

"Yes, yes," said the woman hastily, "I knew
it; the hand of Providence is in this; you were
sent here to-night for a purpose!"

"The hand of Providence may generally be
said to be in everything," returned Ralph lightly,
"but you will excuse me for saying you have
evidently mistaken me for somebody else."

"You shall see that I am not mistaken. It
may prove that I know more of Ralph Dexter
than he does himself."

"That might easily be without your being a wiseacre," said Ralph indifferently.

"Come in," continued the woman eagerly, "I have something to say to you. You need not suspect me, I have nothing in view but your own good."

"I might naturally suspect anybody who made such a declaration, but," continued Ralph, entering and removing his hat, "I have no objection to hearing what you have to say. Your knowing my name is queer, and your profession of interest in its owner still queerer."

"You shall judge as to my interest in you, presently," repeated Madame, trying to make out Ralph's features in the dark hall. "Walk in here and sit down," she continued, opening a door, "I will join you as soon as I have cared for this foolish child."

A purple gloom pervaded the room in which Ralph found himself; carpet, hangings, and furniture were of the same sombre hue; there was a sumptuous atmosphere, a sense of purple velvet in the very air, due perhaps partly to the obscurity,—a shaded silver lamp upon the centre table furnishing the only light.

Ralph had scarcely finished his survey of the room when a heavy *portière* between the folding

doors was raised, and a remarkable-looking person advanced to meet him — a small, shapely
woman with large, faded eyes, snow-white hair
turned back from a furrowed brow, and a face
that showed extraordinary quickness of perception united with extreme emotional sensibility ;
the face was otherwise grave and sad in expression, and bore traces of great suffering.

Dressed entirely in white, even to the rich
white lace that draped her head, her figure stood
out in dazzling relief amidst the voluptuous
shadows of the room.

Seating herself in a low chair by the table,
she beckoned Ralph to a place near her ; then
shading her eyes with her wasted hand, she
studied his face attentively for several minutes
before speaking.

"Ralph Dexter," she said at length, " with one
exception I am now probably the only person
living who knows the secret of your birth. The
one person who shares this knowledge — if indeed she be any longer alive — is your unhappy
mother."

Intense curiosity and interest struggled with
a not unnatural suspicion in Ralph's face as he
sat gazing fixedly upon his new acquaintance.

" In saying this I assume you do not know it

yourself; I have reason to think you do not.
Mr. Dexter's sudden death prevented the disclosure he might have made; Mrs. Dexter, I
have cause to believe, is entirely ignorant upon
the subject; there remains but your mother, and
she — even if she were living, even if chance
had thrown you together — would have stifled
her maternal longings rather than imperil your
happiness by a disclosure of the truth."

Ralph sat in almost breathless silence, seemingly fearful by a word or movement of interrupting a recital of such vital interest to him.

"It is not unfit," pursued Madame Velasco,
"that you should hear the truth from my lips.
You say you do not know me; that you never
saw me before. Alas, my dear boy, memory is
a feeble faculty; it does not stretch back to the
beginning! I was present at your birth; you
were handed naked into these arms; I dressed
you and laid you upon your mother's breast, and
often since I have nursed and borne you in sickness and health. I tell these things to show
you that I am not speaking at second hand; to
prove to you that I am one of the oldest, as of
late I have been one of the very few, friends that
remained faithful to your unfortunate mother;
and I would now prove the sincerity of my

interest in you by striving to reunite you with
her and your little brother and sister."

"What," cried Ralph, with an involuntary
start, "have I a brother and sister, as well as a
mother, living?"

"I do not know; I cannot say now what may
have happened. They *were* living but a short
time ago, — living here with me. They disappeared suddenly and left no trace behind. I
have never heard a word from that hour. Your
mother was suffering from a mortal illness. I
dare not expect, I can only hope, that *she* may
yet be alive, that there may yet be time for her
to see and recognize you once more; but the
children were well and strong; I will not believe
anything has happened to them."

"And are there no means — can you give me
no clue that would lead to their discovery?"

"I fear not; I can think of nothing; my hope
has been that she would send to me when the
end draws near."

Almost overcome by the suddenness of this
revelation, and by the conflicting hopes and fears
which it awakened, Ralph rose and paced the
room in silence.

"But," he continued, at length resuming his
seat, "knowing my mother all these years, you
must have known my father too?"

"I did," replied Madame Velasco, in a changed voice.

"And is he living?"

"He is not."

Rising again and walking to the other end of the room, Ralph wheeled about suddenly and exclaimed : —

"How do you account for my mother's disappearance?"

"I can only surmise ; your father and she had a difference ; in fact, a serious quarrel, in which they parted, never expecting to see each other again. It was a terrible blow to her. A victim of a fatal disease, she saw her life ebbing away day by day ; she saw the time fast coming when her children must be deprived of her care and protection, and she pondered upon all this until, overcome by a sudden morbid feeling of desolation and wretchedness, she ran away like a hunted animal to hide herself, trusting alone to the mercy of God, as Hagar did of old in the wilderness."

"Hagar?"

"I do not think," pursued Madame, without noticing Ralph's curious tone and look, "that she was in danger of immediate suffering from want ; she had husbanded her means, but what is to

become of her children if she dies among
strangers is a matter of sore anxiety to me."

" How old were they ? "

" The girl was nine and the boy five."

" Did my mother know of my whereabouts ? "

" She did."

" Why did she not communicate with me ? "

" Your father prevented her."

" But after his death ? "

" She left my house before his death."

" Did he then die so lately ? "

" Very lately."

" But who — what was he ?   And my mother,
tell me about her.   Do not leave me in this suspense ?   Why did they send me to the Dexters' ?
Why, if they had any natural affection, did they
give their own child to be adopted by strangers ?
My brain whirls with questions.   Do you know
all these things ? "

Madame Velasco's face fell ; she bit her lip
and hesitated.

" Yes," she replied, after a moment's pause,
" I *do* know ; but I hesitate to tell you.   I hesitate to awaken in you feelings of shame and,
perhaps, of anger."

" I demand to know the truth," pursued Ralph,
" you have no right to withhold it ; I am prepared for anything ! "

" Perhaps you are right," said Madame, doubtfully, " but if I speak, I beg you to exercise your
largest charity. For those that are dead, let us
suspend our poor human judgment ; for those
that are alive, let us have sympathy and compas-
sion ! "

Madame paused a moment, and putting her
hand in her bosom, drew forth a heavy gold
locket, beautifully wrought and jeweled.

" It is best you should know," she continued,
in a low tone, as she opened the locket, and with
her delicate handkerchief gently wiped the pictures within. " I do not fear the influence of
this disclosure upon you. It may be a shock,
but it will also be a lesson ; a bitter, but perhaps a memorable and salutary one. This was
your mother's jewel ; she left it for me when she
went away ; it contains the pictures of both your
parents. Honor and respect what in each of
them was good, and forget the rest ! "

With these words she closed the locket, and,
handing it to Ralph, left the room.

Pausing a moment to control his agitation,
Ralph, with trembling hand, opened the locket,
and in an instant a crimson flush covered his
face. After recognizing his father's picture, he
looked long and earnestly at his mother's, as if

17

haunted by something familiar in that also. He was still intently absorbed in its study when Madame Velasco returned.

"I have seen her, surely," he muttered, as if talking to himself. "I cannot be mistaken; but she was thinner and paler than this."

"Yes," said Madame.

"I *have* seen her, then?"

"Yes."

"Where — when?"

"At your own home — at your father's house" —

"Yes, yes; the strange woman — I touched her hand, I lifted her; she leaned on my arm — Great God, why did I not know! . She trembled when I touched her; she put me away; she was afraid she should betray herself — Oh, if I could have said one single word, if I could but once have called her 'mother'!"

"She went to the Dexters' resolved to exhaust every means, to expend her last strength in the effort to see you; she told me of it all — she accomplished her purpose; but almost at the cost of her life."

Ralph made no reply, but walked back and forth a long time in silence. Stopping at length in front of Madame, he said abruptly : —

" Her name " —

" Was Rebecca Hoyt."

" ' Rebecca Hoyt ' — Merciful Heaven — that name, I have heard it ; I have seen it ; and associated with *his* death. — It was she ! She, too, is gone. — God in His mercy prompted me ! "

Ralph threw himself into a chair and covered his face, while his whole frame shook with emotion.

After he had become a little calm, Madame asked softly : —

" Have you any cause to believe her dead ? "

" Yes, yes ; I know it. I myself stood over her ; I threw flowers on her coffin. I saw her grave. I saw the children. I comforted my own sister, and all within the hour in which I had seen *him* laid to rest."

" Strange chance," exclaimed Madame, " but God ordained it ; and doubtless suffered her from some spirit height to look down, a rejoicing witness, upon it all."

As he became more composed, Ralph described the scene of his mother's funeral, and the appearance of True and his wife more circumstantially.

" These people, then, probably still have the children in charge, or at least know their whereabouts — could you identify them ? "

"I think so ; they were both noticeable."

"What shall you do ?"

"Apply to the police first ; if that fails, then advertise and employ private detectives."

Promising to communicate with Madame in case of success, Ralph now took his leave. The moon was gone, a dense sea-fog hugged the earth, and a midnight bell boomed weirdly from a distant steeple as Madame Velasco let him out to grope and shiver his way home.

CHAPTER XIX.

THE "JIBBENAINOSAY."

B Y dint of economy and the exercise of sound business principles, not forgetting "the fundamentalest," Rachel found herself in possession of a considerable sum as the net profit of her first year in business.

This, as True many times explained to her, was "no fancy assets," but "clean hard savin's" left after deducting the small weekly sum which he wisely charged her for the board of herself and Baby, saying : —

" Pay as you go, Titania ; don't go to gittin' into debt, my dear, or you'll never be a Rothschild ! Debt's a horrid black pit 'thout any bottom, that folks tumble into mighty easy, but th' ain't many of 'em git out 'thout boostin'. We don't begrudge you the vittles, Lady Pamela an' me ; but don't you take no favors from nobody ; keep your head straight up in the air like a *gi*raffe an' then you'll know where yo᠁᠁ !' "

Although, of course, she could not understand

how largely her success was due to the constant watchfulness of True, who went with her to buy her stock, taught her how to sort and dispose it, and kept her from being imposed upon, Rachel nevertheless regarded her shrewd protector with increasing respect and admiration, and did such credit to his training that she soon learned to work off her poor stock upon the street boys by the artful temptation of a small discount, in a manner that won the unbounded applause of True, and led him to indulge in the most glowing prophecies as to her future.

That must have been a very obdurate fairy who could have looked on, evening after evening, and seen Rachel and Baby, as soon as the supper table was cleared and Lady Pamela had reached down the cracked blue-and-white teapot, sit down and count over their little savings, striving by different countings and new combinations to make a different and larger sum-total, — that, we say, must have been an uncommonly stony-hearted little fairy, who could have refrained at sight of this from slipping in a magic penny among the shining silver dollars, every one of which had been polished to an equal brightness by rubbing on the parlor carpet.

True Blue, however, was not a fairy, but a

flesh-and-blood creature of business principles, and so he looked on with only an occasional wag of his head or a sly wink tipped at Lady Pamela, and let things take their course.

The children's interest in their hoard, however, is not to be credited entirely to business enthusiasm, for every day and every added penny brought nearer the time for the fulfillment of True's promise of the night at the "Bowery." But now the stipulated sum was at length saved, and the long-expected time had arrived; True put the money into the bank, handing back to Rachel the little blue book in which the deposit was entered, which she received as a rather doubtful equivalent for her shining specie.

The morning after the deposit, True consulted the paper and announced that "NICK OF THE WOODS" was "on the bills" for that evening, and as he pronounced it "a bang-up blood-curdler," the hopes of the children rose to the highest pitch. All day long poor Rachel was almost beside herself with anticipation; recklessly disregarded every business principle; infringed even the sacred fundamentalest; put nothing down in black and white, and altogether behaved in what True called "such an uneddi-

cated way " that only his threat of "givin' up
the Bowery an' stayin' home to review the principles " quite brought her to her senses.

But notwithstanding his assumed severity,
True evidently had a fellow-feeling for his little
ward, for besides overlooking many shortcomings
during the day, he hobbled home at night much
faster than was his wont, to accommodate her
uncontrollable impatience. And when they arrived, there was Baby already quite tired out
waiting for them, dressed in his holiday suit, sup-
plemented by a new neck-ribbon made by Lady
Pamela ; and there was Lady Pamela herself, in
a new alpacca dress, with her hair twisted up
into a shower of corkscrew curls in front and
fastened behind by the most wonderful of white
ivory combs ; and last, but by no means least,
there was the supper — and such a supper : roast
chicken, cranberry sauce, hot muffins, and a little
round mince pie for each one's dessert — all
ready to be served.

True and Rachel changed their clothes in a
twinkling, and presently they all sat down, the
merriest party that ever was heard of inside or
outside a book. Baby laughed and talked and
was too excited to eat. Rachel plied True with
questions as to what sort of a place the " Bow-

ery," was, who "NICK" was, and whether there would be "real woods;" to all of which True gave evasive answers, and chuckled and joked and made so many funny rhymes that Lady Pamela grimly remarked that there wouldn't be any "Bowery" or any "NICK OF THE WHAT'S-ITS-NAME" for anybody *that* night until every crumb of their supper was eaten, if she had to lock the door and put the key in her pocket. With that they all fell to, and made short work of the eatables, and when supper was over True smoked his pipe while Lady Pamela washed the dishes, the children watching the clock and wondering at the imperturbability of their elders.

At length all was done, and Lady Pamela arrayed herself in a grand bonnet with red roses inside and a waving plume without, and True put on his Sunday coat, with a shiny stove-pipe hat, which was brought out from a box under the bed, and they set forth, leaving a light in the window, as Lady Pamela said, " to keep away the thieves."

If they had not all been so preoccupied when they at length filed out the area door, they might have noticed a policeman across the street, engaged at that very moment in pointing it out to a quiet-looking young gentleman by his

side ; and if the children had not been so excited
by thoughts of what was in store for them, or if
True and his careful spouse had not been so
intent upon the children, they might have seen
the same quiet-looking young gentleman get on
the car which they took to go down town.

But they were too much engrossed in their
own merry little party to take any thought of
strangers, and when they had got comfortably
seated in the car, True gave the children tickets
to pay their fare, which Baby was so eager to do
that he held his out to every passenger who
came in ; this kept Rachel laughing until she
was quite out of breath ; and the time thus
passed so quickly that before they suspected it
there they were away down town, at their desti-
nation.

And when they got out, Lady Pamela was so
afraid of soiling the new alpacca that she let go
Baby's hand, to take up her skirts, and Baby was
so astonished at the big building, all blazing
with light, that he did not see the others had
left him, and he might perhaps have been run over
by a passing express wagon, if the same quiet-
looking young gentleman had not just then come
out of the car and lifted him over to the sidewalk.

They were all so alarmed at this incident, and so glad at Baby's escape, that they failed to thank the young gentleman or notice that he looked at them very earnestly, followed them into the theatre, and took a seat in the row close behind them.

Indeed, the children were so taken up with the great theatre, with its painting and gilding, with its huge crystal chandelier and the big green curtain, and the funny figures painted on the proscenium, and the queer little cubby-holes which True called boxes, and where he said only nabobs ever sat, and with the people coming in and the noisy boys up in the gallery, so high that Baby wondered how they got up and how they were ever going to get down, and True Blue was so busy answering their innumerable questions, and Lady Pamela was so rapt with admiration of her husband in his holiday attire, that they soon forgot all about the strange young gentleman, and it is even doubtful whether they would have recognized him if they had chanced to turn around and see him with his eyes fastened on them, listening with absorbed attention to everything they said.

" Do you see all those fellers down there with the fiddles an' things?" said True. " Well,

that's the orchestry ; by an' by they 'll strike up
a tune — they're the boys to rattle out the
music !

> " With fiddle an' flute
> They 'll whistle an' toot.
> With cymbals an' drum
> They 'll make the thing hum ! "

" What are all those funny little green
things ? " asked Rachel.

" Them are the lights, Titania ; pretty soon
they 'll shoot up, an' then the fun 'll begin."

" Shall we see ' NICK ' then ? "

" You 'll see ' Nick,' my dear, when he appears,
an' he appears, generally speakin', when he takes
a notion ; an' you ain't always sure w'ether he's
Nick or w'ether he's the "Jibbenainosay," or
Bloody Nathan, or The Avenger, or the Spirit of
the Waters — for they're all mixed up an' boiled
down together ! But how's my fair one?" he
continued, turning to the silent Lady Pamela.
" Have a peanut, my love, an' don't talk yourself
hoarse ! Here, youngsters, divide them between
you," he concluded, producing a paper of fresh-
roasted nuts. " But there goes the bell, so now
stand from under ! "

The great curtain rolled up at last, and Rachel
and Baby, perched on the very edge of their
seats, transfixed with astonishment and delight,

followed scene after scene with breathless interest, now laughing at Roaring Ralph Stackpole, now falling in love with beautiful Telie Doe, and anon trembling with awe at the "Jibbenainosay."

Lady Pamela, too, was interested, but showed an uncompromising hostility to the Indians.

"Never oughter 've been born," she suddenly cried; "nasty, snaky things enough in the world 'thout them. *I'd* take the tongs to 'em!"

At length, when the action culminates in the grand scene where the Jibbenainosay goes over the cataract in a flaming canoe, amid clouds of fire, Baby's short hair perceptibly rose all over his little round head, and Rachel, in her fright, clung to Lady Pamela, who, in a burst of indignation, exclaimed:—

"Oughter know better 'n to scare folks out of their seven senses! I sh'd like to have old Triton get one spurt at that; she 'd canoe 'em!"

Strange enough it seemed to the children after such an evening to come out into the real world, where it was so cold and dark, and where everything was so dwarfed and noisy and sharp-edged; and it is no wonder that they went off into dream-land as soon as possible after they got into the cars, propped up between Lady Pamela and True.

No one will be surprised to hear that the quiet-looking young gentleman above-described might have been seen the next morning ringing the bell at No. Five Putney Place, or that Zilph hailed him, when she opened the door, with : —

" Hullo, mister! I got all over that — say, do you really think I can lick that boy ? "

" Oh, yes ; but now you 're sure you can, I guess I wouldn't ! "

" Why ? "

" Think of his mother's feelings when she sees him reduced to a pair of shoe-strings ! "

" He, he ! 'T'ud be the best thing she could do with that brat ; shoe-strings 're some good ! — I 'll run an' tell Madame you 've come ; you jes' wait ! "

And away she ran to announce " that gen'leman that brung me home in the hack, you know."

Madame soon appeared and greeted Ralph cordially.

" I have found them."

" Your brother and sister ? "

" Yes ; I think there can be no doubt — the two children, the cripple, and the funny little woman ; the same group that stood round the grave. He was well-known to the police, and I soon found where they live, and now I have

come for you to go with me, that there may be
no possibility of mistake."

Madame Velasco readily assented, and as
soon as she could get ready they started.
Arrived at the area door, it was only after much
vigorous knocking and pounding that it was at
length opened by the mistress of the house.

"We came to see Rachel and Baby Hoyt,"
said Madame Velasco, in her gentlest tone ; "do
they live here ? "

Lady Pamela nodded silently.

"Can we see them ? "

Lady Pamela shook her head.

"Why not, if you please?" interrupted Ralph.

"'Cause they're both engaged!" returned
Lady Pamela, shortly, bristling all over with suspicion.

"Engaged?" repeated Ralph, in an amused
tone.

"Yes ; gittin' their eddication."

"Gone to school, you mean?" suggested
Madame Velasco.

"No, I don't mean," retorted Lady Pamela,
tartly.

"My good woman," began Ralph, in a propi-
tiating tone, "we are friends of these children ;
we have come to visit them. If they are not at
home, we will call again."

"Didn't say *they* warn't at home — ye can't trap me, young man!"

"You said," returned Ralph, hesitatingly, "that they were getting their education, I think."

"An' so they be; girl's gone to business; boy's at his blocks."

"And cannot he be interrupted for a few minutes?"

"No; *his* eddication can't be interfered with."

"But will you tell us where we can find his sister?"

"She's with my husband."

"And where is he?"

"He's at his business, w'ere other folks oughter be; more's the pity they ain't!"

Saying these words the triumphant Lady Pamela shut the door with a significant slam, and left Ralph and Madame Velasco to their reflections.

"So," said Ralph, turning with a half-vexed, half-amused air to his companion. "We can do nothing with this watch dog of a woman. We must hunt up her husband — luckily the police gave me his address."

Ralph handed Madame back into the carriage, gave the driver the necessary directions and they drove away.

"There they are!" cried Ralph, as they turned into University Place. "There's the cripple at any rate!" he continued, pointing to True, who was busy with a customer.

They alighted and approaching True's stand stood waiting for an opportunity to speak with him, when suddenly Rachel, whom they had not seen, rushed out of her booth with a cry of joy and flung herself into Madame's arms.

Ralph kept in the background while they retired into the booth, whither True came hobbling over suspiciously to have a look at the strangers, under pretense of arranging the fruit.

At length Madame and Rachel appeared, and the latter, approaching Ralph timidly, said in a low voice :—

"Madame says you can tell me all about my brother that is lost."

"Do you want to see your brother?"

"Oh yes ; mamma said when she died perhaps he would find Baby and me sometime and take care of us."

The lost brother caught the wondering child to his arms, scarcely able to articulate :—

"He *has* found you ; he *will* take care of you!"

18

CHAPTER XX.

BABY'S BROTHER.

WHEN Lady Pamela heard that the villainous-looking young man whom she had
described as having come to kidnap Baby had
turned out to be Baby's own brother, she fell to
rubbing her nose with a vigor that nearly excori-
ated that sharp-pointed member, and muttered
something about "the sun bein' in my eyes, an'
he might be better lookin' with his hat off."

And when True afterwards let fall a hint that
the same villainous-looking person might drop
around that very evening to see Baby, she smug-
gled the latter into the kitchen and prepared
him for the visit by washing his face with soap-
suds until his cheeks and the end of his nose
shone like a china doll's. And when at length
a loud knocking was heard from the direction of
the area, she flew to open the door with a re-
doubled alacrity, to make amends for her former
suspicions.

"Hooray!" cried True as Ralph appeared. "Here you are, sir, on time like a sun-dial! An' here *we* are, sir, all united an' delighted to welcome Titania's brother.

"Welcome to bed an' welcome to board,
Welcome to all ' Beals an' Bilgo ' afford.

My better half, she stands behind you. — Come forth, my dove! This, sir, is the Lady Pamela, my wife an' the most extraordinary of women; an' this is Titania, queen of the fairies, who you 've met before in the busy walks of Trade; an' this is — Eh, w'ere 's the Commodore?" cried True, looking around at the bashful Baby, who, after sitting an hour in eager expectation of his coming brother, now dared not approach the grown-up and mustachioed stranger.

"Ship ahoy! The hour of joy — Is come, my boy! Run up your signal and fire a salute!" cried True, with an encouraging swing of his crutch.

Thus summoned, Baby sheepishly advanced and suffered himself to be lifted into the stranger's lap, where the mysterious appearance soon after of a box of soldiers, with a real cannon that shot off wooden balls, won him over into an enthusiastic admirer of his new-found brother.

"Here we are, you see," continued True, as Ralph settled himself in an easy-chair on the other side of the hearth, with Rachel and Baby on either knee, "snug as pigeons in a pie. The pie may have an upper crust, but we know nothin' about it ; we ask no odds of it. If the upper crust likes to be the upper crust, let it be it. We don't care. Draw up, sir, and have a pipe.

> " A friend indeed
> Is the fragrant weed.

Eh?—My love, do the honors!"

Ralph took the pipe which the Lady Pamela filled and handed him, and busied himself as he smoked in trying to make out his odd host and hostess.

"I have been thinking," he said at length, with a watchful eye on them both, "what we ought to do about sending this young lady to school."

In a moment True's face fell, and Lady Pamela's face fell, and Rachel, looking from one to the other, evidently did not quite know whether to let her face fall or not.

True puffed away vigorously for a full minute before answering : —

"Hm-m-m, — I don't want to offer any advice,

an' I ain't goin' to offer any advice, though her mother *did* make me her guardeen ; but if you want my opinion — my honest opinion is that if you interrupt her eddication now, to send her to *school*, it 'll be the ruination of her ! "

" How so ? " asked Ralph in surprise.

" ' How so ? ' W'y this way : What 'll she learn at school ? Two times two is four, an' not be sure o' that either w'en she comes out. W'at else 'll she learn ? A lot of stuck-up airs ! Now the question is : *do* you want her to have an eddication, or *don't* you want her to have an eddication ? "

The Lady Pamela nodded approbation at this masterly presentation of the case.

" Why, it is hardly necessary, I hope, to say that, after her health, her education will be my chief care."

" An' w'at is eddication ? " asked True. " It is learnin' how to *do* things, an' to make your way in the world ; an' w'at is she learnin' every day but *that* ? she is gettin' her eddication, an' a good one, too. An' if she 's left alone, she 'll turn out somethin' ; she might get to be fore-woman in an establishment ; she might set up for herself in the produce line ; she might go into anything," he cried, with a sweep of his hand that was doubtless meant to cover the whole commercial world. "An' that's my plan; I teach principles,—principles that'll apply to any branch of trade; an' she's gittin' hold of em!"

Lady Pamela wagged her head again approvingly at these educational views.

"Now the fundamental principles of business ain't easy to git hold of," continued True, filling his pipe, "but w'en they *are* once got hold of, they're *got* hold of! an' there's an end of it!"

Ralph avoided, for his own reasons, entering into present discussion of the educational question with his host, and for the same reasons made no answer to Rachel's petition, as she whispered in his ear:—

"Oh, please do not send me to school! I want to go to business and earn money, and put it in the bank to buy a house for Baby and me— and you can come and live with us too."

Baby catching the words, "money in the bank," in connection with which he had but one idea, cried:—

"Oh, we went to the Bow'ry an' saw Nick, an' we're going again as soon as Rachel gets ten dollars more in the tea-pot."

This speech so tickled Lady Pamela that she

burst into a hoarse little laugh, which was, however, so dry and choking that it ended in a fit of coughing.

"Hello," cried True, turning around in astonishment; "the Lady Pam. hilarious? Go it, my dear; it is better to laugh than be sighin'; only don't choke yourself; take it easy; let it ripple out itself! My wife," he continued aside to Ralph, "don't laugh; she does the heavy dignity for the family; and so you see I take my ease,

> "I laugh an' I chuckle, I giggle an' grin,
> I keep myself fat an' she keeps herself thin.

"A streak of fat an' a streak of lean, you see; that's good in meat, an' why not in life? Do you sing, sir?"

"I do not."

"Mr. Blue does," cried Rachel. "Oh, sing 'The Bay of Biscay, O!' Do, Mr. Blue, won't you?"

"Of course I will, Titania, my dear; anything in the world to keep the pot boilin'. W'en work's done it's done; that's my principle; then's the time to live, an' home's the place to live in — eh? W'en I get home, then horray for the song an' the dance, *I* say. I ain't much on the dance now," he said with a rueful glance at his legs, "but I used to be, an' I b'lieve in goin'

'it w'ile your'e young, an' renewin' your youth an'
ev'ry loved scene that your infancy knew.' Ring
in the orchestry, my dear!"

Lady Pamela repaired to the seraphine and
played a few opening bars, when True, straight-
ening back and throwing his head the least bit
on one side, made the very rafters ring with the
well-known and stirring ballad Rachel had called
for. Baby kept time with a spare crutch, and
involuntarily joined in the chorus. And when it
was over, he begged for "that tune about the
shovel and tongs," at which Lady Pamela showed
signs, for a moment, of becoming hilarious again,
but controlled herself, and presently struck up
the lively ballad of "Widow Machree," which
True sang with peculiar unction. Then Baby,
after taking a final ride around the room on
True's crutch, and thanking Ralph for the
soldiers, which he insisted on taking with him,
went off to bed with Rachel, who, on kissing her
new-found brother "good night," begged him
again not to send her to school, but to come and
live with them all at "Beals and Bilgo's."

Ralph had now an opportunity for a talk with
True and his wife, in which he learned the particulars of his mother's death and her wishes
with regard to the children. He listened with

intense interest to the recital, and when he took his leave assured them that he should let everything remain as it was for the present, and make no change without first consulting them; and finished by thanking them so warmly for all their care and kindness, that Lady Pamela was obliged to resort to the kitchen, and relieve herself by a clatter of tin and crockery.

"Come ag'in, sir, w'enever you'd like; w'enever you feel like eatin' a bit of humble-pie!" cried True, heartily, but with an odd little touch of pride in his tone, as Ralph rose to go.

And Lady Pamela, when she went to let him out, condescended so far to apologize for her brusqueness of the morning as to say:—

"It might 'a' been you an' it mightn't 'a' been you; an' if anybody thinks I'm goin' to sweeten on strangers, I ain't!"

CHAPTER XXI.

THE UNBIDDEN GUEST.

A PASSING angel stirred the pool; Ralph blundered into the troubled waters, and came forth from the involuntary baptism shocked and bewildered. And why not shocked? All new life and new experience must primarily be shocking. The butterfly coming forth from its dark chrysalis must at first be merely shocked at the overpowering glory of his new life. Birth is a shock which the suffering babe has neither tongue nor memory to record, and getting to Heaven — to those happy souls who compass it — will assuredly prove a shock outdoing all before.

As for Ralph, he looked and acted like one just awakened from a nightmare; the weight of the incubus was still upon him. With the horrid discords of the old life still ringing in his ears, he resolutely strove to attune himself to the harmony of the new. Night and day he pondered over the situation, looking his new future in the face, scanning the widened horizon that unfolded so suddenly before him, brightened by incalculable possibilities and shadowed by inscrutable doubts and difficulties.

The problem before him was not of easy solution; it involved several important questions. How without means or resources of any kind was he to take upon himself the charge of the two young lives that had been so providentially given to his care? Even granting that by great energy and good fortune he succeeded in the near or distant future in getting a home for them, what in the meantime was to become of the children? Were they to remain under their present strange guardianship? Was his gently-bred, delicately-organized sister to be left at the most impressionable time of childhood, to the perilous surroundings of her street life and occupation?

On the other hand, had not his mother, with the shadow of death hanging over her, with all a mother's natural solicitude, voluntarily chosen the present guardians of her children? Must *she* not have had confidence in them, — a confidence singular and unusual, — to warrant such an unlimited trust? But again, did not his mother have an ulterior purpose? Did she not — warned by the wretched splendor of her own

life — deliberately seek to sink her children in
the social scale, in the hope that they would be
surer of leading upright and honorable lives in
their humble station ?

Blindly but persistently Ralph groped among
these doubts and queries, going each day to
study more carefully the home life at " Beals and
Bilgo's," going to see Rachel nestled into her
niche in the wall and looking like a little fairy
behind her store of fruit and sweets, going to
consult Madame Velasco, who had conceived a
not unnatural prejudice against the Ballous, and
who was very positive in her opinion as to the
wisdom of immediately removing the children
from their charge.

But when Madame generously followed up this
advice by offering them a home at her own house
until he could make more permanent arrangements, Ralph recoiled from the proposal with an
instinctive shudder. Was it that he would not
bring those pure, innocent children back again
under the shadow and curse of that old life ?
Madame, whose extreme sensitiveness to impression caught every impalpable shadow of meaning, must have detected some such thought in
his face, for she delicately refrained from pressing the matter. But perhaps this very sugges-

tion forwarded the decision to which Ralph was inclining; perhaps it now for the first time occurred to him that his mother might have yielded to such an impulse in going away. Should he defeat her purpose? Nay, should he offend those generous hearts who had opened their doors to her fugitive feet, who had given her a refuge, who had received her children as a sacred trust from her dying hands, and who now, to the best of their power, were trying to carry out her wishes?

Influenced by these or whatsoever other considerations, Ralph now speedily decided upon his course; and his resolution once taken, he proceeded to carry it out with his old-time energy.

He arranged to leave the children for the present as they were, saying nothing of his future plans or purposes. He gathered together his effects and sold such as he could turn into money. He went to the old office where he had studied his profession, and brought away his books and drawings, which he packed up with his clothes and a few valuables. He gave up his rooms. He called upon the one or two old friends whom he still cared for, and all was done. He was ready to go; to go to a fresher field, where he might find purer air to breathe, more room to expand and to grow in, less overwhelming odds to struggle against, and a better chance of success.

But was indeed every chord loosed, was every anchor weighed that held him to the past? Did no regret mingle with the hopes with which he looked forward to his new life? During the bustle of preparation these questions were kept in abeyance by the necessity of action or by the resolute dominance of will; but on the eve of departure came an hour of rest and reaction, when they thronged upon him with resistless force. Then was fought the real battle; after hours of vain struggling he flung himself down at a table, seized a pen, and with reckless haste wrote the following somewhat incoherent letter: —

" MY DEAR MISS DIGHTON : —

"When we parted at your door the other evening, I was mocked by a fleeting hope that you would add one word to your mother's invitation to me. It was for you to speak that word. I could not go in without it; it would have been impertinence and intrusion, after what had passed between us. I waited anxiously for you to speak; I waited in vain. Your silence was as cruel as

it was significant. How could you reconcile it
with what had gone before — with your noble
interference in my behalf a half-hour previous?
Were you still angry at my rudeness? Could
you not forgive a few irritable words? Could
you make no allowance for my wretched, pitiable
state? I was pained and sorry for my offense;
I apologized; what could I do more?

"Our talk had reached a point when everything
seemed on the eve of being cleared up. I fretted
at the interruption; I burned with impatience to
go on. A few words of explanation from you
would have made all right. I had begged for
that explanation, and if I have still any claim to
the slightest consideration, I had a right to it.

"But do I make a mistake in all this? Am I
so obtuse as to want explained what ought
already to be clear to me? I have heard your
noble aspirations for reform; ought I long since
to have seen that your interest in me was simply
philanthropic; that I am merely one of the great
army of unfortunates whom you would make it
your mission to uplift? Have I been pre-
sumptuous in thinking I might be anything other
to you than the humblest of these? Have I
attached an unwarrantable significance to our
relations? Am I not worthy to be answered as
to all these things?

"But why do I hesitate; why do I study phrases? I *must* be answered; it is necessary to my peace; it is necessary in the work that is before me, that I should be relieved from this suspense! It is better to know the worst than fear it! And yet, like a coward, I sh˙ink from the very answer I invite. For my sake, for humanity's sake, for God's sake, then, I beg, I implore that it may be nothing worse than— 'WAIT.'

"Oh, if I could but *say* these words; speak them to your very face! If I could take your hand and look into your eyes, I might, perhaps, make you feel how deeply, intensely, how, beyond all power of speech, I mean them. But twice that privilege has been denied me; I dare not venture it again.

"You have told me that I must have an object in life, a motive for effort, something to care and work and live for besides myself. Thank God, I have at last found it! Whether I shall prove equal to the task, whether I shall prove worthy of this new responsibility, time only can show. My purpose now is strong and I hope for the best. Am I wrong in thinking you will be glad to hear of this; that I shall have your sympathy and your best wishes for my success?

"I took up my pen simply to say good-by; and you see in what it has resulted—my heart would out. I am going away; where, or for how long, I do not know. I must begin anew, amidst new people and surroundings, far away from any reminders of what has been, untrammeled by any of the influences that have so long weighed me down here.

"And so, once more, good-by! whether we ever meet again must depend upon you; but whether we meet or whether we part—I tremble to write the word, I shudder at the thought— my honor, respect, my gratitude and love for you will be eternal as my being.

"Yours ever and always,

"R. D."

Folding and directing this letter, Ralph took his hat and went out to mail it. He walked on and on, past one street-box after another, without dropping it. After he had gone a long distance, he at length stopped on a corner and stood irresolutely several minutes, holding the letter in his hand. Presently he turned and began slowly to retrace his steps. Again he stopped; again turned, and now, moved by a sudden determination, walked rapidly on without

further pause or hesitation, until he came to Mr.
Curley's door. Once more he halted to deliber-
ate, once more regarded the letter, idly weighed
it in his hand, tapped it against his nervous
fingers, looked up at the lighted windows, and
then, as if wresting himself by a violent effort
from the further hold of doubt and misgiving,
he suddenly thrust the letter into his pocket,
quickly mounted the steps, and rang the bell.

He found the brightly-lighted drawing-room
filled with strangers. Mrs. Dighton was holding
a reception, and Dorothy was helping her mother
entertain.

If the latter felt any surprise at seeing
Ralph, she did not show it. She received him
easily and cordially, but not so warmly as her
mother, who took especial pains to entertain
him and introduced him to her most agreeable
guests. Whether Mrs. Dighton would ordinarily
have had the courage and independence thus
freely to introduce one under the ban of society,
is aside from the question ; her present purpose
overrode every other consideration.

But Ralph made poor work of trying to talk.
The discord between his mood and his surroundings could not have been heightened ; it amounted
to absolute pain. Dorothy did not avoid him.

It would have been better if she had; her manner to him was quite undistinguishable from her manner to the other guests. Perhaps he would rather have seen her cold or angry. He sat for a while growing constantly more and more uneasy; the object of his coming was plainly defeated; the restraint of his position at length became intolerable, and he rose to go.

Having taken leave of Mrs. Dighton and her brother, he approached Dorothy, who stood near the door. She expressed a polite surprise at his short stay, but did not oppose his going. She advanced several steps with him as he moved towards the door, but with an instinctive obedience to etiquette stopped on the threshold and held out her hand.

" I came here to-night to see *you ;* I wanted to have a talk with you, Miss Dighton," said Ralph, in a tone so sudden and intense that it sounded almost fierce.

Dorothy looked at him in grave silence ; perhaps she was too much startled by his vehemence to reply ; or it might be she had nothing to say.

" I am going away. I came to say good-by," he went on in the same tone as before.

Dorothy's face changed unmistakably at this

unexpected news, and she made a little half-
appealing motion with her hand. But with his
glowing eyes fixed steadfastly upon her, intent
only upon *her* looks, *her* thoughts, and *her* words,
Ralph was now oblivious of the place, oblivious
of the company, of everything but the one purpose that possessed him.

With a quick furtive look around as if fearful
that his manner might excite remark, Dorothy
stepped out with him through the open folding-
doors into the hall, where, although not free
from observation, they were out of ear-shot.

"I could not go away without seeing you,
without knowing on what terms we stand, without doing everything in *my* power to clear up
the misunderstanding between us!" continued
Ralph.

"I know no reason why there should be any
misunderstanding. I cannot guess the nature
of it. I hope I have given you no cause to
doubt that I am your friend," returned Dorothy,
a little coldly.

"'Friend,'" repeated Ralph with a suppressed
sneer, "friend is a very fine word, but unfortunately it is a little vague; it seldom means
much."

"That depends, I suppose, upon who uses it."

"Precisely; and what you say to me now you might say to any man in yonder room."

"Perhaps I might."

"Do you think, then, that you have treated me quite justly?"

"I hope so; I have tried to."

"You do not answer my question," he said half sternly.

"I do not understand it."

Ralph looked at her a full minute in utter silence, as she stood before him in her rich evening toilet. The soft overhanging light glinting in one bright broken ripple through her hair, and streaming in white gleams along the shifting, silken folds of her dress, brought out in almost majestic relief the sweeping lines of her figure. It is doubtful if she had ever looked so beautiful to Ralph; it is doubtful if she had ever seemed so exasperating.

"Good-by!" he said at length, in a hoarse voice.

"Good-by!"

The two stood for one little moment hand in hand. On the one side, a witness of their parting, stood the fair, mute Hero. On the other, across the threshold, stood anxious, watchful Mrs. Dighton, a society smile in her eyes, a

passing compliment upon her lips, but in her
mother's heart an agony of suspense.

Why could not that brazen image, like Galatea
of old, have waked in that moment to conscious
life and told her secret? Why, occupied eter-
nally with her own selfish sorrow, did she stand
and hold her peace, and suffer those good-bys
to be said? Why did that cruel little woman
look implacably on from among her chattering
guests, and forbid not that parting?

But nor image nor woman spake. No voice
was lifted and no hand was raised ; and so the
last words were said, and the unbidden guest
strode down the hall and out into the night.
And when he reached home and stood before
the smouldering fire upon his hearth, he drew
his own letter from his pocket, and with a bitter
smile tore it into tiny shreds, muttering as he
watched them blacken and shrivel among the
embers : —

"Only a few more ashes."

CHAPTER XXII.

SCHOOL VERSUS "EDDICATION."

TO follow Ralph in his wanderings; to watch the development of his character; to record his successes and failures, is without the limitations of our plan. Happily it is not necessary. We need only with flying pencil chronicle the outcome of it all; tell in a word in what his new life had been fruitful to himself or to others.

Going from place to place through the far West, he at last settled in a young and thriving city, where there seemed a promising field for his work. He there resumed, with characteristic vigor, his abandoned profession, for which he had a fair but by no means an extraordinary talent. There was nothing noteworthy in his experience except the singleness of purpose with which he persisted in his work, the unremitting concentration of thought and effort with which he encountered difficulties, and the triumphant energy with which he may be said to have fairly conquered success.

"It is easy to write phrases in a novel; it is easy, with prodigal hand, to invest this or that fictitious personage with unusual or extraordinary qualities, — it is the trick of the storyteller," will perhaps be the reflection of hardworking but unsuccessful mediocrity. But we reject the imputation; the qualities we have mentioned belong to Ralph no more than to scores of young men who go forth year after year to do battle with the world. All experience proves that Fortune yields more often to Persistence than to Talent, and that, in fact, she has never been known to hold out long before a fixed will and a tireless energy.

What matters it how long Ralph waited; how long he worked? Divisions of Time are ideal and arbitrary; Time itself is a fiction which yet we teach so categorically to our children, that the ordinary intelligent school-boy would doubtless stare to be told there was no such thing as a year; that life is truly measured by events; that we are really older or younger in proportion only to what we have seen, done, and suffered.

But Ralph's thoughts were not so fixed on his work as to cause him to forget the object of it.

He wrote constantly to the children, telling them
of his health, his hopes, and his increasing success. At the end of several months there came
for the first time a letter addressed to True.

He found it awaiting his return one night, and,
as a letter was to him an important event, he
deferred opening it until he had eaten his supper, and was comfortably fixed for the evening
with his pipe, easy-chair, and slippers. It was
then that the children gathered around, and Lady
Pamela came in from the kitchen and stood listening with intense interest while True very
slowly and in a quite unnatural and rather orac-
ular tone,— which, in common with many other
and better-schooled people, he always assumed
when he had occasion to read, — proceeded to
declaim the letter.

It ran as follows : —

" MY DEAR MR. BALLOU : —

" I am very much obliged for your various kind
messages through Rachel, and I am very much
indebted to you and your excellent wife [ahem !
that is you, my dear,]' your excellent wife for all
your kindness and attention to the children since
I have been gone. I am happy to say to you
that, after long waiting, many reverses, and much

disappointment, I have at length succeeded in establishing myself in business, so that I now feel justified in assuming the charge and support of my brother and sister.

"I shall still, if you are willing, leave them with you — at least until my prospects here warrant me in making more definite arrangements — confident that they will have the best of care and treatment. But I now wish to carry out a purpose, of which I spoke to you briefly on the occasion of our first meeting, but which I have not hitherto been able to realize. I told you, I think, that my first care, after their health, was for their education. The time has come for that to be attended to. I now wish them both to be put to school as soon as practicable.

"While I am conscious of the many advantages of a business education, and have no doubt that Rachel has made great progress under your tuition, I have concluded that, as she is not to be a business woman, as her life will, I hope, be a private and domestic rather than a public one, she had now better give up her present employment and fit herself for the station which I hope to see her occupy.

"I wish, therefore, you would make arrangements as soon as possible to give up her booth —

[Here True's face fell ; he gave a long "m —
m — m " of doubt, and Lady Pamela wagged her
head ominously, while True, after various clear-
ings of his throat, very slowly and distinctly read
over the last paragraph to make sure there was no
mistake,] — "to give up her booth, and, together
with Baby, to go to some good school.

" In the choice of a school you will oblige me
by consulting Madame Velasco, to whom I have
written upon the subject, and who will doubtless
call upon you immediately.

" Inclosed you will find money for the children's expenses, in the disbursement of which
I rely entirely upon your good judgment. [True's
face brightened at this personal tribute, while
Lady Pamela bridled and rubbed her nose with
an embarrassed air.]

" I wish you would write me at length as soon
as you get these arrangements completed. I
hope to be able soon to return to New York,
when we will settle upon our plans for the future.
Meantime I leave all the details to you. I
inclose a letter to the children, which please
hand them with my love. Also oblige me by
giving my compliments to Mrs. Ballou ; — assure
her that I realize and appreciate all her services

in behalf of my little ones, and am deeply grateful therefor.

"Very truly yours,

"RALPH DEXTER."

"A very fine letter!" exclaimed True, folding the sheet and assuming again his ordinary tone; "and scholarly, too; that last passage now: 'My compliments to Mrs. Ballou, and assure her that I realize and appreciate,' etc. That is eloquent, down-right eloquent. Yes, that letter might go in print; the style of it is good, but"— True assumed a most august expression, and sank his voice to an impressive whisper, as he added, "it's all wrong in principle! Mind, Titania, I don't blame your brother; he *thinks* he's doin' all right, an' it's very han'some of him, an' all that, but he's wrong — dead sure — in principle! What's he goin' to do?" he continued, re-filling his pipe. "Take you away from business, interrupt your eddication, an' send you off to school, where your brains 'll git muddled with 'rithmetic an' jography, all your good habits 'll be rooted up, an' you 'll forgit your fundamental principles."

Lady Pamela heaved a deep sigh and closed her eyes with an indescribable expression, while

Rachel looked very grave and sad, to think her brother should be so wrong-headed.

"Still, my dear," continued True, "your brother is your own flesh an' blood, your natural gardeen, an' we must do as he says. He *means* well, but I can't help thinkin'," he went on shaking his head dolefully, "what 'll become of you w'en you git goin' to them schools!"

"Can't I go to business never any more?"

"Never more!" echoed True, tragically.

"But what will become of my booth?"

"I shall have to sell it out to somebody in the business."

On hearing this Rachel's eyes moistened, and one or two tears rolled slowly down her cheeks.

"Then I can't ever put any more money in the bank!" she continued, contemplating the remoter consequences of this ill-advised step.

"An' we can't go to the Bow'ry any more," chimed in Baby, with a very indefinite notion of what was under consideration.

To these and other similar reflections True only replied by a solemn shake of the head, repeating at intervals, with much emphasis: —

"Your brother *means* well, my dear, but he is young, and he is wrong in principle — *dead sure!*"

Nothing, however, could long cloud True's spirits, and having reduced the whole family to a satisfying depth of misery, he called aloud upon his spouse to "touch the lyre" as usual. But poor Lady Pamela was quite unequal to the task; she was busied with her own private thoughts and conclusions over what she had heard, and calling Rachel aside she told her confidentially to put on her best dress in the morning, and braid her hair in ribbons, for "there's no tellin' w'en that person, Madame Thingumy'll be round," — from which may be gathered Lady Pamela's opinion about consulting an outsider.

"She *may* know a wonderful sight, but she don't look it, that's all I've got to say!"

"My dear," interposed True, pacifically, "it isn't everybody that is capable of expressin' that wealth of intelligence in their face that you are; we must pity the poor lady in this respect; no doubt she knows more than she seems.

> By the looks of a frog,
> An' the looks of a log,
> You can't tell that the frog
> Can jump over the log;

which is to say, appearances are deceitful. As speakin' as *your* countenance is, my dear, nobody'd ever know what tremendous accomplishments you're mistress of."

"Guess I don't look quite like a fool !"

"If any nigh-sighted person ever entertained that wild delusion, my dear, he'd wake to a stern reality w'en he got his goggles on."

With sorrowful heart Rachel saw True go off to business without her the next morning. She sat all day in state, in her best gown and ribbons, awaiting the possible coming of Madame Velasco, reflecting with horror upon the prospect of having her brain muddled with "them schools," and firmly resolving, whatever might come, to hold fast to the "fundamental principles."

Lady Pamela put the little parlor in its best trim, adding several treasured ornaments from her private hoard, and lastly — what she was never known to do except on the rarest and most momentous occasions — brought forth from its hiding-place, between the mattresses of her own bed, a flannel bag from which she produced the "Testimonial," a resplendent silver bugle, which she disposed upon a special silk mat of its own upon the centre-table, first removing everything that could prevent an uninterrupted view of its splendor.

As the day slipped by, however, and Madame

Velasco did not appear, Lady Pamela expressed herself in very vigorous terms about "folks that didn't keep their engagements;" which, considering that the expected caller had made no engagement, was, to say the least, not very consistent; but it was one of the good woman's faults, as True often reminded her, that where it touched a matter upon which she felt strongly, Lady Pamela could not be counted upon to be strictly consistent; in which we leave it to be estimated how much she differs, after all, from the world at large.

The next day Rachel and Baby were attired as before; and once more the bugle was brought forth, and this time, sure enough, about noon the expected knocking was heard at the area door. Lady Pamela dropped her broom and dust-pan, and enunciated with much decision the proposition that she guessed "they would pound till she was ready to let 'em in," with the added corollary that they "*probably* wouldn't git in till she *was* ready." And, accordingly, not until she was duly arrayed in the alpacca and the comb, and had viewed herself, full face and profile, in the kitchen mirror, did she at length repair to the door, where the unfortunate Madame Velasco was on the point of going away in despair.

Lady Pamela conducted her visitor in silence to the house, ushered her into the parlor, and after satisfying herself by a hasty glance that the " Testimonial " was still safe, placed a chair for her guest where she could have the best view of that exceptional piece of plate.

After greeting the children, who were very glad to see her, and commenting on their health and growth, Madame was going on to tell about her letter from Ralph, when she was interrupted by the dry remark from Lady Pamela : —

" We 've *heerd* the news."

" Indeed ? " returned Madame, " then I suppose you are very glad," she continued, turning to Rachel, " that you are going to school."

" Oh, no ! " said Rachel, with a troubled look.

" Why not, my child ? "

" Because — because I don't want to get muddled."

" ' Muddled ? ' " repeated Madame, with an amused look. " Oh, everything will be clear very soon. You will learn a great many things at school. You will learn how to read and write and keep accounts better than you do now. You will learn about your own wonderful body, about this beautiful earth and all the strange plants

20

and animals upon it. Don't you want to know all these things?"

"Yes; I suppose so," answered Rachel, rather doubtfully.

"And you will learn how to use your own language, and how to read and write foreign languages"—

"I hope *not*," interposed Lady Pamela, emphatically, "none o' that for *me*; no foreign gibberish nor foreign anything else: give *me* pure native!"

"But, my good woman," objected Madame, gently, "it might often be advisable to teach children what we would not choose to study ourselves."

"*You* may do that, Ma'am," retorted Lady Pamela, with increasing vehemence. "*You* may teach *your* children to walk a tight-rope, or jump over the moon, or any other hey-diddle-diddle-cat's-in-the-fiddle thing that *you 're* ashamed to do, but none o' that for *me*—not if *you* please!"

"Then," continued Madame, turning again to Rachel, "don't you want to learn to draw and to sing and to dance, so that you may grow up an accomplished as well as an intelligent woman, an honor to yourself and your brother?"

"If you *do*," broke in Lady Pamela, whose

zeal had now quite got the better of her prudence, "*if* you do, I say, I wouldn't give a fig for
your principles!"

This speech greatly alarmed Rachel, for nothing had been inculcated with such force and fre-
quency by True as strict adherence to principles.

"Oh, I mustn't do anything, if you please,"
she faltered out, "to go against the fundamental
principles."

"'Fundamental principles?'" repeated Madame with a puzzled look. "Why, certainly not,
my child. I want you always to observe the
fundamental principles, and all other rules and
principles that are good; your own conscience
will enable you to judge of all that, as you grow
older. But I must go now," she continued, seeing perhaps the uselessness of further discussion
in the presence of her hostess; "I came to tell
you that I have found a school for you and Baby,
where you will be taught only good and useful
things, and if Mr. Ballou will bring you to my
house, I will take you there as soon as you get
ready to go; and I hope you will prove a very
prompt, clever little scholar."

"What is a scholar?" asked Baby, clinging to
Lady Pamela's skirts and regarding Madame
doubtfully, as she held out her hand to say good-
by..

"It's a muddle-head!" said Lady Pamela emphatically.

After this Parthian shot she showed her visitor out in a quite cheerful state of mind, and returning, smiled grimly to herself as she packed the bugle in its flannel bag and tucked it away in its old hiding-place between the mattresses.

CHAPTER XXIII.

THE UNRETURNING LEANDER.

MEANTIME Hero stood awaiting her unreturning lover; stood day and night in her dark corner, wearing ever on her bronze face the same mingled look of hope and foreboding; stood holding in her drooped hand the burning beacon for him who, somewhere in the wastes of night, amidst the storms and buffets of Time and Things, was bravely struggling against adverse tides and fates to come to her embrace.

To Mrs. Dighton this heathen maid wore another guise; to that wretched woman, despite the classic beauty of her figure, despite the winsome sweetness of her face, she became a haunting horror, a pursuing shadow of retribution, a sight, a form, more terrible than the midnight-conjured spectre.

Perhaps, after self-preservation, the most active motive-principle in the human breast is the thirst of discovery. Life is a struggle after revelation. The intellect seeks to unearth new facts, the soul to penetrate new mysteries. In great things and little it is the same. If we have buried in our hearts one poor shivering little secret, Chance and Design straightway conspire to wrest it from us. The criminal flies in vain from the detective eyes of man and nature, and finds peace only in death or confession.

If an instance be wanted of the truth of this, Mrs. Dighton's experience will supply it. Her normal state seemed now one of warfare. The hall, which heretofore had been the one neutral place in the house, a mere passage-way from room to room, became now the scene of perpetual ambush and sortie, where Chance led on his viewless forces to insidious attack, where Design opened masked batteries and plotted stealthy charge and countermarch.

Two or three incidents will show this better than a thousand words.

One evening Mr. Curley announced at the tea-table that he proposed taking up the carpet and laying a new floor in the hall.

"I hope you will do nothing of the sort, Samuel," said Mrs. Dighton quietly.

"Why not?"

"I prefer the carpet," she said more positively.

"But the carpet has grown very shabby, and you yourself proposed a long time ago to get a new one."

"I have changed my mind," she answered with increasing decision.

"But, if we are going to change, it will be cheaper, cleaner, and in every way better to have the floor."

"I dislike a floor; it is cold and noisy."

These short and very decided answers from his sister, who was wont to be so yielding, surprised and perhaps irritated Mr. Curley, for he answered somewhat curtly : —

"I am sorry, my dear; I thought you would be pleased; but it is too late now to object. I have already ordered the tiles for the floor; they are very beautiful, and I got them at a bargain."

Mrs. Dighton electrified her family by immediately rising from the table with a very pale face, and saying in the greatest agitation : —

"Then I hope you will instantly countermand the order. I have a very decided objection to the carpet's being removed, and I request as a particular personal favor that you will not touch it!"

With these words she walked quickly out of the room, leaving her brother and daughter in speechless astonishment.

It is hardly necessary to say the floor was not laid.

Again it was Dorothy who was the innocent offender.

Lying awake one night with her tormenting thoughts, Mrs. Dighton heard her daughter, who slept in the adjoining room, moving softly about. She listened at first carelessly, but when, presently, she heard the chamber door open, and Dorothy, with stealthy steps, stealing along the hall, she became instantly alarmed. She rose, quaking in every limb, opened her door, groped through the hall, stole down the stairs, turned, and saw a sight that must well-nigh have frozen the blood in her veins — *Dorothy, in her night clothes, standing directly before the bronze image!*

With a piercing scream Mrs. Dighton rushed towards her.

"Hush! Hush! It is only I!" cried Dorothy, turning and catching her mother in her arms.

"Wretched girl, what are you doing here?"

"Bugaboo; what a horrid little Lady Macbeth you are getting to be, Rhody," cried Dorothy laughing; "it's enough to make one's blood run cold! 'Wretched girl,' indeed! Wretched mother, you mean; wake-up, goosey-gander; it is only I, I tell you, come down to get a glass of water!"

"Oh, my dear," cried Mrs. Dighton, with a gasp of relief, "how you have frightened me! Why will you do such things?"

"'Such things'?" repeated Dorothy, almost choking with laughter as her mother clung to her spasmodically, 'Banquo and Donalbain,' 'A deed without a name,' and all the rest of it. Oh, please, *don't* be so absurd, Rhody! 'Such things,' indeed; pray was I to lie and parch all night for a drink?"

"But why didn't you knock at my door and say you were going down?"

"To be sure; why didn't I wake you up, and wake Uncle Curl up, and say: Your daughter, ma'am; your niece, sir, — drinks — drinks, an't please you, a glass of water. 'The King doth wake to-night and takes his rouse!'"

"You wouldn't trifle so, my dear, if you knew the state of my nerves."

"Well, there, then, go back to bed and to sleep," said Dorothy, kissing her mother good night when they reached the latter's room, "and don't go prowling any more! After this when I go down I will lock you in."

Next, it was the housekeeper who threatened her peace.

Winter had rolled away, spring had come, and the annual domestic upheaval, the war with dust, was in order. To the first suggestion of this Mrs. Dighton opposed a firm objection. In vain the methodical housekeeper urged the necessity of carpets and curtains being removed and cleaned; it was deferred from week to week until the time came for the family to go to the seaside, when, to the surprise of all, Mrs. Dighton insisted upon sending the officious housekeeper with Dorothy and her uncle, to get things at Windmere in order, while she stayed behind to attend to the shutting-up of the house in town.

She had never been known to do such a thing before. She gave no reason for it now; but she had latterly grown so restless, peevish, and capricious that, although Dorothy held various private consultations with her uncle about Rhody's incomprehensible freaks, they agreed to make no objection and Mrs. Dighton was accordingly left behind with two of the servants.

Her purpose in all this now appears. The night that Dorothy and Mr. Curley left, she rose from her sleepless bed, stole down stairs and again, with beating heart, stood before the hated image. Seizing it with desperate clutch she swung it to the floor;—there, underneath, still undisturbed, lay the little white parallelogram, the cause of all her misery! The time had now come to put an end to that misery; with one bold simple act to purchase peace! Time, place and solitude, all concurred in promising success. She stretched forth her hand to take the letter; but in that moment a sudden tremor seized her; she looked around with quick, startled glance as though the air were full of sudden noises. She clutched the image again, to replace it; to her horror she could only lift it an inch or two from the floor. She struggled; she wrestled with it as though it had been a creature of flesh and blood, intelligently hostile; but all in vain, her utmost strength did not avail. She walked the floor in an agony of fear and helplessness. Suddenly an expedient occurred to her; she arranged hassocks and chairs in a series of steps from the floor to the table. She began again, and after a frantic struggle of half an hour succeeded, at last, in replacing the statue, and then dropped exhausted and half-swooning upon a neighboring sofa. Cowardly little woman, why did you hesitate! What flimsy, worthless distinction did you make between concealing and destroying!

Defeated in her purpose, Mrs. Dighton flies,

the next day, to join her family at the seaside, where, in the enjoyment of a few months of assured peace, she hopes to find relief.

But who can escape from his shadow! " They change their sky and not their mind who run across the sea." The same conscience, the same heart — bearing the same burdens — adhere there as here. Mrs. Dighton had left the dumb image behind ; was she to find a living Hero here? Was another face, ineffably dear, to bear the same look ? Were other eyes, whose every turn she knew and loved, as she watched them gazing off upon the heaving sea, gazing up into the star-lit sky, gazing out over the wind-blown forest, to wear the same look of foreboding, of yearning, of waiting for another Leander unreturning, — unreturning now for days and weeks and months, and well-nigh years ! Unreturning and, perhaps, tossed with spent strength upon the flood of some dark Hellespont of sin and trouble !

CHAPTER XXIV.

THE "Lightning Express" came rushing and thundering into the station. One man got out upon the platform; not to say that there were not hundreds of other dusty creatures, each with his errand of business or pleasure, of life or death. But we have no concern with these; they are colorless entities; our interest and sympathy are not big enough to embrace them all, except in a cold, general way. By which we mean — dear philanthropists, do not take alarm! — that we cannot be weighed down by the aggregate woe, we cannot be elated by the cumulative joy of all these; our little gill-measure of Being is not equal to it; and so we can only say: "God-speed!" to the Good and "Confusion" to the Evil.

But for our one man we have a necessary and especial interest, and we keep a careful eye upon him as he crosses the ferry and goes stalking up Broadway.

"Who is he?"   "What is he?"—Whisper;
a word in your ear!

"Eh, what?—With these broad shoulders,
with these bushy whiskers?" Why not? Times
change and we change in them, we hope. The
world moves; men come and go; the babes of
yesterday rise up and flout us to our faces, call
us dotards, and "push us from our stools." And
we give way perforce—alas! the fleeting years,
O Postumus!

But here is nothing strange—the stripling has
become a man. In less time than he has been
away Alexander overran Asia; Cæsar conquered
the Gauls; Wellington cooped up "the little
Corporal" in Elba; and many other as great
things were achieved.

Meantime we approve our pilgrim in his brawn
and dust. We are a little sorry for the whiskers,
perhaps, for they cover up a mouth whose tricks
of sensibility, decision, humor, satire, indifference, and what not, used by turns to fascinate
and exasperate us.

But for Ralph himself—beshrew our tell-tale
pen; we were keeping the name for a more
effective introduction upon the next page!—you
may be sure he is avalanched by thought, remin-
iscence, regret, remorse, and so on to the end

of the chapter. It is enough to make the poor fellow lightheaded, and he does indeed walk a little unsteadily, but then, he has hardly got his land-legs on yet, nor deadened the whirring in his ears of a three days' journey by what our dear old English wit would have called "a flash of silence."

But there are offsets now to be made — thank Heaven! There is a goodly lump of sweet to neutralize the sour, and — to speak with an excusable violence — Ralph's reflections must have been of the bitterly-happy sort.

Bitter or sweet, however, he keeps them under healthful control, and loses no time in depositing his traps, shaking off some of his dust and getting around to a certain little area-door we know of, where he stands listening to "Wild George" and "Jumping Jacob" stamping impatiently in their neighboring stalls, while Lady Pamela takes her own time to draw the bolts and present at length a not-very-gracious visage to his view.

"Good evening!"

"W'at d 'ye want?"

"Don't you know me? I am Mr. Dexter."

"So you be!" she exclaimed, darting at Ralph and seizing his hand in both her own with a rapturous squeeze; "oughter known it. — Sakes alive — sh-h " —

With many mysterious signs and winks she led the way through the yard, turning around at every step to shake a cautioning finger.

"There!— Sh-h!— Don't stir!" she whispered, when they reached - the stairs. "*My* soul 'n body, they 'll jump out of *their* skins! I 'll go in jes' though 't 's nobody, 'n by 'm-by you come."

Breathless with excitement Lady Pamela disappeared and left Ralph alone on the dark staircase, with no very definite notion of the part he was to play.

Marching into the little parlor where the family was assembled, Lady Pamela grumbled something about the nuisance of "folks goin' round knockin' at other folks's doors," and having diverted suspicion by this clever strategem, seated herself at the seraphine, whence she had been summoned by Ralph's knocking, and struck up the well-known ballad of "Somebody's Coming," in which, as she evidently expected, True presently joined.

But when, at the end of the second stanza, Lady Pamela heard a faint click of the outer latch, and the next minute, to the utter amazement of True and the children, somebody did come, and they all stared, and didn't know him until he spoke, and then both children recognized him at once and sprang forward, crying, "Brother Ralph, Brother Ralph;" and Ralph laughed and cried, and True laughed and cried, and there was no end of commotion, — when, we say, all this happened, the Lady Pamela had become quite beside herself, and choked and coughed, put her apron over her face and turned pirouettes in the corner till True feared she had lost her reason.

Baby and Rachel forthwith perched themselves on Ralph's knees, while True went off with such a string of rhymes as was never heard from mortal man before.

> "Oh, welcome from the ragin' sea;
> Oh, welcome back to 'B. & B;'
> Behold your shattered bark once more
> Safe anchored on her native shore.

That's right, my love," he continued, addressing Lady Pamela, who was slipping out unobserved, "seek your native heath, give vent to your feelins', an' make the welkin ring.

> "Go quick an' kill the fatted calf,
> The chicken, or the cat,
> Or other dear domestic beast
> You soonest can come at!"

"I almost didn't know you—wasn't it funny?" said Baby, looking admiringly at Ralph. "I've

been up to the head in my class lots o' times, an'
I 've got a medal, and Rachel can write best of
any one in the school, and can draw *be*-autiful
maps."

"We 've got all your letters in a box," chimed
in Rachel, "and we 've read them over every
night till they 're almost torn to pieces."

"Yes, and I 've got those soldiers, you know,
only I 've knocked the general's head off, but
Mr. B'lou says he can stick it on."

"Madame Velasco teaches me to sew every
week, — she sews beautifully — and she has given
me a linnet in such a pretty cage — there it is
hanging in the window, and lots of pretty things
besides."

"We can't go to the Bow'ry now; Mr. B'lou
won't take us. He says we 're going to be
swells 'cause we go to school, and we mustn't go
to the Bow'ry."

True coughed nervously and affected to laugh
at this remark.

"What *are* swells, brother Ralph?" pursued
Baby.

"I hardly know; very weak and foolish people,
I fear."

At this answer True coughed harder than
before, but was saved from further embarrass-

ment by the timely appearance in the doorway
of Lady Pamela, who said something incoherent
about a bite and a journey, from which it was
not at all clear whether she expected somebody
to take the one or the other.

Ralph, answering her looks rather than her
words, endeavored to excuse himself on the plea
of a late dinner, but in vain ; he found no alternative but to follow his enthusiastic hostess to
the kitchen, where stood a table that — if ever a
material plank did become vocal — should have
groaned under its load. Plied with one delicacy
after another, Ralph only escaped from the table
when he had been brought to the verge of
apoplexy.

When they gathered again in the parlor, Lady
Pamela asked suddenly : —

" Tell him about the medal ? "

" Yes."

" And the maps ? "

" Yes."

" Might's well see 'em, I s'pose," she continued,
producing a key and opening the table drawer,
from which she took a shining silver medal, and
hung it by a ribbon about Baby's neck. The
look of pride and reverence with which she
regarded the medal showed that she held it in

only less estimation than the "Testimonial." It was the map, on the contrary, that awakened True's enthusiasm, and he was evidently a little disappointed at Ralph's quiet commendation.

"That's science, I call it! Them cross lines now, longertude an' latertude, every one true ; an' the rivers an' mountains an' capitals with a ring round ; an' the little ladder of inches at the bottom, — Columbus might have discovered Ameriky with that."

It was evident, by their hearty and unaffected interest in the children's progress, and the pride which they took in their acquirements, that the prejudice against schools had somewhat worn off with the worthy pair.

And when late in the evening Ralph withdrew, leaving behind on the table a small parcel marked : —

"For Mr. and Mrs. Ballou,"

which True, on opening, found to contain a handsome meerschaum pipe in a case lined with blue satin, and a beautiful set of cameo jewelry on a red velvet cushion, in a morocco box, the gratitude and satisfaction of that happy pair may be imagined, but can only be very inadequately described in words.

"Put 'em on, put 'em on!" cried True, impatiently.

"Hair ain't curled nor nothin'," objected Lady Pamela.

"Never mind your tresses, my charmer, don the gems! Assume the sparklers!

> "In jewels bright, in jewels rare,
> Oh, deck thyself, my Lady fair!"

"Might slip on my alpacca in a minute," muttered Lady Pamela, quite overcome by the splendor of the jewelry.

"Tut, tut, never mind your robes of state, my Cinderella; on with the scintillators."

. Thus persuaded Lady Pamela nervously pinned on the brooch and put in the ear-rings, when True, rising, cried rapturously : —

"Hooray, Queen of Sheby, come to the arms of your Solomon!"

With a cautioning "Look out for them earrings," Lady Pamela walked blushingly up and submitted to the usual embrace.

True then filled his new pipe, while Lady Pamela retired for a private inspection of herself in the kitchen mirror. Coming back presently to find her spouse's head almost lost in a cloud of smoke, she said with a wag of her head that made the cameos rattle : —

"I ain't no prophet nor no *clairvoyant*, but take my word, Tru' B'lou, *that* young man is goin' to be a statesman!"

CHAPTER XXV.

FOR WEAL OR WOE.

R ALPH'S announcement of his purpose to
take the children back with him cast a
profound gloom over the household of " Beals
and Bilgo." · True was not heard to make a
rhyme from morning till night, and the disconsolate Lady Pamela had no longer any heart to
"touch the lyre," but shut herself up in the
kitchen, in a stony silence upon which no one
dared intrude.

Ralph's visit had already extended to several
weeks, when one morning he received a business
letter summoning him home immediately. Inclosed was a note from one of his Western
friends, commissioning him to buy various knick-
knacks, including some books and stationery,
sportsmen's traps, a pistol and cartridges, etc.,
that could be got at better advantage in the city.

He sent word at once to Lady Pamela to have
the children ready to start the following day ; he

made a short farewell call on Madame Velasco, and spent the rest of the morning running about the town, executing his commission.

Coming out into the street after making his last purchase, he looked at his watch and found it was nearly twelve. Calling a carriage he hurried to the depot, and arrived just in time to catch the noon train for Windmere as it was moving away from the platform.

Although apparently acting upon a sudden impulse, he may perhaps have had this in view from the first. Perhaps he wanted to see his old country friends and neighbors, or go over his old haunts in field or wood, or simply to take a bath in the sea before going back upon the prairies. It is no business of ours what he wanted. It is enough for us to know that he went; went and found the place for the most part unchanged; found his old village acquaintances very glad to see him after he had introduced himself, for what with his shoulders and his whiskers, not a mother's son of them knew him.

The beasts were more intelligent; the old coach-dog at the little tavern recognized him at once, as also, to his great delight, did his own old saddle-mare, which, on leaving the village, he had sold to the tavern-keeper. The faithful creature whinnied when he went into her stall, and exhibited every sign of equine delight. Nothing in all his coming back had so touched Ralph as this. He petted and talked to the animal a long while, and ended by ordering her to be saddled for a ride. When she was ready he mounted and cantered off along the old familiar turnpike.

Familiar enough the road and familiar every object upon it, and more and more familiar with every step he advanced, until the faithful mare turned of her own accord into the entrance to the well-known grounds, and without let or hindrance from her master trotted confidently along the avenue between the overhanging elms, up to the very door.

The very door indeed; the *scabies* of decoration had not yet appeared upon the outside. Ralph sat in his saddle and glanced furtively about. Everything was in extreme order; the trim shrubbery, the closely-shaven lawn, the carefully-kept flower-beds. It was mid-afternoon. There was a dead silence everywhere, and upon Ralph's strained ears fell only the sound of his own loud heart-throbs, mingled with the soft soughing of the ocean breeze.

He sat in his saddle as though rooted to the

spot. Unobserved he had come ; unseen he had seen ; he had been blest with a dream of home. Should he go? He might yet do so without detection. Slowly he gathered up the reins, but his eager mare had tasted the fresh green grass — an unaccustomed luxury — and ravenously clung to it, giving no heed to the tightened rein. Did her gluttony then decide the matter? Or did a fatal spell hang upon each nerve and muscle of her master? In a moment it was too late. A noise was heard. A step approached, and the next minute a man-servant appeared in the open door.

Ralph awoke from his lethargy ; he jumped off his horse and mounted the steps.

" Is Miss Dighton at home?"

" Yes, sir ; will you walk in ?"

Shown into the darkened drawing-room he handed the servant his card. The man had hardly withdrawn to pursue his leisurely course up the back-stairs and beguile the time by a chance gossip with any intra-mural wayfarer he might meet on the road to his young mistress' room, when a rustling sound caused Ralph to look up.

Through the open door he saw a tall figure in a cloud of white drapery come floating down the

broad staircase, floating along the hall, and floating at last into the room where he sat. He rose
to his feet breathless. A well-known face flushed
and paled. A fair hand was outstretched half
eagerly, half coldly. A frank, clear voice said :

"Why — Mr. Dexter — I am surprised — I am
glad to see you."

There was no tardy recognition here. What
was instinct in the brute will perhaps be called
intuition in the woman. Amuse yourselves with
your names, good philosophers!

"You are looking well — I need not ask after
your health."

"And *you* are much changed; have you been
away ever since" —

"I saw you? Yes!"

What was the tall barrier these two were talking over? Their voices came from afar; their
words from no deeper down than their throats.
Whence came that barrier? Was it glass that
would break or ice that would melt? It was
something transparent, for they could see each
other through it; could see perhaps each the
other held fast in the clutch of pride — oh, cruel
Pride! Oh, foolish pair!

"I have been away a long time, — time enough, it seems, to be forgotten in. It is amusing to find how after a few months' absence, more or less, one's memory is so nearly obliterated that he is called upon to establish his identity."

"But when one disappears and chooses to give no account of himself, his friends can hardly be expected to know of his whereabouts by intuition."

"True; but one may be restrained from being more communicative to the world by the indifference with which the world regards him."

Dorothy had seated herself in a quaint old chair of black oak with a high carved back. Close beside her was a table on which stood a jug-full of roses. She stooped down and inhaled the perfume of the flowers as she replied:

"I am not reproaching you, Mr. Dexter."

The acute reader must make out for himself why Ralph flushed a little as he pondered this speech; pondered it while he attentively regarded the speaker, still bending over the crimson roses, her head and arms and white-draped figure showing in vivid relief against the dark chair, while every voluminous fold of her dress seemed redolent with the delicious aroma of the flowers.

"I dared not flatter myself you were," he returned very quietly, "I was only generally justifying myself, or, if you please, moralizing and making a bore of myself — I beg your pardon, I have not asked for your mother."

"She is very well, thank you!"

"And your uncle?"

"Quite well also; unfortunately they are both absent in the city. Mamma had some errand to do, and went in with my uncle this morning."

A pause here of several minutes marked the first stage of the interview. The barrier still stood intact, the glass unbroken, the ice unmelted. Ralph, absorbed in intense watchfulness of his companion, was unconscious and composed. Dorothy seemed struggling with embarrassment. She caught at the first commonplace.

"Does Windmere look naturally to you?"

"So much so that I can hardly realize it is no longer my home."

"I hope you will feel at entire liberty to go where you like and do as you please. I am sorry my uncle is not here to go about with you."

"Thank you, it is only the atmosphere I care

for. I should rather dread to see changes even
if they were improvements."

"There have been very few changes made outside the house."

Another pause ; the glittering barrier seemed
by impalpable cristallization to rise higher and
higher, and the voices to come from farther and
farther off. Dorothy, yielding helplessly to the
increasing restraint, floundered in distress.

"The weather has been " —

"Miss Dighton, perhaps I ought to apologize
for making this call. You may consider it an
intrusion or a presumption."

Dorothy took a half-opened rose from the jug
and pulled it to pieces as she replied : —

" I cannot conceive any reason why you should
apologize, Mr. Dexter ; at the same time I will
be frank enough to say that I am very much
surprised to see you."

" That is evident ; but if you are surprised to
see me and are willing to confess it, my visit
cannot then be quite customary or proper, or
whatever is the society cant. But why ? I do
not know ; I cannot see. I was once on visiting
terms with you. You have even called yourself
my friend. What, tell me, has changed all this ?

I have not consciously done anything that could have injured or ought to have offended you."

" Then you consider me the cause of the change ?"

"Entirely ; I am surprised that you can ask the question."

" You cannot be more surprised than I am at such a charge. I am sorry if I have been remiss in the matter of hospitality or friendliness — perhaps your expectations of me were unreasonable !"

" Perhaps they were," returned Ralph, bitterly ; " so many of my expectations in life have been thought unreasonable, it may indeed very well be ; if so, my punishment has been in proportion to my presumption."

" Is not that a little ill-natured ? "

" Doubtless ; I dare say I am as ill-natured as unreasonable."

" You will certainly prove both, Mr. Dexter, if you maintain that tone."

" I beg your pardon ; I fear I have lost the power of distinguishing my ill from my good-natured side, — if indeed I have one."

" But whether your expectations were large or small," continued Dorothy, coming back to the point, " whether they were disappointed or not,

I hope you do not think I have ever failed to give you a cordial reception, or to do all in my power to " —

" Do you then think you *have* always given me a cordial reception ? "

" Certainly ; if I know what cordiality is."

" Miss Dighton, I would ask if when I — but no " —

" Why do you hesitate ? "

Ralph pondered a moment in silence.

" No," he said at length, " let bygones be bygones. All these considerations are little and trivial compared with your meaning and intent. If you have always *felt* cordially towards me, that present assurance will outweigh every past impression."

" I have never had occasion to feel otherwise ' " said Dorothy, simply.

" God knows you have not," cried Ralph, fervently. " Miss Dighton, whatever you may think of me, whatever you may ever have thought, however much your feelings may have changed, or whatever misconstruction you may have put upon my words or actions, I at least have but one feeling with regard to you, — a feeling of profound gratitude ; a feeling of most tender friendship, of respect, of admiration, of — yes, you cannot help it — of unalterable love ! "

"Stop, Mr. Dexter; I beg. I implore you!"

"I cannot, I will not until you have heard all I have to say; until you have heard it and considered it, and answered it. It was you who first stretched out to me a hand of sympathy; it was you alone who, when all the world had turned from me, remained firm in the faith that there was any good left in me; it was you who made any effort to save me from a life and a state worse than death. It is you whom I associate with the great change in my life; you whom I associate with every good purpose and impulse; you who pointed out the way; you who lighted that way with hope; you whom I have grown to think of as my savior, as the inspiration of my hopes, of my faith, of my fortune, of my all in this life."

Dorothy had risen and stood, white and trembling, supported against the tall chair, her eyes downcast upon the bare stem of the late lovely rose, which she twirled vaguely in her fingers. Was the glass of the barrier at last breaking down? Was the ice fast melting away? or did a relentless pride still whisper in her ears:—

"Who is this man that he should trifle with you; that having spoken thus to you once he should wait for years in silence, expecting you

to catch eagerly at the offered prize of his love ;
that having gone away for all these changing
seasons without one word, one letter, one message, in the meantime, he should come back
and expect to find you eager to meet and welcome him ; even waiting like ripe fruit to drop
into his arms at the first shake of the tree ?
What claim has he to such favor, an outcast, a
man who has forfeited the esteem of his friends,
and the respect of the world, by the most lawless
courses ; a man who gets his living by means
abhorrent to every honorable and respectable
person ; a man so proud and passionate that he
yields to no control, acknowledges no authority ;
who, to-day, may love and admire you, and to-
morrow cast you off, — a man without honor,
name, or character ? "

Did any or all of these thoughts pass through
her mind as she stood motionless there, grasping
the old chair, and saying with half-stifled voice :

"Oh, spare me, Mr. Dexter, spare me and
spare yourself the trial, the pain of this " —

"I cannot ; I must not ; if the worst must
come, I will know it now and here. Dorothy
Dighton," he exclaimed, advancing and resting
one hand upon the table, and striving to read
the downcast face before him, " I love you as

few men can love a woman. You have saved my
life, my honor, nay, my very soul from pollution.
I cannot bear the thought of life without you.
If I am to be anything in the future, if my life is
to bear any fruit of good, it must depend on your
answer to me now. Do not be hasty! Do not
rashly speak words that will entail upon me an
eternity of desolation. Is it — can it be possible
that I am consumed with this living flame of
love for you, and you have no answering glow,
no faint little thrill or throb in your heart in
answer to these words? Has the Almighty been
so cruel? Is it so? Tell me! Speak" —

"Oh, Mr. Dexter, I do not know — I" —

"You do love me, — it must be" — cried
Ralph, springing forward and seizing her passive
hands. "Do not deny it! Let me have one
moment of such pure happiness as I thought
only angels could know!"

"Mr. Dexter," cried Dorothy, striving to control her great agitation, "whatever feeling I may
have for you, whatever feeling I may have had
for you in the past, I cannot, I dare not let them
influence me here. I do not understand you;
we do not understand each other. I dare not
place my life's happiness in your hands. I have
no right to imperil not only my own but my
mother's peace by so rash a venture."

"I will not listen to these considerations;
they are timid cautions; I will blow them away
with my breath. If you love me, have faith in
me! If your heart was on fire like mine, you
could not stop for these cold calculations. Follow the voice of God in your heart, and leave the
rest to the future! Do not speak again until
you say yes! Look up in my face and let me
read your eyes! Come, — come to me; now,
here! Come to me for life! Come to me forever!"

His whole frame shook and his voice grew
husky with the resistless force of his passion, as
he drew Dorothy gently towards him, and put
his strong arm about her waist.

"Be one with me in effort and trial! Be mine
to cheer and comfort and help! Be mine to
guide me through darkness and trouble and suffering! Look up — look up in my face! Speak
— speak at last — I cannot wait! One word
— one — yes! yes! yes!"

"Mr. Dexter," said Dorothy, at length, releas-
ing herself with difficulty from his hold. "I
have spoken; I speak again. We can never
— be — anything different to each other — than
— we — are — now."

Shaking in every limb, she supported herself

by the chair, raised her ashen face, and with a breathless voice, continued : —

" I am sorry if this causes you suffering. I am sorry if it disappoints hopes you may have cherished. I wish you every blessing, every success, every happiness, but I — I — cannot share them. I know the effect of this upon you ! I know I shall never see you again, but I — I cannot do — I cannot say anything else. And so — Good-by ! I — I shall — always be your friend ! "

She turned and walked slowly towards the door. Ralph stood rooted to the spot. A film came over his eyes, he saw the white figure float far — far — far off and then up — up — up, and with it the light and joy and cheer floated out of his heart.

CHAPTER XXVI.

A BEATEN army, disorganized and demoralized, melts into helpless units. No longer dominated by a controlling will, moved by a common purpose, cheered by a common hope, pressing on to a certain objective point, — all its centralizing influences lost, it succumbs to anarchy and flies in panic.

A man in like state, with shocked senses, with stunned faculties, with defeated purpose, yields to a like despair.

Stupefied and benumbed, Ralph walked out of his old home. The hope that had beguiled his long, weary term of work and waiting, the dreams that had filled his imagination, the inspiration that had spurred him on to success, the guerdon he had fondly promised himself — where were they ?

And what was left ? Duty ! For Love and Hope — Duty ! For guide, counsellor, and friend — still Duty ; ever and only Duty. With

that one stern figure moving by his side, with
that one pitiless voice ringing in his ears, he
mechanically mounted his horse and drove away.

Some instinct prompted him, as he came out
upon the road, to turn from the village ; to keep
clear of curious eyes and idle tongues.

After riding for several miles along the highway, he struck off into the woods through an
unfrequented road that led to the sea. The
coast in this direction was rugged and precipitous, and everywhere densely wooded, the trees
coming close up to the edge of the cliff for a
distance of many miles.

It was midsummer. A severe drought, like a
burning fever, had dried up the soil and left
thirsting vegetation to live upon its own vitals.
The dust lay white and thick upon the turnpike.
In clayey beds the earth cracked and yawned,
open-mouthed, for drink. Even into the dense
woods the unalleviated heat had penetrated, —
licking up the brook, the rivulet, the subterran-
ean spring, and squeezing from the spongy moss
its last drop of moisture. Dry and whitened
stones marked the beds of the purling sylvan
stream. Deciduous trees cast down their pre-
maturely-yellow leaves, and waved their naked
branches above the ground strewn with their own

decaying vestment. Earth lay gasping in the torrid air beneath a cloudless sky. Heat reigned supreme — a demon - king. The heavy atmosphere weighed down like an incubus upon every square inch of oppressed vegetable tissue, of human nerve and fibre. The approach of night brought no promise of relief ; the sun burnt red in a brazen sky, and the far-off sea reflected the hot hues from its glassy surface.

But what heeds Ralph air or sea or sky ! What heeds he aught in earth or heaven save the ache in his own heart ! The sun at length is gone, the long twilight spent ; night is coming fast, and still he goes on and on through the darkening woods, the hollow ground resounding beneath his horse's feet, the dreary tree-toads singing above his head, and the yellow leaves falling all around.

Night closes in at last, and darkness settles in massive shadows through all the woods. But hush ! — far off there is a faint stir in the air. In the tense silence moves a spirit of something ominous and evil. It comes nearer ; seeming now to take shape in sound — a faint, confused, uncertain murmur, like an echo, or the dream of some past tumult. *Crescendo ;* — coming nearer, rising louder, it sounds now like the hollow roar of waters beating upon a distant shore — but not in the direction of the sea.

A sudden breeze springs up before the unconscious rider, and blows back athwart the hot face of Night; blows back stronger, — stronger and swifter, — swifter, as if sucked into the maw of some great vacuum.

Swifter and stronger, stronger and swifter the movement behind — now no longer faint and far-off — comes near and loud; comes with the on-rushing of a tempest, with a force that shakes the earth. The wind grows to a gale that rocks the forest, dense clouds shut out stars and sky, and the blackness of darkness palls the earth.

Waking at last as from a sleep, Ralph looks about in amazement. Familiar as is the locality, he can find no landmark or bearing in the rayless darkness. He tries to soothe the terrified mare; he turns instantly about and gives her the rein, trusting to her keener sense to retrace the path he can no longer see.

Snorting and quivering the scared animal flies along the homeward way; the tall trees around them bend as reeds before the furious wind, and huge boughs are twisted off and flung like straws athwart their path.

Suddenly Ralph reins up with an involuntary

cry of horror — the cause of the tempest is
revealed. Nature's dreadest force is abroad, and
sweeps the earth like a besom of destruction.
Looking up into the black sky he sees a dull,
angry glow — in a moment more some flying
sparks — the awful truth flashes upon him —
THE WOODS ARE ON FIRE!

With momently-increasing fury the flames are
sweeping towards them. Behind is no escape —
the frowning cliffs overhang the very sea. To
ride on and find some side path leading to the
right or left, by which to outflank the coming
danger, seems the only hope. The mare needs
no urging; she flies through the darkness. With
every step the sparks fall thicker; the smoke
becomes denser. Still on and on they go; no
path opens on either side; they dash into the
underbrush, the mare stumbles over fallen logs
and old stumps; falls to her knees; gets up,
rears, plunges, and sticks fast in the thicket, —
it is impassable. They return to the main road,
and in the feeble hope of being able to reach the
highway rush on, as it were, into the very jaws
of death.

The heat, the blare, the stifling smoke soon
stay their course. Winged with swiftness, like
a gigantic spirit of evil, the fire comes roaring

and crackling through the trees, withering to cinders and ashes alike the lofty pine and the tender sapling, with its scorching breath, and licking up everything within reach of its myriad fiery tongues.

To retreat is deferred, but certain destruction. Ralph presses forward still a few rods, to a point where a small clearing gives hope that he may face and ride through the flame. But as the dense black mass of smoke, and the towering fiery waves roll nearer, he sees the futility of the hope. Indeed, he is no longer able to control the ungovernable terror of his poor beast, as, blinded by the smoke and scorched by the intense heat, she whirls around, fairly screaming with fright, and rushes frantically back towards the sea.

Swift as they fly, the fire comes fast upon their heels. On and on they rush, until now they hear the surf beating upon the rocks close before them.

Turning, Ralph tries again, by riding along the edge of the cliff, to outflank the fire. But there is no path ; rocks are thrown in wild confusion on every hand ; the terrified beast rears and plunges and, at length, falls with torn and bleeding legs among the sharp stones.

Meantime the flames come every moment nearer; the heat grows every moment more intense, and the whole air is filled with falling sparks. Ralph stops and looks around; at once the utter hopelessness of the situation is revealed : to the right, to the left, before, and all around, the furious conflagration rages. The black smoke shuts out heaven and earth, and leaves but a vision of flame — an infernal prospect. Dismounting, he turns his horse's head from the awful sight, and the poor creature utters a pitiful sob and lays her face upon his arm as though appealing to his higher power and intelligence. He puts his arm about the faithful creature's neck, caresses and talks to her as he looks anxiously about for some means of saving her life.

But the wind drives the choking smoke down upon them in stifling masses, and the increasing heat now grows intolerable. The suffering animal rears and screams in pain. As Ralph raises his arm to stroke her head, he is sensible of something heavy in his pocket. It is the pistol he had bought in the morning. A thought flashes upon him. He draws it quickly out. He tears open the box of cartridges with hasty fingers, and fits one to the barrel. Once more he turns about; once more realizes that there is no hope; death, in its most horrible form, is inevitable for the poor beast; death with untold agony. He hesitates no longer, leads her to the brink of the precipice, caresses her for the last time, puts the pistol to her ear, and shoots her through the brain.

Standing now free upon the edge of the cliff, he, for a moment, surveyed the scene. The sea, lashed to fury by the wind, rose in huge waves and thundered upon the rocks, uniting with its sister elements in a carnival of license. Ralph grew calm amidst the uproar—an undismayed intelligence amidst the whirl of things. Exhausted by the experiences of the day, indifferent to what might come, he stood with the yet smoking pistol in his hand, looked at it a moment curiously, and then, with a quick impulse, threw it far out into the seething waters.

But, in another instant, a cloud of smoke swept down upon him, and a tongue of flame almost wrapped him in its fatal curl. He stooped down, let himself over the edge of the cliff, and began climbing slowly down its precipitous side. Relieved here from the scorching heat, he was exposed to the new peril of climbing in the darkness over the wet and slippery rocks. Letting

himself down carelessly upon a seemingly secure
foothold, he felt the rock suddenly give way, —
crumble to gravel beneath his feet ; he began to
sink ; for one terrible moment he clung with
desperate fingers to the smooth wet surface
above him, and then — fell ; fell out of the darkness, out of the disappointment, out of the wrong
and cruelty of life, into the hands of God !

CHAPTER XXVII.

HERO SPEAKS.

MRS. DIGHTON was waiting as usual at the bottom of the stairs as Dorothy came down to breakfast.

" My dear child, what is the matter ? "

" Nothing ! "

" What makes you so pale, and your eyes so heavy ? "

" I am a little tired. "

" Drop down on the sofa in this cool corner and get a rest ! "

" I do not want to lie down. "

" Then sit in the big easy-chair by the door, and I will bring your breakfast ! "

" I do not want any breakfast. · I will sit on the piazza. "

" What harum-scarum thing were you doing yesterday to upset you so ? "

" Nothing unusual. "

" Where did you go ? "

" Nowhere. "

" Did you have anybody here ? "

" No — yes."

" Who ? "

" Please, mamma ; do not tease me now ! "

At length Mrs. Dighton understood that her daughter wanted to be left alone. Accordingly, having settled her in a willow chair on the piazza, folded about her an unnecessary wrap, brought her a superfluous footstool, vainly tempted her appetite with every available delicacy, and annoyed her with various other little motherly attentions, she went away to join her brother at breakfast.

" I 'm troubled about Dorothy," she said, dropping one, two, three sugar cubes into her brother's cup.

" What 's the matter ? "

" She 's all out of sorts ; won't eat her breakfast, or say or do anything but mope."

" Humph ; it 's the heat. She 'll come around all right by and by."

" I hope so, but she is so seldom ailing that I am a little anxious. Were there any callers yesterday, Thomas ? "

" Yes, Ma'am ; one."

" For me ? "

" For Miss Dorothy, Ma'am, — a strange gentleman."

" You took up his card ? "

" Yes, Ma'am ; but I didn't notice the name."

" Take this cup of tea out to Miss Dorothy, on the piazza, and say I wish she would try to drink it ! "

The man withdrew, bearing the dainty cup upon his tray.

" Wonder who it could have been, Samuel ? "

" Who ? "

" Dorothy's caller."

" Oh, one of a hundred people. What a woman you are for riddles ! Do you know I have just made out why this coffee tastes so much better than the restaurant coffee yesterday in the city ; it 's the Blue Meissen ! "

" Pure Java and rich cream may have a little to do with it," returned Mrs. Dighton, tartly, irritated, perhaps, by her brother's indifference.

But Mr. Curley was not so indifferent as he seemed. For without appearing to pay any attention to Dorothy, he really contrived to devote the day to her. He made her nosegays, swung with her in the hammock, played cribbage, enticed her into taking a ride, and all the time asked never a question, nor said a word about his favorite hobby. And after tea he read the evening paper aloud on the piazza, while

Mrs. Dighton unconsciously kept time with a
troubled fan.

"Tremendous storm last night," he began,
skimming the paper in the style of an expert
getting the news and skipping the comment.
"Immense damage — effects of storm at Roches-
ter, Buffalo, Albany, Windmere — here we are!"
he continued, as his busy eye-glasses flew up
and down one long column after another.
"Great fire in the woods! Ha, that accounts
for the smell of smoke this morning. Thirty
thousand dollars' worth of timber destroyed!
Casualties: Body of a man found at foot of
Trap Rock — half burnt carcass of horse on the
top of cliff — Schooner Betsy from Portland sent
boat ashore — man still alive, but unconscious —
leg broken, violent contusions in other parts of
body — taken to New York and sent to hospital
— proved to be Mr. Ralph — what? Eh?"

"Samuel, Samuel — quick!"

Mother and uncle sprang forward with outstretched arms.

"What's the matter?"

"Sh" —

"Nothing."

Dorothy put them both aside and staggered
towards the door.

23

"Let me go with you!"

"I can go alone."

And she did go alone; went up alone to her own room that night and came down alone in the morning. And nothing *was* the matter! Nothing that she could tell. Nothing more than has been the matter with women before and since. Nothing that prevented her from going about day after day like a living ghost, with fixed eyes and closed lips, resolutely performing every accustomed duty.

Nothing; but enough nevertheless to make her watchful mother determine to take the family back to the city in the very midst of the hot weather.

As for Dorothy, she asked no questions why or wherefore. She went back to the city because she was told, because the rest went,—as a matter of course. And when there, she went to ride in the Park, went to sail up the river, went to concert, church, and theatre, to be sung at, preached at, and played at; went as the patient horse goes up and down in the treadmill.

And day by day, up and down, march, march, always moving, never advancing, she worked in her treadmill, and thought, as she heard the whir of the wheel and the rattle of the harness, that she was living and moving and having her being as usual, and that the great world knew nothing of the treadmill.

But the treadmill is not renewing to the hopes nor recuperative to the energies, and so what wonder that day by day the mill turned slower, slower, weaker, weaker! What wonder that mother and uncle grew alarmed ; that physicians were summoned who examined the patient and agreed with her that—nothing was the matter.

At length anxious Mr. Curley came home one evening with accounts of a wonderful woman-doctor who had made some extraordinary cures in such cases. He gave his sister a card bearing the address. She determined to go at once and take Dorothy. The next morning, as she sat in the carriage with her daughter, she read to the waiting driver from the card her brother had given her : —

"No 5 Putney Place."

Madame Velasco was at home. On coming into the room where her visitors were waiting, she glanced hastily from one to the other, and without speaking went directly and sat down by Dorothy's side.

Mrs. Dighton made some preliminary explanation, to which Madame paid no attention.

"Please remove your glove! Now give me your hand!"

Clasping the proffered hand closely in her own, the new doctor sat regarding her patient for a few moments in silence. Then shutting her large, tired-looking eyes, she said presently with a wave of her hand towards Mrs. Dighton : —

"I must see the patient alone."

"No, no," returned Mrs. Dighton, quickly, alarmed perhaps at this unexpected suggestion ; "I am her mother ; she is my only child. You may speak as freely before me as if you were alone."

Dorothy, working ever wearily up and down in her treadmill, looked on indifferently.

Madame still sat with closed eyes, holding her patient's hand.

"Have you anything to say to us?" asked Mrs. Dighton, impatiently.

"I cannot say what I wished."

"Say whatever you wish! Do not mind me, I repeat ; speak! My daughter will tell you the same," returned Mrs. Dighton, irritably.

Madame shook her head, but made no reply for several minutes.

"The trouble," she began at length, addressing Dorothy and paying not the smallest heed to her mother, "is partly here," — raising her hand to her head, — "but mostly here!" — shifting her hand to her heart. "There is something pressing down upon you *here;* something large and hard and cold and frightfully heavy. It is tall; it looks like a woman, a dead woman."

"You must not talk in that strange way to my daughter! She is too ill to bear it. We came to you for advice, for medical treatment," interposed Mrs. Dighton, coming forward in great agitation.

"Her feet are standing right *here,*" continued Madame, unheeding the interruption, "*on your heart!* They are hard and heavy and cold. *They are crushing out your life*" —

"Come away at once!" cried Mrs. Dighton, vehemently, as she seized Dorothy's arm. "Come, come, my dear; she is crazy; you shall not listen to her!"

Dorothy sat motionless, looking from her mother to the strange woman in listless wonder.

"But under those feet is a balsam — a salve — a cure for you" —

"Stop, Madam!" cried Mrs. Dighton, seizing the passive hand from the clairvoyant's hold. "Come, my dear, quick, let us go! How could your uncle send us to such a place!"

Mrs. Dighton dropped a banknote on the table and hurried her daughter away, showing herself far more agitated by the strange doctor's talk than the patient herself; so much agitated indeed that she could not repeat it at all coherently to her brother when they got home, but described it generally as "just such stuff as you might expect from that sort of people."

Mrs. Dighton now prescribed for the patient herself, and decided upon a trip to Europe. They were to start as soon as possible. She made all haste, but with two houses to shut up and arrangements for a long absence to be made, there was much to do. And so for two weeks she was very busy, going and coming in her numerous preparations, and left Dorothy to her brother's care.

Arriving home one evening, from a day at Windmere, she found the two in the hall; Mr. Curley busy inspecting some pieces of old armor that had just been sent him, Dorothy standing listlessly in the dining-room door, looking on.

After greeting them and giving some little account of her day in the country, Mrs. Dighton turned to go up stairs, when Mr. Curley said casually : —

"I was just speaking, my dear, of moving things about here a little " —

A nervous look came into Mrs. Dighton's face, but was instantly repressed as her brother continued : —

"But it is hardly worth while now we are going away. I thought that by moving the clock up to the turn in the stairs, where we could see it from both halls, putting these antlers over there, this bench here, the umbrella-stand there, and the chairs here and here, it would give us much more room and produce a much better effect. As for this armor, I really don't know what to do with it."

At this moment a servant appeared in the hall to speak to Mrs. Dighton.

"Stay, to be sure," continued Mr. Curley, enthusiastically, advancing to the corner and laying hold of the fateful Hero, " this is the place of all the world, just over the table ! "

Mrs. Dighton turned in time to see the act, but not to hear the words.

"Stop," she cried in a voice that rang through the hall, as she started forward with outstretched hands and a look of deadly pallor ; " do not touch that statue — I beg, I implore you ! "

It was too late. Mr. Curley's back was turned,

he could not see his sister's face, the heavy
bronze was already in his hands, it was easier to
set it on the floor than replace it on the table.

"Do not be childish, my dear," he replied
placably, as he took his breath, "I will put it
back again directly."

Only Dorothy had seen her mother's look and
attitude as she stood rooted to the spot where she
had turned, staring wildly at the corner.

Following the direction of her mother's gaze,
Dorothy looked curiously down upon the now
vacant table, where the long-lost letter lay revealed.

Mr. Curley, mounting a chair with a piece of
armor in his hand, was about to step upon the
table.

"Eh, what's this, — a letter directed to you,
my dear? Why, it has never been opened!"

Dorothy took the letter with idle curiosity,
looked at the strange handwriting a moment,
and carelessly opened it.

She read at first with a puzzled air; then a
faint flush began to creep over her face and
neck; deeper it grew, and deeper still, until it
burned in intense crimson in her cheeks. A
mysterious force seemed to run through her
inert frame and strain every nerve to rigid ten-

sion, while the whole expressive force of mind and body centred in her burning, wondering eyes.

Twice, thrice she read the letter; turned it blankly in her hand, looked at the dusty envelope, turned confusedly towards the table and the statue and at length to her petrified mother, who stood regarding her in dumb, agonized suspense.

In a moment a flash of intelligence shone in the daughter's eyes; she paled as suddenly as she had flushed; she bent upon her mother a look that grew every moment more cold, collected, and accusing. Speaking at length in slow, repressed tones the daughter said : —

" *You* did it ? "

The craven mother, quailing before that accusing look, strove in vain to frame a word of denial with her palsied tongue and nerveless lips.

" He — came — and — asked — for — me ! "

The guilty mother made an appealing movement with her quivering hands.

" *You* — sent — him — away ! " pursued the daughter with unchanged voice.

The accused woman waited as the criminal waits for the axe to fall.

The daughter folded the letter and advanced

up the hall towards the stairs. The mother flung herself in the way and held her fast.

"Oh do not — do not go yet! Hear me — hear me, my child. It was for you — for your good alone I did it. I could not part with you. I could not let you go with — with that bad, reckless man!"

The daughter made no answer. Her face was fixed and stern. Calmly, inflexibly she released herself from her mother's detaining arms, and proceeded on her way. Again, with frantic movement the mother seized and clung about her, crying piteously : —

"Oh, no, no, no, Dorothy! Do not, do not look like that! Speak to me, forgive me! One word — my child, my child — speak!"

Again the daughter gently but relentlessly unfolded each clinging finger of her mother's hand, and passed out of reach up the winding stairs, giving back no pardoning word, turning back no pitying glance.

And when in the still watches of the coming night the penitent mother stole to her daughter's bed-side, crying still for pardon, only the un-touched pillow stared blankly in her face, and only a mocking echo rang through the empty room.

CHAPTER XXVIII

QUADRUPEDS.

IF we were suddenly called upon to describe Ralph's feelings when he opened his eyes and looked about his large, airy room in the hospital, with its bare white walls and hard wood finishings, we should say he must have felt very much like a bundle of sticks on fire. But as this is a mere matter of the imagination, — having never ourselves had the complex physical experience of a fever and a broken leg, — no reliance is to be placed upon it as authority.

But, finding himself, in some inscrutable way entangled amongst these sticks, Ralph, doubtless, first busied himself speculating as to how he came there. How long he was puzzling it out, and how much of it he recalled, we, of course, can only surmise ; but when he began to realize his present position and note his surroundings, he must have remarked in the cool professional faces of the doctors and nurses a look, which, though naturally unmingled with any anxiety and solicitude, still betrayed an unmistakable interest and doubt as to what was to become of the bundle of sticks. In short, the impression must soon have been gathered from the experienced eyes that hourly came and glanced at him, and went their way, that nothing but a miracle could save his life.

But a miracle is nothing but a wonder, and the world is bristling with wonders; our daily walks are hedged thick with them; and so we may as well say, in a word, that a happy alliance of good doctors, good nurses, and good vitality carried the day, and his life *was* saved — saved, but how?

The visiting surgeon, a man of eminence in his profession, but with a cold manner and a voice like the clink of a hammer on an anvil, announced the result to Ralph, one morning, in reply to the latter's daily question : —

" How are we getting on, doctor ? "

" Not very well! "

" How so ? "

" You are in a very critical condition ! "

" I understand that."

" It will be necessary for you to submit to a severe surgical operation before you can get better."

"Anything you advise, doctor," said the patient cheerfully.

"I had hoped to be able to avoid it."

"What is the nature of it?"

The careful surgeon put his fingers upon the patient's pulse and looked keenly in his face, as if testing his strength before replying: —

"I am sorry to say you will have to lose your leg."

Ralph had been prepared, and had doubtless braced himself for the announcement, but, in his weak condition, he certainly showed praiseworthy firmness in suppressing every trace of emotion at these shocking words. He turned his eyes towards the window and remained silent several minutes, while the watchful surgeon studied his face.

"What will be the consequence of my declining to submit to the operation?"

"Death!"

"On the whole," returned Ralph calmly, "I think I should prefer that."

"Pooh, pooh; a leg's not such a great loss. You are a young man; you'll soon get used to an artificial limb; your usefulness will not be greatly impaired. Seventy-five per cent. of the community are wanting in some of their limbs or senses."

"That may be; seventy-five per cent. of the community are wanting in common sense or honesty. I find no comfort in the reflection."

The doctor did not *say*: "It is my business, sir, to give advice, not to argue about the expediency of following it;" but he *looked* it plainly enough, as he drew out his hard shining gold watch, and, fixing his hard shining eyes upon it, said briefly: —

"My time is limited; I will leave you to reflect upon it!"

"One moment; how soon, in your judgment, should the operation be performed?"

"Immediately!"

"To-morrow?"

"Yes."

"I shall require concurrent opinion before consenting to such a mutilation."

"As you please; the superintendent will attend to that!"

The superintendent did attend to it. In the course of the day a consultation of doctors was held. After a careful examination, they unanimously agreed with the visiting surgeon. Ralph then spent a sleepless night in making up his own mind. What thoughts of Rachel and Baby, of his unfulfilled mission, of his duty to himself as well as to others, determined him, it is of no moment to inquire. It is enough to know that he decided, that he consented, that the thing was done.

And when it was all over and he began to grow better day by day, he sent word to " Beals and Bilgo," and as soon as he was able caused himself to be removed thither, where one and all so vied with each other in care and attention that he only saved himself from being literally nursed to death by the exercise of the greatest firmness and the employment of the most ingenious tactics of defence. The children would scarcely allow him to raise his arm for himself; True sang and told stories for his entertainment, while Lady Pamela outshone and surpassed herself — and, as a matter of course, all other merely mundane cooks — in the concocting of delicacies to tempt his appetite.

And so it was not long before he could go about a little with crutches, and many were the jokes cracked between him and True about their being quadrupeds and having a crutch-race in the back yard as soon as he was able.

Madame Velasco came often to see the patient during his convalescence, bringing him books, flowers, and other dainties — attentions which

were regarded with evident disfavor by Lady
Pamela, for that worthy woman seems never to
have conquered her first prejudice against Madame, calling her, in contra-distinction to the rest
of the feminine world, "she," and never failing, at whatever inconvenience to herself, to
appear in state on the occasions of Madame's
visits, saying confidentially to True: "If '*she*'
expects to cut *me* for a green cheese, she'll find
skippers."

As Madame, however, in her gentle way, ignored this latent hostility, outward peace was
maintained.

But another visitor one day surprised Lady
Pamela as she was washing the walk in front of
the area door. A fine carriage with a coachman
in livery drove up, and a lady speaking from the
carriage window asked for Mrs. Ballou. The
latter in her momentary flustration incautiously
acknowledged herself to be the person in question, which admission she afterwards bitterly
bewailed to True, saying: "I hadn't a minute to
slip on my alpaca or git the Testimonial out or
nothin', but jest had to take that kerridge company right in to Mr. Ralph, an' he with his hair
all crumpled up from a nap."

But Mr. Ralph was too much surprised to see

the carriage company to think of his "crumpled" hair, and the carriage company was too intent on seeing Mr. Ralph to take note of Lady Pamela's toilet.

"I am shocked to see you in this condition, Ralph!" said the strange visitor, as the latter hobbled up to shake hands. "I have only just heard of your sad accident; a person calling herself Madame — Madame Something-which-I-have-forgotten, was good enough to come and tell me about you; also about your finding your brother and sister, and your very praiseworthy life of late — it seems like an answer to my prayers."

The old voice and manner, there was no mistaking them, else Ralph might not at first have recognized Mrs. Dexter in the woman before him, so incredibly old and infirm had she grown in the comparatively short time since they had met. Mayhap Ralph had misgivings as to his treatment of Mrs. Dexter; mayhap her changed looks affected him; at any rate his own voice and manner perceptibly softened as he thanked her cordially for her visit and sympathy, and inquired after her own health.

"My health is very much broken, but God

still gives me strength to attend to my duties, and that is all I can ask or expect."

Ralph began to express his great sorrow to hear it, when Mrs. Dexter continued with the old martyr-to-duty tone : —

" I came here to see you ; to see what I could do for you ; to express my sympathy for your affliction. I am grieved, but I cannot say surprised, that you did not send for me ; that you did not at once come to my house, and spare me the pain of finding you in such a place as this."

It was unfortunate that Mrs. Dexter, with perverse ingenuity, should always hit upon topics and adopt a tone that infallibly aroused antagonism.

"Thank you," returned Ralph, struggling to maintain his kindliness of manner, "I was in no condition to send for any one at the time of my accident, and now I should make a poor return for all the goodness of my friends here if I took any exception to their style of living ; and, indeed, I have every comfort and attention I could wish."

"I am deeply mortified," continued Mrs. Dexter, "that you should have thought it necessary to trespass upon the kindness and hospitality of strangers, when, as I have before taken pains to assure you, my house is always open to you."

"I am no longer trespassing, thank God, upon the hospitality or kindness of any one. The accommodation I find here my good host and hostess are willing I should pay them for; and for the constant attention they bestow upon me, I am the more ready to receive it that it is simply and spontaneously rendered, and affords them the most evident pleasure."

"I am doomed again, I see, to be disappointed in the hope with which I came to see you; in the hope that your hard experience of the world since you left the shelter of my roof, that your ample opportunity for reflection, might have somewhat softened your strange prejudices." .

"And I had hoped, Mrs. Dexter, you might have learned by this the futility of such discussions between us. Our views are hopelessly adverse. I beg you to consider that I have arrived at man's estate, and that it is natural I should exercise a man's right to independence."

"But do you think of the future?"

"I do."

"What can you expect to do in your maimed condition, when you have found it so hard to succeed with your unimpaired strength and vigor?"

"I have no doubt that in some humble way

I shall be able to earn a living for myself and the children."

" But if you will not accept help yourself, I am willing to make a reasonable provision for the children."

" I thank you again for them and for myself, but we need not for the present and we will not for the future, if my health is spared, trespass upon the bounty of any one."

Mrs. Dexter sighed and remained silent some minutes before rising to go, when she said : —

" How long do you expect to be confined ?"

" The doctor says for some weeks yet. I am then to have an artificial leg, and must learn the use of it."

" And in the mean time I scarcely dare offer to contribute anything to your comfort or entertainment."

Ralph flushed a little as he replied : —

" I fear it will be useless for me to try to convince you that I have declined the offers you have hitherto made me on motives of principle, not that I wish to disoblige you or decline all friendly intercourse with you or kindly offices at your hands. For the matter of my comfort here, it is, so far as I can see, perfect ; but I trust that from you or any other I should receive any simple attention or offering in the spirit with which it was tendered."

Without attempting a reply, Mrs. Dexter said good-by and withdrew.

Ralph took leave of her very cordially, thanked her again for her kindness in coming, and was very happy afterwards to remember that he had done so, that they had parted from each other in greater kindliness, and that he came nearer a feeling of respect and liking for her as he watched her down the yard and out the little door, than ever before in his remembrance.

CHAPTER XXIX.

SUNBEAMS ON THE WALL.

R ALPH was getting on. Every day he was gaining strength. But strength is not the whole of health ; as in the sunshine besides light and heat there is also cheer ; as in wine besides nourishment there is flavor and sparkle ; as in the rose besides beauty there is surpassing fragrance, so in health, besides the normal action of vital organs there is something of all these — a cheer, a sparkle, an aroma — which is its better part. And it was precisely in this better part that Ralph was lacking, and it was for precisely this reason that he crept so slowly on through the weary stages of a long convalescence.

"If he'd only jes' git a little chipper he'd go it double-quick!" said Lady Pamela, as she sat watching him one day while he took his after-dinner nap upon the sofa.

Lady Pamela was "tidied up," as she called it, for the day, and was busy "settin' a stitch" in a

pair of True's pantaloons. The little room was
in perfect order save for a space about Ralph's
corner where his books and papers were scattered ; the summer breeze played idly among
the tendrils of the trailing window vines, above
which the linnet hung in his gilded cage, and
the slanting sunbeams danced in golden cotil-
lions up and down amongst the paper flowers on
the wall.

Suddenly there comes a knocking at the area
door. Lady Pamela sits with rigid countenance
and affects not to hear it until a second and
third repetition compel her at length to rise,
muttering impatiently : —

" *She* again ! "

But when, instead of " she," there appears a
strange young lady asking for Mr. Dexter, Lady
Pamela becomes, as usual in case of strangers,
very suspicious, and replies shortly : —

" He is asleep."

" If you please I will come in and sit until he
wakes."

There is something in the quiet, decided manner in which the strange young lady says this
that overawes Lady Pamela, who, without further
demur, conducts her to the house, ushers her
into the little parlor where Ralph still lies sleep-

ing, and then withdraws into her own stronghold.

The visitor seats herself in the chair vacated
by the mistress of the house, and gazes anxiously at the sleeper's wasted face. Presently
he stirs; he raises his arm. The color comes
and goes in the visitor's face and she holds her
breath in suspense. Another stir and the sleeper
turns over upon his side, and with a deep sigh
opens his eyes.

He sees the figure sitting motionless before
him; he stares at it in bewilderment; he looks
confusedly about the room, then back at it again,
but neither moves nor speaks.

The visitor softly approaches and takes a chair
by his side.

" I hope I have not disturbed you."

He looks intently into the speaker's face and
gives no sign of having heard her words.

"I shudder to see how you have changed; to
think how long and terribly you have suffered."

The sick man coldly turns away his head
without a word or look of answer, and fixes his
eyes upon the shifting sunbeams on the wall.

"Mr. Dexter, I have come to ask your for-
giveness. I have done you a great wrong, but I
did not know what I was doing. I was inno-

cent, I was deceived — will you not speak?
Will you not hear me?"

The restless linnet chirped and twittered in
his cage, the vines rustled in the casement; it
was long before a husky voice replied : —

"Why do you come to mock .me *now* with
explanations?"

"Because I did not know before; because I
have only just learned the truth."

Again the sighing breeze, the singing bird,
filled in a painful pause.

"If you wish to disturb my peace by futile
words, if you wish to rouse in me again the
storm of passion that has but just been stilled, if
you wish to draw me back into that darkness and
despair from which I have scarcely risen, speak !
I cannot prevent you!"

"One word from you will prevent me."

"I shall not speak it."

"You do not need to speak it. I do not come
to disturb your peace; to cause you pain or
trouble. I come to atone for whatever part I
may have had in all your suffering in the past.
I must speak, — at some future time if not now.
You would be doing me cruel injustice to forbid
it. If you are too ill to-day"—

"I am not ill."

The averted face did not soften ; the tones of the repressed voice were chill and measured.

"Are you unwilling then to hear that every cold word I may have spoken to you in the past, that every indifferent look, every harsh or unjust thought, have all been actuated by blindness and ignorance ; that I have been the victim of a cruel trick, a wicked deception ? Are you unwilling to hear that I am not so unworthy, so unwomanly, so capricious as I seemed ? "

Still the flickering sunbeams danced their golden changes on the wall, and still the stern eyes of the sick man fixed upon them never wandered.

"Are you unwilling I should remind you that when you first — that once, a long time ago, you did me the honor to — to " —

The visitor cast her eyes to the floor and struggled with a passing embarrassment.

"To ask me to share your life and fortune " —

"Can you not spare us both the recollection of that scene ? "

"I would willingly spare *you ;* I must not spare myself. Painful, obnoxious to me as it is, I must remind you of what followed ; that I was prevented from answering you then ; that you wrote me a letter to which you have never received a reply. Recalling all this, will it make any difference in your feeling towards me to know that I never received that letter, that I never knew of its existence until within the past forty-eight hours ? "

He half-turned his head ; a look of interest and attention dawned in his face ; but after a moment he said in his former voice : —

" I called to see you before writing that letter."

" Yes."

" You refused to see me."

" I never did."

For a moment he turned his head quite around and looked full in his visitor's face.

" I sent up my card, you returned a message that you were engaged."

" I never received the card. I never sent the message."

" Who then dared " —

" The message was sent, the letter was intercepted by the same person — do not ask me who, do not ask me for what motive it was done, spare me that part of this confession ! "

His eyes wandered slowly back upon the sun-lighted wall and he mused a long time in silence.

When, at length, he spoke, his tone and look were much altered.

"I thank you for telling me this; it lifts a great shadow, a great burden from me. I could not bear to think you were capable of such — such — that you were other than I believed you. I rejoice to hear that you are all I once thought you. It will always be a consolation to me to know that I was not deceived in you; to feel that I have met one such noble and disinterested woman. Now I can think of you with pride and satisfaction as having been true to yourself in the past as you are true to yourself now."

"And is that all? Can you not forgive me?"

"I have nothing to forgive."

"Yes, oh yes, you have much, very much; I doubted you, I feared you, I did not know you. Now I have heard all; the noble life you have lived, the struggle you have made, the victory you have won. I have heard the whole bitter story, — all that you were too proud to tell me. Can you now forgive me for so long doubting, so long distrusting and fearing you?"

"You had cause enough for doubt, for distrust, and even for fear."

"You do not answer; you will not speak the words that are necessary to my peace!"

"If such idle words can gratify you, I say with all my heart I forgive you; with all my heart I wish you the happiness that you deserve."

"But you speak as though you were far away from me, as though we were about to part."

"I am far, very far away from you; we are about to part."

"Why cannot we still be friends? Why cannot we forget the past? Must this one mistaken act of another's build up an eternal barrier between us?"

"There is no barrier. I shall be proud and happy still to think of you as my friend. But to be near you, to see you and speak to you, I could not bear that. It would destroy my peace — such thoughts, such temptations I must forevermore put out of mind!"

"You say you forgive and yet you banish me — can it be that your feelings are so changed?"

"They can never change."

"But you said once that I was dear to you, that I was necessary to your happiness."

"You were, you are, but I shall never — all is changed now."

"But when you spoke those words I did not know you, I did not know myself. And now,"

—she continued, kneeling by the sofa, clasping his hand tightly in her own, and looking close into his face, "now, when my eyes are opened, when it is all made clear, am I, must I be bound by that answer?"

"Dear, generous girl," he cried in great agitation, as he gently pushed her from him, "I see your meaning; in a moment of impulse you would make amends for an innocent error by a sacrifice of your life. I will not suffer it. The temptation is terrible," he continued, as, with averted eyes, he still firmly thrust her away, "but I must, I *can*, I WILL resist it!"

"Oh, you *could* not thus drive me away if I were still dear to you!"

The pent tide could no longer be restrained; all the laboriously-built barriers of pride and reason were swept away in an instant.

Whirling about he caught her to his arms in a swift, passionate embrace; the next moment a great sob broke from him, and his whole frame shook with uncontrollable emotion as he again thrust her off, crying wildly:—

"There, there, go; go at once; do not stay, do not speak, I cannot — oh, I cannot bear it!"

"Do not — do not drive me away! Let me stay; let me stay with you now"—

"Dorothy — Dorothy, if you have any pity; if you have any mercy — stop!"

"And forever!" she concluded, overcoming his resistance and winding her arms closer about him.

"Oh God, oh God, that it might — that it might only be! But no, no; it cannot, it must not; it is too late, too late now for that! Such a life, such a future are no longer for me. When I begged for your love, when I asked you to share my life, I was a *man!* Now," he continued, almost fiercely, as he threw aside the light wrap that covered him and exposed his deformity, " I am a wretched cripple; a maimed and mutilated creature; *an object of pity!*"

"No, no; an object of greater love, of better respect, of higher honor," returned Dorothy, gently replacing the wrap, "dearer to me, infinitely dearer and more precious" —

"Do not — do not tempt me!" he cried, striving once more to thrust her away; "I must not yield to you. I must not take you from your home to share a life like mine!"

"You must; you have! This is henceforth my home, here — here *upon my husband's heart!*"

And now the sunbeams danced madly up and

down and all over the wall ; the rustling vines seemed trying to clap their green hands for joy, while the linnet, hopping upon his topmost perch, poured forth a glad epithalamium over the two hands clasped, the two hearts united, the two lives at last made one.

CHAPTER XXX.

TRITONS.

MEANTIME Lady Pamela, shut up in the kitchen, became uneasy ; became, in fact, very much agitated. She paced up and down the floor, rubbed her nose, wagged her head, and gave expression to her feelings in very vigorous whispers :—

" Who 's she anyhow, juggerknotin' it over me with that fine an' mighty air ? She 'll come in an' wait, will she ? Who asked her to, that 's what I want to know ? I give you fair warnin', you an' all of you," she continued, shaking her fist towards the parlor, " that your shadders don't darken that airy again. Hark, now they 're talkin' ; sunthin 's wrong ; folks don't talk in that low, squeezed kind of a way for nothin'. There, hush, hark ; they 've stopped ; w'at 's that mean ? Pr'aps she 's flew at him an' throttled him. Pr'aps she 's shot him with an air gun an' then hung herself to the door. If she thinks I 'm goin' to have ' Beals and Bilgo ' made a mor-gu'

25

an' cemetery of she's mistaken, I tell her that!"
With these words Lady Pamela resolutely strode
up to the door leading to the parlor, paused,
gave one or two loud warning coughs and a
startling "ahem," stretched forth her hand to
turn the latch, when suddenly the door opened
in her face, and the strange young lady stood
before her.

But Lady Pamela's soul was nerved up to
resolve-pitch and she did not flinch.   She only
retreated a step or two, and stood grimly regarding the intruder, as if prepared to resist any
further invasion of her stronghold.   The strange
young lady, however, was too absorbed with
something else to notice all this, as she stepped
out into the kitchen, shut the door softly behind
her, and beckoned the little woman into the
farthest corner of the room.

The Lady Pamela followed suspiciously, and
listened, in an attitude of defense, to a long
whispered communication from the stranger; at
the end of which, the astonished little woman
stood for one moment as if petrified by surprise,
and then ejaculating with a gasp: "My soul 'n'
body!" flew into an indescribable and desperate
fit of activity.

She darted from room to room, indoors and

out, up-stairs and down, and in her one little
person seemed to fill the whole premises with
a prodigious stir of preparation. When the
children came home, they, too, immediately
caught the fever of excitement and went flying
off on errands to every point of the compass.
True was sent for and came skipping home in a
breathless condition, and what with his irrepressible voice and clattering crutches, added tenfold
to the noise and confusion, while the ubiquitous
Lady Pamela, without for a moment intermitting
the rattle of preparation in the kitchen, seemed
to pervade every distinct and separate part of the
house at one and the same instant of time — the
presiding genius of the turmoil.

With the approach of evening the bustle
gradually decreased. Order came forth out of
chaos. The little parlor was lighted and decorated with flowers. True and the children came
in one after another in their holiday dress, and
when Ralph at length woke to a consciousness
of the unwonted stir, and asked what it all meant,
and Dorothy whispered a few words in his ear,
a beautiful flush crept over his face, a beautiful
light came into his eyes, and he answered the
speaker in a way we do not feel called upon to
describe.

Presently a step was heard on the stairs, a rustle in the passage, the door opened, and Madame Velasco appeared, all in white, in such a wonderful toilet that True and the children gazed at her in speechless admiration, while Lady Pamela cast a dismayed look down at her own kitchen apron, and put her hand to her head in consternation, to find that the comb was not there.

But Madame brought such a beautiful basket of flowers to put on the centre table, and kissed Dorothy so heartily, — saying something about not having seen her since morning, — and shook hands with the busy little hostess so cordially, that the latter quite forgot her prejudices in the overpowering enthusiasm of the moment.

And when, presently, Baby came in from answering a knock at the door, and announced a carriage for Mr. Ballou, the alert Lady Pamela hurried her spouse out of the room, produced his stove-pipe hat from the box under the bed, handed him a thick envelope with particular directions to "put 'em on in the kerridge," and followed him out upon the landing with a parting injunction not to let the grass grow under his feet. And when, half an hour afterwards, True returned with a pair of white

gloves on, and came ushering in a reverend-
looking gentleman with a white necktie, and
Rachel came smiling up and placed a wreath
of flowers on Dorothy's head, and True, muttering something about " City Hall " and "certifi-
cate," produced a legal-looking document from
his pocket, which the reverend-looking gentleman said was quite right; it was all at length
explained.

But when the consecrating words had been
said, and Madame Velasco had kissed Dorothy
again and again, and Rachel and Baby had
kissed their brother and new sister, True, unable
any longer to restrain himself, to the astonishment of Dorothy and the reverend gentleman,
broke forth : —

" Hooray, the thing 's done ; two times one is
one. The knot 's tied. A strong knot, a hard
knot, a double-and-twisted knot, a knot withstand-
ing and notwithstanding.

> ' Let the loud trumpets ring,
> Let the little birds sing,
> And every live thing
> Dance the Highlander's Fling ! '

Or anything else they can twist their toes to.
On with the song and dance ! This is revelry,
sir, this is glorification. These ancestral walls,

these marble halls, with vassals an' serfs by your side, never looked down upon a scene like this! Another Triton! Two more Tritons! Half-a-dozen Tritons—the world is turning to Tritons!

> ' We 're birds of a feather,
> We all flock together
> On our own native heather.'

What ho, my love, where are you? Stand forth an' join in the chorus! Stand forth an' welcome the new Tritons!"

The Lady Pamela thus summoned advanced stiffly with her hand mysteriously held behind her, and said grimly:—

"Might be a good many wuss things 'n Tritons!"

"Hooray," cried True, with enthusiasm, "there hain't been a female head her equal for out-'n-out dead-levelness since Mrs. X. Socrates floored 'Old Soc' with the hemlock."

"You 're right, my dear friend," said Ralph, warmly, "there not only might be, but there are, a good many worse things, and very few better things, and we are proud of the title."

Lady Pamela advanced a step nearer and looked more mysterious than ever, as she pronounced in broken and spasmodic clauses the following longest sentence she was ever known to utter:—

"I ain't a Cresis — never said I was — ain't a beggar neither — know w'at a weddin' is, I guess. 'T sha'n't never be said — bride went empty-handed out o' Beals an' Bilgo's — w'ile *I* live! 'Tain't much to give — didn't say it was — but it's all I've got — an' — 'f you could be — kinder, sorter careful — *I* use 'silver white;' whitin' scratches — I sh'd like it!"

With these incoherent words she brought her hands quickly to the front, held for a moment before the eyes of the wondering bride and groom the glittering "Testimonial," then dropped it into Dorothy's lap and darted into the kitchen, whence presently arose such a tremendous clatter as was never before heard even in Beals and Bilgo.

"The' won't be a whole dish left in the house to-night!" muttered True, as he wiped away a furtive tear upon his coat-sleeve. "But go it, my dear, go it! Never mind a few pots an' kittles! Strew your conquerin' way with crockery, an' deuce take the odds!"

But Lady Pamela proved that there was not only a whole dish but a good many whole dishes left, by very soon opening the door and inviting the company out to such a feast as has seldom been heard of outside the "Arabian Nights."

And while they were all assembled around the board, and had satisfied, as well as they were able, her exhorbitant demands upon their appetites, True arose and, clearing his throat, gave utterance to the following sentiment : —

" Here 's to your health an' happiness! Here 's to your peace an' prosperity! May you always have good luck, an' if you have bad luck may you come up smilin' an' never give in! May you always stick to each other like the bark to a tree! May you always remember the extryordinary felicity of this *festive* hour! May you always count on a welcome at ' Beals and Bilgo's,' an' never, never,

> W'ile water flows,
> Or wind blows,
> Or grass grows,

forgit that you are

TRITONS!"

CHAPTER XXXI.

F ROM a quadruped Ralph now soon became a triped — a very common species of the genus mammal which has never received due notice at the hands of the naturalists. He threw away his crutches and got a cane. It was, of course, pretty hard, painful work at first, limping about on the shapely tapering pin which the artificial limb-maker had furnished him, but with Dorothy walking by his side up and down the yard, with the children running on before, and True at the head of the stairs crying out : — " Hooray, you go it like a drum-major ; you 'll soon be able to kick a foot-ball ! " he had every incentive to improve that a reasonable man could ask. Now, moreover, having received from some mysterious source that " better part " of health that had been so long wanting, there was nothing to hold him back, and he accordingly made such rapid strides towards recovery as justified Lady Pamela's happy compliment that he looked like " a new man."

It was wonderful, too, to see how Dorothy adapted herself to the life at "Beals and Bilgo's," entering into it to such a degree that True enthusiastically declared she must have been born a Triton, and had never got her wings fledged until now — showing a sorry confusion in that worthy's mind as to the natural history of the Triton, which he persisted in regarding as some sort of a mythological bird.

Lady Pamela found her duties much increased with such an addition to the family, but she proved herself fully equal to the situation, and even found time to "touch the lyre" when True felt in the humor for singing.

It was on one of these occasions, when they had been cheering the spirits of the company with "The Heart Bowed down, etc.," that a loud knocking at the door summoned Lady Pamela from her post at the seraphine. Rising with a mumbled "wonder who on earth that can be," she went to answer the call, and presently came back, ushering in a shrewd-looking little gentleman, who gazed about with an astonished air as he walked suddenly into the brightly-lighted parlor from the dark landing.

The new-comer did not have time to recover from his astonishment before he found himself in Dorothy's arms. The latter, after she had embraced the little gentleman over and over again, at length turned with a proud look towards Ralph, who was standing in the background, blushing in the most delightful way, and said simply :—

" My husband."

And strange to say, when the little gentleman advanced towards Ralph, calling him a rascal, a black-hearted villain, a kidnapper, and saying he never would forgive him, while all the time they were vigorously shaking hands, Ralph laughed and Dorothy laughed, and embraced the little gentleman again with renewed rapture.

But when the latter presently, with a look of uneasiness, took Dorothy aside and whispered something in her ear, her face suddenly changed, and she hurriedly left the room. Then there was an awkward pause for a moment, till Ralph bethought him to present True and Lady Pamela to the little gentleman, who at once won their hearts by a chance but most happy compliment to " Steamer No. 10," which he had seen through the open engine-house door as he came in, standing in glittering readiness for service. He made friends with the children, too, by a narration of the thrilling adventures of " Sinbad the Sailor," in which, be it said, True and his wife soon showed themselves quite as much interested as the youngsters.

So absorbed indeed was the eager group of listeners, that not one of them noticed the pale little woman who came in clasped in Dorothy's arms, and went up and said something in a low tone to Ralph; not one of them noticed the kindly, hearty way in which Ralph answered as he gave his hand to the little woman : —

" It 's all right now. I deserved it ; I can forgive anything and anybody, now that I have the most precious jewel in the world for my own."

Not one of them noticed all this, for the sufficient reason that at this very particular moment Sinbad was having a hand-to-hand conflict with at least forty of the most desperate pirates, each bristling with at least a dozen cutlasses, and we dare not say how many revolvers, howitzers, and other necessary accoutrements of the regular business-like roamer of the main.

But when the story was done, the story-teller rose and went and kissed Dorothy again, and said with a very noticeable air of relief, whether on account of the pirates Sinbad had sent to their just reward, or on account of something else that had been said and done by the little group in the corner, " Now, you graceless runaway, when are you coming home to the bosom of your family?"

It was then first that True and the rest of them noticed the pale little woman, and remarked the look of trembling anxiety which she fixed on Dorothy as she waited for the latter to answer Mr. Curley's question. Perhaps Dorothy also noticed that look, and perhaps that is why she answered so tenderly yet significantly and firmly.

"This is my home!" she said, taking Ralph's arm and nestling close to his side. "And this," she continued, turning and putting both arms about Rachel and Baby, "is my family!" But seeing the look of distress upon her uncle's face, and the pitiable misery upon that other face, she instantly added: "But we're coming to see you very soon, all of us, to make a visit — a long visit perhaps."

"Cozy little snuggery you've got here," said Mr. Curley, turning to True, while those other two were taking leave, "easily made habitable, blue-gray paper, slate-colored dado; piece of felt over that abominable carpet, strip off this horrid horsehair, cover your chairs with blue cloth, paint your doors a warm gray, put a valance on that mantle-piece, and hang up half a dozen heliotypes in plain oak frames."

All this was Greek to True; indeed the speaker had muttered fully half of it to himself, as his eyes wandered about the room. Nor did he wait for an answer. He shook hands with Ralph, and moved impatiently towards the door. Those two were a long time taking leave. Would they never be through? Mr. Curley went out the door, down the steps into the yard. The two came slowly after, and but that Mr. Curley made a desperate effort at cheerfulness and kept up his old serio-comic tone to Dorothy, that parting at the area door might have been much more prolonged and painful.

"There, there, go back to your Pyramus! Don't come blarneying your old uncle, you wretched hypocrite! Go along back to your Pyramus, and send him to me one of these fine days; I shall have some business with the young scapegrace!"

But Dorothy understood her uncle, and kissed him over and over again, as smiling through her tears she whispered that all the Pyramuses in the world could never drive her dear old cross-patch from his corner in her heart.

It was only a few days after this that one

morning, just after the postman came, Dorothy saw Ralph get up and go out with an open letter in his hand. He went down into the yard and limped back and forth upon the brick walk a long time by himself. At length he came in and handed the open sheet to her, and she saw by his face that he was very much shocked and saddened. The letter contained a brief announcement of Mrs. Dexter's death.

Dorothy went with Ralph to the funeral, and although he spoke not one word to her about it either before or after the ceremony, she knew well enough what were his feelings, knew what associations were awakened within him at sight of that still stern face, at sight of every familiar object within those walls — his childhood's home. She knew the scene must make a profound impression upon him, and strove to divert his mind from too constantly dwelling upon it, but an event that occurred about a week after the funeral rendered all her efforts for a time quite in vain.

He received one morning a note from our old friend, the cheerful attorney, requesting him to call, upon a matter of importance.

He went and found the legal gentleman —

save for a slight increase of girth — the self-same smiling, satisfied, astute person as of old. He received Ralph, too, with the same brisk, business-like air as on the former occasion. But this time there was no hesitation, no uneasy hitching in his chair, no premonitory explanation as he confidently approached his subject.

"Take a seat, Mr. Dexter! You're looking remarkably well ; changed some since I saw you. Filled out, — spread ; " he continued, throwing back his own ample shoulders, "very much for the better, — excuse the compliment !"

Ralph bowed silently and took the proffered seat.

"Well, our dear old friend has gone. Death must have come as a relief to her ; suffered greatly towards the end, but if anybody could afford to die, she could. Wish we were all as well prepared, Mr. Dexter! Splendid woman — strong character, strong intelligence ; did an immense deal of good. Very methodical and business-like, too ; made all her preparations very carefully, and left everything in apple-pie order. I asked you to come in this morning, Mr. Dexter, to listen to her will."

The shrewd old lawyer cast a searching look

at Ralph as he took a paper from the table, and perhaps he was a little puzzled at the grave and troubled expression on the latter's face.

"It has been opened and read to other members of the family interested. I didn't know your address or should have sent for you. Mrs. Dexter has left the personal property derived from her husband in part to the charities he proposed endowing, and in part to his family. The real estate in which she had dower also, of course, reverts to them. Out of her own estate she has given bequests to various relatives and dependents, and — I beg your pardon, I may as well read the instrument itself, or that part of it I wish to communicate to you."

The attorney opened the will, turned one or two leaves, and with another quick look at the gathering trouble on Ralph's face, proceeded : —

"'All the rest of my separate estate which I owned and enjoyed apart from any interest and control of my late husband, whether the same be real or personal and of whatsoever nature and description, I give and bequeath to Ralph Dexter, the natural son of my late husband, Sydney Dexter, and I hereby appoint the said Ralph Dexter sole executor of this my last will

26

and testament, and request that no bond be required of him in the execution of this trust.'

"The rest of the will is as I have described — perhaps you would like to examine it for yourself!" continued the lawyer, handing Ralph the open paper.

Ralph took the will and read it over carefully, while the lawyer scanned with a curious air his saddened face.

Folding the paper at length and laying it upon the table, Ralph rose silently and was about to leave the office.

"Excuse me, Mr. Dexter, what do you propose" —

"I beg your pardon ; take any steps that may be necessary ! Direct me in what I must do personally — I accept the trust ! "

The magnanimous offering of the dead woman was magnanimously received. But it was many days before Ralph told Dorothy of it, and it was many more days, aye, weeks and months before she could reason or cheer or drive away the remorse with which this generous act almost overwhelmed him.

But an unexpected ally came to her aid. Uncle

Curl came flying in through the open area-door very early one morning — greatly to the discomfiture of Lady Pamela, who was scrubbing the bricks — and said that he and Mrs. Dighton were going down to the seaside that very afternoon to spend the rest of the season. He had waited long enough for faithless Thisbe, and now he had come after her and she was to go to the seaside too, and bring Pyramus with her, and the children also. Hush! *he* was speaking and wouldn't be interrupted. The carriage would be at the door at four o'clock P. M. precisely, and everybody was to look sharp and be on hand, for he was not to be trifled with. And away he flew again down the wet bricks before anybody could say ah, yes or no.

And after he was gone Lady Pamela came and handed Dorothy a large envelope, saying: "The little gentleman, your uncle, told me to give it to you."

On opening the large envelope Uncle Curl's hurry was all explained, for there was a title-deed signed, sealed, and delivered, conveying "all that piece or parcel of land with the buildings thereon, situate at Windmere, etc., etc., to Dorothy Dighton Dexter; to have and to hold to her and her heirs forever."

And Dorothy looked at it a few minutes in silence, and then one round hot tear fell upon the neatly-written signature of " Samuel Curley," and made a blister on the paper and gave the ink a blurred look from which they will never recover to the end of time. Then she softly rose, laid the paper in Ralph's lap without a word, and went away to get ready.

At four o'clock P. M. precisely, sure enough, up drove the carriage. And everybody was ready, and everbody made haste to get in — everybody, that is, but poor Lady Pamela, who stood alone and disconsolate in the area-door. When Baby saw her and got out of the carriage to run back and give her another farewell kiss, she caught the youngster in her arms, gave him a tremendous squeeze, then rushing in slammed the door with a force that made "Wild George" and "Jumping Jacob" start in their stalls, and flew up the walk in a mood that ought to have caused every pot and saucepan in " Beals and Bilgo's " to tremble.

As for the rest of them they drove off to hold court with Queen Anne. Before long, however, it was discovered that Her Majesty sorely needed a steward at Windmere, somebody to live there all the year round and take care of things when the royal household was away, and so, very strange, surprising, and wonderful to say, True was thought of, and he and Lady Pamela accordingly soon found themselves established in a snug cottage which Dorothy — despite much protestation and many cries of "atrocious, horrible," etc., on the part of Mr. Curley — persisted in fitting up in the most flowery and bowery way, with roses all over the carpet and roses all over the walls. And here True was as happy as a clam, and proved himself a very thrifty and energetic manager of the estate, putting everything down in black and white in the most punctilious manner, and observing all the principles, not forgetting "the fundamentalest." And if his excellent wife was at first a little homesick for "Beals and Bilgo," it all disappeared from the day that Dorothy came in carrying a parcel under her shawl and said she had come down to ask a great favor ; that she had something she greatly prized which she feared might get lost or injured in her own frequent removals back and forth between town and country, and so she had come down to beg Lady Pamela to take and keep it for her so that Mr. Dexter and she might know it was safe, and could come and see it whenever they liked.

Lady Pamela's harsh features relaxed, and a pleased look shone in her eyes as she reverently took the precious " Testimonial" and placed it on the centre-table, where directly it caught a sun-beam from the adjacent window and reflected it straight into the little woman's heart.

THE END.